MORE HARM THAN GOOD

THE KILTEEGAN BRIDGE SERIES - BOOK 3

JEAN GRAINGER

GOLD HARP MEDIA

To my mother, who is always with me.

PROLOGUE

*T*he story so far...

Beautiful Lena O'Sullivan is only seventeen when she falls passionately in love with Malachy Berger. But Malachy's father, a Nazi living in Ireland, posing as a war hero, August, maliciously tells his son that Lena is seeing other men.

After Malachy abandons her and disappears to America, Lena finds out she is pregnant. She goes to Wales to have her baby in secret, and there she meets Eli Kogan, a Jewish doctor. They marry and return to Kilteegan Bridge with "their" baby, and Eli takes over the local medical practice from Lena's dying godfather, Doc.

A year later, Malachy returns to be at his father's death bed, and more terrible lies are told. August Berger claims Malachy's mother Hannah didn't die of a heart attack, but hung herself. Also, he tells Lena that her father's death wasn't a shooting accident; he was murdered by Berger's companion and fellow Nazi, Phillippe Decker, who has fled the country.

Malachy, who still loves Lena, asks her to leave Eli. When she refuses, he returns to America alone, where he buys an engineering company with the inheritance his grandparents have left him from their wine business in Alsace. He also leaves Kilteegan House to his son, Emmet. However, when Emmet is seven, it turns out that August Berger willed Kilteegan House to Phillippe Decker, so it wasn't Malachy's to give. Decker gets in touch; he wants his house back.

Lena is glad Decker has resurfaced. She wants him arrested for her father's murder. She tracks him to Strasburg where she confronts him. He tells her that it wasn't him but August Berger who murdered her father, Paudie Sullivan. And not only that, but Berger murdered Malachy's mother, Hannah.

Lena has something to tell Decker in return. He believes his "friend" August rescued his Jewish girlfriend Rebecca from a concentration camp and organized her to go to America. Decker longs to find Rebecca; somehow he imagines when she sees him, she will forgive him his Nazi past.

Lena takes Decker to an historian who reveals Rebecca was cruelly murdered, her body intended for display in a Nazi museum. Realizing he has lived his life in denial, Decker commits suicide.

Meanwhile, Malachy has arrived in Kilteegan Bridge. Lena's mother Maria is minding Lena's and Eli's children, including Emmet, because Eli has gone to find Lena. She invites Malachy to visit, and Emmet realises that Malachy is his biological father.

Malachy invites Emmet to America, but although seven-year-old Emmet is very impressed by Malachy's enormous wealth, he opts to stay with his "real" Dad, Eli Kogan, and all the rest of his loving family in Kilteegan Bridge.

Now read on...

CHAPTER 1

*L*ena Kogan loved Friday evenings. She and Eli usually spent them in the small sitting room off the library, reading the papers or a book. It was so cosy in there with a fire crackling in the grate. It wasn't cold during the day, but there was a chill in the evenings. Now that the children were older, it was also peaceful, which made it easier to talk about important things. Like the idea she had been mulling over in her mind for the last few days, ever since Mrs Shanahan apologetically handed in her notice.

She turned to look at her husband. He was reclining beside her on the sofa, his long legs stretched out towards the fireplace and a glass of whiskey at his elbow. He looked tired after his long week, and she noticed his blond hair could do with a trim. Eli Kogan had more patients these days than he could handle. The Kellstown patients kept coming to him instead of to their own doctor, and when he said he couldn't take another doctor's patients, they told him such heart-breaking stories – Dr White dismissing a lump in a woman's breast as an abscess until it was too late, or refusing to give morphine to a dying grandmother because 'it might kill her' – that he hadn't the heart to send them away. Dr White should have been struck off, and Eli had reported him to the medical council on several occasions, as had Dr Burke in Bandon, but it seemed to come to nothing. The man was a menace.

Outside the sun had gone down but it was not yet quite dark, and even through the closed window she could hear the rhythmic thud of a ball against a wall. Pádraig had convinced Lena to let him paint a goalpost on the gable end of the stables so he could practise taking frees all day long. He was a fine footballer, and though his sport wasn't rugby like his father, he was shaping up to be the best the Kilteegan Bridge team had.

In the distance came shouts from the upper paddock, where sixteen-year-old Emmet was teaching his younger sister, Sarah, how to handle Molly, the fourteen hand chestnut he was rapidly growing out of. Ollie, the pony, was still alive and much loved, but nobody could ride him now; Sarah was too tall and her feet were nearly on the ground with Ollie, so Emmet had finally allowed her up on Molly.

'Emmet will need a new horse soon,' Lena said absent-mindedly, thinking aloud. She knew her oldest son had his eye on a beautiful glossy black stallion that Skipper was working with for some businessman from Meath, but she also knew the owner wasn't selling. Once Skipper had soothed a powerful horse – he hated the word 'broken' – they often went on to become prize-winning racers that earned their owners a fortune.

'Can't he and Sarah just share Molly?' asked Eli lazily. He had never really understood why anyone would want to ride a horse. 'All those vet and farrier bills add up, you know.'

'No, Eli. He's too big for her already and still growing. But that's not what I wanted to talk to you about.'

He tilted his head to one side to smile at her. 'So what have you decided, Mrs Kogan? And do I have a say in it?'

She laughed. 'Of course you do.' Eli often made out like he was henpecked, but she knew he was joking. He respected her judgement but would never do anything he actually thought was wrong just to please her. She grew serious again. 'I'm thinking of employing Mrs Moriarty as our new housekeeper.'

Eli sat up on the sofa with a start. 'Mrs Moriarty, the Mouse's wife?

I mean, I know she's a lovely woman and all that, but do you seriously want to risk drawing the Mouse down on top of us?'

Everyone called Mrs Moriarty's husband 'the Mouse'. Lena wasn't sure why but assumed it was because of his beady eyes and pointed nose, and the way he bared his sharp yellow teeth when he greeted someone in the street. He was an annoying little man, always playing pranks and telling tall tales. She found him insufferable; he thought he was hilarious. 'I know he's an awful man, but...'

'Can't you persuade Mrs Shanahan to stay on?'

'Eli, of course I'd rather have Mrs Shanahan, but she's set on going to live with her son and his wife. It's been years since she was able to climb our stairs, not that I minded one bit – it was good for the children to do their own bedrooms – but his house is all on one floor, which she says is better for her knees. And she's been very lonely in the old place since Mr Shanahan died, God rest him, and she's looking forward to having her grandchildren around her.'

'Well, I suppose we have to have someone new then, but why does it have to be poor Mrs Moriarty?'

Lena sighed again. 'Because precisely that. Because everyone, including you, calls her "poor Mrs Moriarty", and she is. She has that horrible little man as her husband to contend with, who spends all the money he can earn in the Donkey's Ears and then goes home and gives her dog's abuse. And despite the awful hand she's been dealt, she is so kind and giving to the whole parish.' Lena was warming to her theme now, she knew that everyone avoided the Mouse, for good reason, but that wasn't his wife's fault.

'She does Meals on Wheels for the elderly, she does the flowers in the church, she helps Bridie O'Loughlin in the little playschool, and everyone loves her. She's such a giving person. And they have no children because she keeps having miscarriages, even though you've specifically told him how dangerous another pregnancy would be for her. I just thought she needed a safe place to come, Eli. I'm even thinking that Mrs Shanahan never let us put up her wages because of not being able to clean upstairs, so we could afford to pay Mrs Moriarty more without making the Mouse suspicious. She could give half to him, because he'll take it from her, but she can keep some for herself – I can even keep it here for her – so one day when she has the courage...' Her voice trailed off.

'She can leave him?' Eli's eyes twinkled.

Lena blushed. 'Well, I won't say that to her. She's very devout, and the idea of divorce or even separation would only horrify her. But at the same time, maybe one day she could just go on a long holiday to her sister in England and not come back, she could divorce him over there maybe.'

'Ah, the English with their heathen ways, allowing people who are miserable to legally separate. I don't understand why it's illegal here, honestly, it seems cruel to me. Anyway, that's a good plan, Mrs Kogan.'

Lena's heart flooded with love and gratitude. 'So you agree? You don't think I've lost my mind?'

'I do. And I love your mind. Almost as much as I love your...' He pulled her towards him, but at that point, their fourteen-year-old daughter came bursting into the sitting room and they had to spring apart. She told them a breathless story about how she had jumped Molly over a two-foot hurdle and Emmet had said she was 'quite good', which was high praise indeed from her older brother.

'I'll continue my admiration later,' Lena's husband whispered in her ear as she sat nodding and smiling at Sarah, and Lena felt a warm glow. Her whole life was so perfect: a husband she loved beyond measure, three happy, healthy children, her whole family around her.

On Sunday they were going to lunch at the farm, where her mother would cook one of her legendary roast dinners followed by apple pie and cream, and Jack and Skipper would tell them what had been going on at the farm that week. Her twin sisters, Molly and May, would go on about sheep and their madcap plan of moving to New Zealand, and Emily and Blackie would be there and Klaus as well, the Cork historian who was like one of the family now.

Things were so much better with Maria these days, and Lena no longer felt she had to walk on eggshells around her mother. That new drug, lithium, made such a difference. Maria still had manic depression – she always would – but it was over two years since she'd had to go into St Catherine's, the psychiatric hospital run by nuns in Cork. And the whole family was more open about her illness now, which also helped.

Eli had been the one to start it, as he overheard Lena and Emily murmuring about it one night. She would never forget what he'd said.

'If your mother had a heart condition, or emphysema or ulcers, would you be whispering in corners, like it was shameful? No, you wouldn't. It wouldn't be her fault, just bad luck, and this is the same. She has a mental illness. It's not her nerves, and she's not a bit low, or a bit high. She has a chronic physiological disease that will need to be managed and medicated for the rest of her life, just like anything else – diabetes, arthritis, whatever. But it doesn't help her to have you all afraid to mention it, or skulking around the issue like it's something to be ashamed of.'

They'd decided then to be more open, and Eli was right – it was all much easier. It meant her mother could be more honest with them all about her needs and the way she was feeling at any given time, which gave Eli a chance to adjust her medication before anything too bad happened.

Tomorrow, Lena decided, she would talk to Mrs Moriarty about the housekeeping job. She had a feeling the Mouse wouldn't object to the new arrangement. It would give him more time in the Donkey's Ears, which had gone downhill since Twinkle's time, and more money to spend there.

Her mother had said not to bring the children on Sunday – apparently there was something to be discussed – so maybe that could be a start for Mrs Moriarty. She could come up after Mass to get to know Emmet and Sarah and Pádraig, and Emily's Nellie, who would be here as well. Of course all four children already knew Mrs Moriarty and liked her as well as pitied her, just like everyone else in the village, but it would be nice if they got used to having her around the house. And that way Lena wouldn't have to worry about cooking them a meal before going up to the farm.

CHAPTER 2

'So what do you think of her?' Sixteen-year-old Emmet was spread out on the soft grass of the orchard, a straw hat tipped over his eyes. His cousin, Nellie, swung idly to and fro on the old wooden swing that Mr Shanahan had made for them years ago, hanging it on two ropes from one of the sturdier apple trees.

'I think she's very nice,' said Nellie, 'and she's a great cook.'

'A great cook?' He raised himself on one elbow to frown at her, his hat tipping off his head, revealing his dark-red hair. 'How on earth do you know that?'

'Sure, didn't we just have the dinner she made, shepherd's pie and buttered carrots, and then rhubarb crumble.'

'Oh, stop messing, Nellie.' With an exasperated sigh, Emmet threw himself back down on his back, adjusting his hat again against the sun. He was pale-skinned and burnt easily. 'You know I mean Isobel Lamkin.'

'Oh, *her*.' Nellie, who'd clearly known perfectly well who he meant all along, grinned. 'She's such an airhead, you'd hardly think she was sensible enough to be allowed out on her own, let alone inviting you to go hunting with her. Though why anyone sensible would want to go hunting in the first place…'

'It's the sport of kings, Nellie.'

'It's "the unspeakable in pursuit of the uneatable" more like. That's a quote from the great Oscar Wilde, the only thing I remember from Mrs Edward's snoozy English class. Thank God we won't have her next year – she's having another baby.' She grimaced. 'Can you imagine Mrs Edwards "doing it"? Urgh! Still, she must have.'

'There's something wrong with you, you know that, don't you? Thinking about our English teacher like that! Anyway, maybe she's racier than we think. I don't believe the new Monsignor would approve of her teaching us about Oscar Wilde. He was on about Sodom and Gomorrah and the sins of the flesh this morning.'

'I know, sure wasn't I there? For a fella who has never laid a hand on a woman, he sure talks about it a lot. Between sex and the dangers of the demon drink, he's like a broken record.'

Emmet lolled his head to one side to look at her. She sat on the swing, her toes resting in the daisies, gazing off at the distant fields. 'Ignore him. I do. I'm in my own world when he's rabbiting on.'

She shrugged, tossing back her long fair hair. 'I just hate the way he lectures us like we're all going around committing mortal sins morning, noon and night. Chance would be a fine thing.'

Emmet laughed. Nellie was always moaning about how Kilteegan Bridge was so boring, with no fanciable boys or anything to do.

The very popular Father Otawe had returned to Uganda, and the parish was heartbroken after him. He'd served in Kilteegan Bridge for twelve years, and in all that time, nobody had anything but the highest regard for him. He was the only African priest in the diocese, and Kilteegan Bridge was proud of their exotic cleric. He'd baptised the babies, married the couples and buried the dead with grace and kindness. He had been available to the people of the parish at all times; it was never a problem. People called for Father Otawe in the middle of the night to anoint the sick, and he had performed all his work with good humour and kindness, dismissing any apologies for disturbing him by explaining that was what he was there for.

Poor Mrs Ormond, his housekeeper, had been so distraught when Father Otawe left that Eli had had to give her a few sleeping tablets.

Apparently, she had recurring nightmares that he was being torn apart by lions, though Father Otawe had told her many times he had grown up around monkeys and elephants and other harmless creatures and not lions. But the poor woman was so lonely after him, she couldn't sleep for worrying about him. She had a photograph of him in her purse, taken when he first arrived, a smiling newly ordained priest. He was the son she never had.

This new man, Monsignor Collins, was a complete contrast to the amiable African. He was a thunderer who talked of nothing but hellfire and sin.

'And did you hear him this morning, going on about how the Jews killed Jesus? And poor Uncle Eli sitting there. The cheek of him.'

Emmet laughed. 'Oh, Dad doesn't mind him. He still likes to come to Mass with us – he likes the peace of the church. I don't think the Monsignor knows he's Jewish any more than most people do. Dad doesn't hide it, but he doesn't go on about it either. Sure, no one pays any attention to the Monsignor anyway.'

He noticed they'd got off the subject of Isobel Lamkin, but he didn't bother to bring her up again. Nellie always complained that the sort of girls he was interested in were boring and stuck-up, but he couldn't help the way every girl flirted with him. And sometimes those girls, like Isobel, were very pretty indeed. Nellie was pretty too, beautiful in fact, but she was a nightmare for her parents the way she rattled around in skimpy outfits, insisted on getting her own way and had opinions about everything. She'd confided in him that she had full-blown plans to go to London to become a make-up artist, though despite all her bravery, he noticed she'd not yet got up the guts to tell his Auntie Emily. Uncle Blackie would be heartbroken, but Nellie could always get around him. But Auntie Em was cut from the same cloth as his mother, and they were not women who took kindly to things that didn't suit them. It would be interesting to see who won the day, Emily or his wild cousin. His money was on Nellie.

'You're not the only one with a love life, by the way,' Nellie said suddenly.

He blinked, coming back from his drifting thoughts. 'Are you talking about yourself?'

She blushed, stirring the daisies with her toes. 'I might be.'

He sat up, feeling a stab of shocked protectiveness. It was like Sarah saying she had a 'love life'. It would horrify him, and Nellie was only about two years older than Sarah. 'Who is it?'

'Nobody you know.' A faint smile played around her lips.

He relaxed and comforted himself that it could only be a boy from the tech school. He and Nellie went to the secondary because it was better if you had plans to go to university, but the tech was where people who wanted to go into a trade went. He was definitely going to university, but Nellie had no interest. The tech boys were all harmless enough, probably too scared to even kiss a girl in case it was a mortal sin. 'Oh, I'll find out. I bet it's Benny McLoughlin, that neanderthal who can barely read or write. Or maybe his knuckle-dragging friend Rob McGrath. Anyway, it's bound to be one of those donkeys.'

Her eyes flashed, and she jumped off the swing in a temper. 'Of course it's not them, and you shouldn't be so snobby about Benny. He's clever with everything but words, and Rob's not had your advantages. His mother is on the gin from morning to night, but he's still a whole lot kinder about other people than you are, and he helps Mrs Bonner with her shopping every Thursday and won't take a penny for it.'

She stormed off towards the paddock, where Sarah was jumping Molly around the arena Emmet had set up for her using planks and blocks from Blackie's farm supplies. Nellie's parents used the sheds of Kilteegan House for storage, and Blackie always insisted Emmet could take whatever he wanted.

Emmet sighed and lay back again, gazing up into the trees, where tiny green apples were beginning to form. This was always how it was with Nellie these days; she seemed on edge. They would be having a perfectly pleasant conversation, and then she'd take umbrage over nothing and go stamping off.

He pitied the poor boy who had fallen for her. Although he loved Nellie dearly, there was no way he'd be able for a girl like her, even if she wasn't his cousin.

CHAPTER 3

*L*ena sat in stunned silence, looking around the big farmhouse table. Emily and Jack were also speechless, though Blackie was smiling broadly. Eli was suppressing a grin, and Skipper seemed to find the bit of lino between his feet absolutely fascinating. Molly and May, her nineteen-year-old twin sisters, both looked completely confused, and Klaus Rizzenburg, who up to that moment had been as serene as ever, now looked like a prisoner in the dock awaiting his death sentence.

The old grandfather clock ticked, outside the chickens clucked around the yard, and a tap dripped where the delft was stacked in the Belfast sink after lunch.

'Well, say something, one of you,' Maria O'Sullivan urged, her cheeks flushed.

Eli nodded at Lena, clearly wanting her to be the one to start the ball rolling, but she...well, she was just a bit taken aback. He raised his eyebrows at her. She cleared her throat and took the plunge.

'Congratulations, Mam, and Klaus, of course. We're very happy for you both.' The words sounded strange to her ears, but as she went on, she found she meant it. 'We had no idea that you two were...well, more than...well, "close", I suppose. We just had no idea that your friendship had turned into…' – she blushed – 'well, anything else. Like, we knew you used to visit Mam in St Catherine's over the years, and that you went out for teas and lunches and things, but we… Well, look, it doesn't matter what we thought. But ah…well…it's very nice news. And, Klaus, we're very…em…very happy to welcome you to the family.'

As soon as she'd finished her clumsy little speech, Eli backed her up. 'Absolutely. It's wonderful news,' he said enthusiastically.

Then the tension seemed to dissipate, and Jack and Emily and the twins were shaken from their shock, and the next few moments were taken up by hugs and handshakes.

Maria was pink with happiness, showing off a beautiful engagement ring, gold with an emerald surrounded by tiny diamonds. She'd kept it hidden in her pocket until the announcement. 'I know you're probably all a bit surprised, and I was myself, to be honest, when Klaus proposed. But as you know, he's been so kind to me, and we've known each other for a good few years now, so he knows me, warts and all.' She gave a rueful smile. 'And still he seems to want to take me on, God knows why.'

Her mother had not aged much over the years, Lena thought. She still looked exactly as she had when Lena was small. Like a mermaid. Tall and willowy, a girlish rather than a womanly figure, long fair hair that she wore down her back. No other married woman in her fifties would dream of having her hair hang loose as it would be a cause for scandal, but she was Paudie O'Sullivan's poor eccentric wife and she was given a free pass.

Perhaps it was the difficulties of her mental illness that kept her mother insulated from the normal day-to-day woes that carved deep lines into the faces of other women. Or possibly it was the fact that the social rules of dress and hairstyle for women of a certain age didn't seem to apply to Maria. She lived life to the sound of her own drum, something that was very unusual in rural Ireland. She was an expert with a needle and wore homemade, slightly ethereal clothes, long aquamarine dresses with gold embroidery or shorter ones with wide-legged trousers underneath, so again, her sense of style didn't age her either. She didn't dress provocatively – that would not have been forgiven – but she was just a bit odd. That was the assessment Kilteegan Bridge had made of Maria O'Sullivan, and Lena had known it all her life.

Daddy had brought her mother here as a young bride – his parents were alive then – and Maria had been able to breathe for the first time; Lena often heard her say that. She had been suffocated in the dark, airless, silent-as-a-tomb house in Cork, her parents mortified at having such an oddity for a daughter. They would have locked her away in an institution if it hadn't been for Maria's older brother, Ted, who fought for her always. He was the rock of her childhood. And then she had found another rock, a big strong farmer's son from West Cork. Paudie O'Sullivan had been the love of her mother's life, and she was his. Despite all her problems, Paudie adored her, and when she was low, or finding it hard to cope, his solid, sensible, loving presence brought her peace.

But he was gone a long time now, murdered back in 1955, and it seemed right that her mother should find happiness again, with another man who fully understood her and her illness. The manic depression would never leave Maria O'Sullivan, but Klaus seemed ready to take it on.

Klaus Rizzenburg looked different in every way imaginable from Lena's father, who had been dark-haired, dark-eyed, big and broad. Klaus had a longish melancholy face, lined with past suffering, and a shock of silver hair that he wore combed back off his high forehead and that curled at the nape of his neck. He was slender and very tall; Maria was easily five foot eight or nine, and he was a good four or five inches taller. He always wore a suit, a gleaming white shirt and a bright tie. On his smallest finger he wore a gold ring with a red stone, a garnet, she thought. It looked like a woman's ring, and Lena considered it strange but had never asked him about it. It clearly meant something to him, but he never said what.

Sitting beside the youthful-looking Maria, Klaus still appeared old for his age. When Lena first met him on the boat to Wales seventeen years ago, she'd thought he was in his sixties rather than his late thirties, so haggard was his face, so grey his hair, but she learnt that he had been a soldier in the German army, then taken prisoner by the Russians, and eight years in a prisoner of war camp had taken its toll. Since moving to Ireland, his biological age had been slowly catching up with his appearance, and he looked much the same now as he had back then.

The history professor caught Lena's eye and smiled, then spoke, his gentle rumble filling the space of the farmhouse kitchen. These days he had only a slight trace of a German accent – he'd worked hard to remove it, she always thought – and now he sounded just slightly foreign and pleasantly cultured.

'Maria, I want to "take you on", as you say, because I love you very much. And if we can have your children's blessing, then I would be the proudest man in the world to be your husband.' He turned to them all sitting around the table; clearly he'd prepared a speech.

'I never knew your father personally, but I feel like I have a strong sense of the man he was from all of you. I know how much you all loved him, those of you who knew him, and I assure you, I'm not trying to replace him in any way. I know what your parents had, and I am glad they knew such love. But I really do love your mother as well, and she loves me – perhaps not in the same way, but there are many ways to love, I believe – and we would like to join two lonely lives and make one happy one if you will all permit it?' He turned to Emily. 'Emily, you're the oldest?'

Lena knew Emily was very fond of Klaus, so she was surprised to see tears build up in her sister's blue eyes.

'Oh, Em...' Maria was upset now. 'I'm sorry. I'm not trying to replace your dad. He will be in my heart, your hearts, forever, but –'

'No, Mam, I'm... These aren't sad tears,' Emily interrupted, her voice choking. 'For so long after Daddy died, you were so, so sad, and you were very low so often. Those were terrible years. But Eli has been doing such a great job with all the new medications available now. Not that Doc didn't try, but there are so many new drugs and treatments, and now we all talk about your illness and there's no more secrecy. It's not your fault, Mam, you just got a hard cross to bear, that's all.'

All eyes were on Emily now, and Blackie put his arm around her. 'And when I asked Lena if the nice man she'd met on the boat might be able to help you find your beloved brother, I never in a million years thought it would lead to this. We all thought that Klaus was just being kind, calling to visit you and trying his best to find Ted. I know now that probably Ted can't be found, God rest his soul, but then Klaus found Eli's cousin Rosa, which was so wonderful, and on top of that, you both found something in each other. You found love out of all that happened and all you endured, Mam, and then for Klaus, after that terrible war... Well, these are tears of joy.' The fat tears flowed down her cheeks freely now as her mother moved to wrap her arms around her.

Then Jack, usually so quiet, found his voice. 'Klaus and Mam, if this is what you both want, then of course we're happy for you. And I know our dad would be happy too.'

Maria smiled gratefully. 'Thank you, Jack. And you should know, myself and Klaus are close to signing the contracts on a house near Blarney, a lovely new build, nothing big or fancy, just a small bungalow with a garden, somewhere you can all visit and near enough to Klaus's work. So this makes no difference to the farm, which you will inherit as your father would have wished. And of course, Skipper has his home here as well. And Molly and May until they're married.'

Skipper squeezed Jack's hand under the table and glanced surreptitiously at Molly and May. Ireland was very much about the oldest son when it came to the family farm, but as an American, Skipper was more equality-minded and clearly wondered if the two young women might be hurt not to inherit any of the farm themselves. Both the girls had abandoned formal education as soon as it was legal; they hated every minute of school. But they loved working the fields, and there was nothing they didn't know about dairy and hens and pigs and lambs. They worked so hard, almost as much as Jack and certainly more than Skipper, who spent most of his time with the horses.

But Molly and May didn't look at all upset; they were used to the rules of rural Ireland. They had converted one of the old sheds into a house for themselves to give Jack and Skipper more room in the old house, and they had plans to head for New Zealand at some stage. The government there were offering incentives for experienced farmers to resettle, and they were seriously considering it. Now the two young women jumped up and hugged their mother and Klaus, speaking at exactly the same time, as they so often did. 'We're both so happy for you, Mam. And, Klaus, welcome to the family.'

'You five are wonderful. Really, I don't deserve such good, kind children, and their other halves.' Maria smiled around the table.

Skipper coloured slightly. He suspected that, though nobody ever said it in as many words, everyone in the family knew Jack and he were closer than pals.

Maria continued. 'And I never imagined there could ever be anyone for me after your dad, and even if I did like someone, well, given the way I am, I just never imagined... But Klaus has seen me at my worst, he knows how bad it can be, and still he wants me and I want him.'

Standing up, Klaus produced a naggin of whiskey from inside his smart jacket. 'I brought this, just in case.' He winked and opened it.

Blackie helped by locating glasses, and Eli took the bottle and poured a little shot into each glass.

Passing them around, Eli said, 'I think we should propose a toast to the newly engaged couple. May they have years of wedded bliss together.'

'To Mam and Klaus,' Jack said happily.

'To Mam and Klaus, to Maria and Klaus.' The voices echoed around the room.

* * *

'So DOES it feel strange to you?' asked Eli as they drove home that night under a full yellow moon.

'A bit. But Klaus is lovely, and he's been so good to her. I'm glad she's found a companion, and for him too – he always seemed so lonely. He has no family left after the war.'

'I think they have more than companionship in mind.' Eli chuckled. 'I'd say…well, I'd say by the cut of them, it's love and passion and the whole nine yards.'

'Well, that's enough of that kind of talk,' Lena said, punching him lightly on the arm. 'My mother pairing up with a nice old man I can cope with, but any thoughts of, well…you know, no thank you. Mam and Klaus can hold hands and have the odd peck on the cheek, and that'll do fine. Sure what more would they want at their age?'

At this, Eli hooted. 'Your mother is only in her fifties! Are you telling me I can look forward to holding hands and a peck when we're that age? Because let me tell you, Mrs Kogan, that will not do me at all.'

'You'll be lucky to get that much.' She laughed. 'On our knees praying for a happy death should be all we'll be thinking about by then.'

'I'm sure your mother has some very different thoughts on that subject. She and Klaus have a lot of lost time to make up in the bedroom department…' Eli was enjoying her discomfort. He always found the Irish very puritanical for a nation where twelve children weren't uncommon. He always joked that in other cultures, there was a lot of talk and very little action, whereas in Ireland the reverse was true.

Lena covered her ears and sang loudly. 'I'm not listening to you,' she warbled as her husband teased her.

CHAPTER 4

$\mathcal{E}$mily sat at the dressing table brushing her hair as her husband lay stretched out on the bed behind her. She knew he was admiring her. He always said watching her brush her long blond hair every night was the highlight of his day.

She also had a feeling Blackie wanted to tell her something. But it could wait, she decided, as she was too busy savouring the day, her mother's happiness, the hope they could put Maria's sad past behind her.

It had been touch and go with their mother's mental health for years, which was why for a long time she and Lena had kept the truth of their father's death a secret from everyone else in the family, even Jack. Nine years ago, Lena had persuaded Emily that it was wrong to not tell Jack, and the twins when they were old enough, and that it might even help their mother to know the truth instead of just suspecting something was being kept hidden from her. The fact was, Paudie had been murdered by Malachy Berger's father. August Berger was dead now, and so was his henchman, Phillippe Decker, so there was no revenge to be taken, only the relief of no longer keeping secrets.

Maria had been amazingly calm when they'd told her, despite

shedding fresh tears for her husband. In a way, it seemed to help her to know the truth, as if she'd suspected it all along and it was only the feeling she was being told lies that upset her.

'I'm still reeling. Mam and Klaus – it's unbelievable, isn't it?' she said, meeting her husband's dark eyes in the mirror.

He nodded, sitting up again and pulling his shirt over his head. Blackie was so-called because when he was small, he was usually covered in coal dust from the shop. But it suited him. His beard, if he grew it, was almost blue-black, and his skin was so tanned, he looked anything but Irish. Dark hair curled tightly all over his bare chest, and he always joked that Emily was his fair lady. He was muscular and strong; years of lifting bags of animal feed and cement kept him fit, though he had silver streaks at his temples now. 'Well, I think it's great. Your poor mam has had a rough old trot, hasn't she? Her own parents were a right pair of cold fish, then she finds happiness with your dad and he gets killed, and the poor woman in and out of hospital for her nerves all these years, and her only brother, the one person who loved her as a child, gone missing. I'm delighted for her.'

'I am too. I just never expected it, I suppose. I mean, it's so amazing all this came out of me suggesting to Lena that Klaus look for Mam's brother.'

'And it's probably a much happier ending to the story than him actually finding Ted,' said Blackie wisely.

'You're so right. I think it's definitely better for Mam that Ted was never found. It would only upset her, I think.'

Emily and Blackie, like everyone else in the family apart from Maria O'Sullivan, were sure Ted must have joined the Nazi party, because the two things Klaus had managed to find out were that Ted's father-in-law, Gunther Kloch, was high up in the Abwehr, the German intelligence service so beloved of Hitler, and that Ted's wife, Christiana, was also a big supporter of the führer, as were the rest of her family. It seemed unlikely Ted would stay with Christiana if he'd disagreed with her politics; he could easily have come back to Ireland to get away. Even so, Maria was still convinced her brother could never have joined the Nazis. She said he had been so kind and loving to her when she was growing up, he just couldn't be that sort of man.

'It's still so out of the blue, though, Klaus proposing,' Emily mused.

'Well, I don't know. He's been around an awful lot this last while.'

'Ah yeah, but just as friends surely?' She turned to face him, holding out her arms for a hug. He came and put his arms around her, and she inhaled, loving the aroma of him. That was what nobody understood. She had loved Blackie Crean all of her life, and nothing had changed. She and Blackie had been sweethearts since they were thirteen years old. Everyone, including her sister Lena, thought she was marrying beneath her station. The O'Sullivans weren't wealthy, not gentry or anything like that, but they were respectable. But the Creans, well, they just weren't. Dick, Blackie's father, was a desperate waster altogether, always bumming money, and a bit light-fingered too. And his brother, Jingo, well, he was plain awful.

Blackie had promised Emily that the terrible reputation of the Creans ended with him, that he would work hard, support her and their family, and never disgrace her. And with Emily's help and support, he'd stuck to his word. He was one in a million, her husband.

Actually, it was Emily herself who had seen off Dick Crean. People thought she was all meek and mild, but underneath she had a temper as wicked as Lena's, just a lot better under control. She'd gone at Dick with a pike when he was about to hit poor Mrs Crean a clatter one day at the back of the shop, and she'd threatened him with guards and courts and all sorts. He knew she wasn't joking or bluffing, so he'd hightailed it and hadn't been seen since. And now he was in England, to the best of everyone's knowledge. Apparently he had another family there, some other poor woman shackled to that eejit.

Blackie's older brother had followed his father nearly nine years ago after, by a miracle, he'd got off with being found with a load of silverware from Professor Lamkin's house. Jingo had blamed it on the maid, and the jury had been divided, although the Lamkins themselves stuck up for the maid. Emily shuddered at the memory. Poor Mrs Crean had been mortified, as the trial had been in the papers. But while Emily and Blackie felt terrible for the poor woman, on the subject of Jingo, they were relieved. At least he was out of their lives for the foreseeable future.

She and Blackie still lived over the shop, Crean's Hardware as it was once called, but now they'd changed the name to BetterBuy Farm and Home Stores. Blackie still was able to supply everything from a needle to an anchor in the hardware side, but four years ago they bought the house next door and knocked through, doubling the shop floor. Now they had home wares, clothes, shoes, toys, even cosmetics. The shop was going from strength to strength, as were their other two shops in Cork and Bandon, which the banks had trusted their business enough to lend them money to buy.

Mrs Crean, Blackie's mother, had moved to a little cottage just up the main street. She no longer toiled in the shop, though she did lend a hand if she felt like it. Now mostly she grew roses and lilies in her little garden and enjoyed a peaceful retirement after years of drudgery. Five years ago, she had taken up painting pictures and had shown a surprising talent, so much so that Emily insisted on hanging several of them in the shop. Peggy was very embarrassed, but they sold immediately, and now she was getting commissions from the local gentry for painting their dogs and horses. Professor Lamkin had even insisted on paying her fifty pounds for a portrait of his favourite greyhound. Peggy tried to turn down the money on account of Jingo having robbed his silver, even if he had got away with it, but Professor Lamkin refused to take no for an answer. And the best thing about it was that Peggy had felt forgiven and able to hold her head up in the village again.

'So I told Nellie I'd leave her to the bus tomorrow,' Blackie was saying. 'I've to go to the mart anyway, but she'll have to get the last bus back. I've to go up to Dinny Ferriter about that bull he's trying to sell. Though what I'm doing stuck in the middle of this deal, I don't know.'

Emily kissed his nose. 'Because you are a kind man and Ann Clancy needs a bull and Dinny is selling one. But everyone knows that pair can't stand the sight of each other since the Legion of Mary dance mix-up in 1950 when Ann thought Dinny was asking her up to dance and he was in fact asking Sheila Murray behind her. Ann walked onto that dance floor with Sheila behind, and Dinny picked Sheila, leaving poor Ann a laughingstock.'

Blackie's arms tightened around his wife. 'And there's nowhere like this place to bear a grudge, is there? I mean, it was only twenty-five years ago. Ann can't be expected to get over it that quickly, can she?'

'Oh, in Kilteegan Bridge, any grudge worth bearing has to last at least four generations. You know that.' She giggled.

They got into bed and cuddled up like they did every night, her head on his chest. They both worked so hard that often they had only the most perfunctory of conversations in the shop, so they made a point of going to bed at the same time every night to spend some time together.

'So I'll collect Nellie,' said Emily, 'though why she's wasting her time going up to Cork every day this summer to learn beauty, I'll never know. All that course is doing is making her look madder every day. She had bright-blue eye shadow and blue pencil under her eyes yesterday, and her hair is so long and hanging down over her face. But she tells me it's fashion and I'd know nothing about it.'

Blackie laughed. 'Sure she's young, and what harm is she doing?'

'But she's so contrary and on edge about everything. Her cousin Sarah is so sunny and sweet.'

'Ah sure, Sarah's only just turned fourteen – she's time enough yet to be a right little madam. Remember we thought someone had replaced Nellie with a changeling when she was fourteen? A right monster she was for a while, but I get the feeling she's calming down again.'

'If we'd had more, we'd be able to compare, I suppose,' Emily said sadly. She'd had lots of miscarriages, two at after three months, and Nellie was their only surviving child.

'I know, love.' Blackie stroked back her long fair hair. 'But she's smashing, and we must be thankful for her, even if she wants to do her eyes up like some fella hit her a clatter, and I have belts wider than her skirts.'

'I am thankful. And for you and for us and our business and everything. We are doing fine.'

'We are, for now anyway.'

Something about his tone made her go up on one elbow and look into his handsome face. 'What? Is something wrong? I thought earlier you had something on your mind, but then you didn't say anything?'

He sighed, pushing himself up against the pillows. 'I didn't know how to tell you, to be honest. I only heard it today, and we were hurrying not to be late for Sunday dinner at the farm. And then there was all the excitement about Maria and Klaus – I didn't want to spoil things.'

'Blackie, you're scaring me. What is it?'

He looked awkward and a bit guilty. 'Well, I hope it turns out not too bad, but Jingo is back from England. PJ Flannery told me and Mam in the churchyard after Mass. Apparently PJ has a sister who works in Dublin airport, and she saw my brother arriving.'

Emily's heart sank. PJ was the local sergeant, and he'd be none too pleased to see Jingo Crean turn up. Blackie's older brother – he must be thirty-seven now – brought nothing but trouble. 'Will he come here to Kilteegan Bridge, do you think?'

'I don't know, and I said to Mam if he came to her house, she was to send him away, but he's her son you know, and blood being thicker than water and all of that. I'm betting she won't refuse him if he does want to move in, and he knows she's a soft touch. We haven't heard from Joanne for years, so she'll cling to Jingo.'

Blackie so rarely mentioned his older sister that left when he was a child and had never returned to the family that Emily was taken aback.

'I suppose so.' she said.

Emily hated the thought of seeing her brother-in-law again – he was so drunk and dirty and foul-mannered – but she tried to see Peggy's point of view. 'I suppose if it was Nellie, no matter what she did, I don't think I could close my door to her.'

'Well, let's hope Nellie stays on the straight and narrow then. She's probably breaking some decency laws, the get-up of her, but as she says, we haven't a bull's notion about style.' Blackie chuckled. He adored his daughter, and she had him wrapped around her little finger for all his giving out.

Emily felt a pang of guilt of her own. She'd still not told Blackie about something shocking that had happened the day before; she was afraid he'd explode over it. But on the other hand, it would be best if it didn't reach his ears from someone else first. 'Blackie, I've something to tell you that isn't great either.'

He turned to her and waited, two anxious lines between his brows.

'He… Well… The Monsignor stopped Nellie in the street on Saturday. She was getting off the bus from Bandon. She went to apply for a weekend job in the hotel there. I told her she could work in the shop, but apparently retail is beneath her and working in a shop is "sooo boooring" and everything we stock is "sooo pathetic".'

'Emily,' he said kindly, 'what happened?'

She sighed. This was hard. 'Anyway, the Monsignor told her that her skirt was too short, her top was too low and she had too much make-up on. He said she was a disgrace and she should go home right away and change into something that wasn't going to cause a scandal.'

As she'd known he would, Blackie exploded, sitting upright in the bed, going red in the face. 'What? Who does he think he is, embarrassing my daughter like that in public! It's 1975, not the dark ages. The cheek of him. He might be a Monsignor and what have you, and I've never spoken harshly to a member of the clergy in my life, but nobody – and I don't care who they are or what collar they're wearing – speaks to my daughter like that. The cheek of him. I'll be having a word, you can be sure of that.' He looked nearly ready to jump out of bed then and there and head over to the parochial house to have it out with the new priest.

'You don't need to "have a word" with Monsignor Collins, Blackie. There's already been plenty of words roared at him,' Emily said rather grimly.

'Roared by who?' Blackie looked a bit piqued someone else had stepped into his role as Nellie's protector.

'By your own daughter, I'm sorry to say.'

'Nellie?' Blackie's eyes widened.

'Yes. Nellie. She snapped at Monsignor Collins that he must be the kind of man who stares at young girls if he even noticed what she was wearing, and that he should mind his own business, and that her legs and boobs were not that.'

For a moment Blackie looked completely shocked; it was very strong language to use on a parish priest. But then he hooted with laughter. 'Did she really? Oh my God, Em, imagine having the guts to speak up like that? I know you're probably mortified, but fair play to her.'

'Fair play to her? Blackie, are you mad?' Emily was flabbergasted. 'She basically called the Monsignor a pervert. How is our family going to live it down?'

But her husband only laughed more and more. Emily didn't know where her own hysterical giggles came from – it certainly wasn't funny to annoy the Church – but before long the two of them were in paroxysms of laughter, wiping their eyes and gasping for breath.

CHAPTER 5

'What's that?' Jack asked Skipper as the cowboy took a large brown envelope from between two books on the shelf and threw himself down on the big old sofa they had beside the range. The envelope was distinctive, with lots of American stamps, and Jack hadn't seen it before. Skipper must have tucked it away as soon as it arrived.

Skipper smiled his lazy smile, the one that melted Jack's heart that first time he met him on the ranch in Montana. Skipper was like something from a comic book: dusty jeans, a checked shirt, a Stetson hat and a belt with an enormous buckle. 'It's my private mail is what it is.'

'Be like that if you want,' Jack said, turning his back and crouching to fill the range with turf.

'So aren't you going to ask me what's in it?' Skipper asked, taking a bite out of an apple.

'Apples will give you a stomach ache at night,' Jack said lazily as he threw in more sod, 'and then I'll have to listen to the moaning out of you.'

'They don't. That's another one of your crazy old Irish ideas. Remember when you told me that you had to cover potatoes with pepper in case I got all backed up? Y'all sure do make up some weird stuff.'

Jack laughed as he locked up the range. 'I didn't make that up. That's what everyone says, have done for years.'

'Well, Jackie-boy, just 'cause somethin's been that way for years don't make it true now, does it?' He opened the envelope and slid a magazine out, holding it out to Jack, who took it after washing his hands. It had a black-and-white cover with a photo of a very attractive man.

Jack scanned the title. 'ONE Magazine? What is it?'

'I ordered it from San Francisco. Well, a friend of mine, Carlos – he used to work on a ranch in San Diego with me years ago, and we've stayed in touch sometimes – I asked him to send it to me.'

Jack leafed through it. There were short stories, poetry, adverts and articles. The title of one caught his eye. 'Jim Foster addresses Democratic Convention of 1972 in Miami, Florida'.

'Isn't he the fella you were telling me about? The one who was thrown out of the army?'

Skipper nodded. 'Jim Foster is making America liveable for people like us. Carlos has heard him speak a few times, and he's joined his party. It's excitin'.'

'If you live in San Francisco maybe, but not in Kilteegan Bridge. There's no change here, I'm afraid.'

'I guess so.' Skipper sighed. 'Don't you get tired of it, though, Jack, all the sneakin' and pretendin'?'

Jack looked at the man he'd loved since he first laid eyes on him in 1958, under the huge, endless Montana skies. He'd gone there to explore new ways of farming without destroying the soil. Skipper had followed him home, and they'd worked the farm together ever since.

'I don't really. I can't imagine how it would be if we could just be as we are, you know, like now, and everyone knew.'

'Carlos says he and his guy, José, just walk around, go to bars together. There was a Gay Liberation parade this summer there, right in the middle of San Francisco. Can you imagine that? People, men and women like us, just walkin' around and not carin' what anyone thought?'

Jack fought down a wave of anxiety. Something about the way Skipper talked about how things were in the States unsettled him. He was happy. He had Skipper and his farm and his family around him, and that was all he needed. He didn't feel any wish whatsoever to walk down a street holding Skipper's hand or kiss him in front of people. 'Do you want to go there to live? To San Francisco?'

Skipper smiled, then took another big bite of his apple. 'What about you?'

'Well, I can't leave the farm, but if you want to go back...' Jack hated the thought of letting Skipper go, but he wouldn't stop him if he wanted to live a freer life. Not that anyone had even bothered them here. The worst fright he'd had was when the new Monsignor came to visit, but it was only about trying to convert Skipper to Catholicism. Skipper told Monsignor Collins his mother was Methodist and his brother went to a Baptist church in Bozeman. He made no mention of the fact his old man worshipped at the bar, but the mere thought of all those Protestants was enough to send Monsignor Collins flying off back down the lane in his posh new Saab like the devil was after him.

'Jackie-boy, you and me are stickin' together, no matter what,' said Skipper. 'I would like the idea of maybe goin' for a visit, just to see it all, but I'm a farm boy and I don't belong over there with those city types no more than you do.'

'But what about the other thing?' Jack asked. 'The draft?'

Skipper shrugged. 'Well it's all over now anyway, but I was here in Ireland since before that nonsense even started, and even if I hadn't been, Uncle Sam doesn't take boys like me.' He laughed. 'Wyatt and Laurie Lee said the guys who drink in the Bucket of Guts joined the National Guard, or even the Coast Guard, 'cause no way they were havin' the government sendin' them to Vietnam. Some just burnt their draft cards or drove to Canada. I ain't the only one who didn't fight, that's for sure.'

'I'm so glad you didn't go.'

'Ain't nobody left over there who supported it, as far as I can see

29

and now it's all over anyway. People got sick of it, and then when Tricky Dicky got caught, well that put the tin hat on it all. And the civil rights movement, the peace movement, the women's liberation, all that, all against the war. It's peace and love these days.' He grinned and made the peace sign with his fingers. 'Walter Cronkite called it in '68, when he told everyone what a shambles it was, that we ain't got no business over there in Vietnam. Well, he was just saying what was goin' on over dinner in homes all over the country. We never lost a war before, and that's gonna be hard to swallow, but American mamas wasn't gonna keep sendin' their boys over there to come back in a body bag, that's for sure.'

'How did Wyatt not get drafted?' Jack asked, coming to sit on the arm of the sofa. 'He'd have been the age, wouldn't he?'

'His leg. My old man made him climb over a chain-link fence to steal some car keys when he was a kid, but there was a dog there, mean old German shepherd, and he grabbed Wyatt's leg when he was halfway up the fence, almost tore his foot clean off. The damage done means he can't run or nothin', so he got rejected.'

'Poor Wyatt.' Jack was shocked. He'd had some hard times in his own family, dealing with his mother's illness and the death of his dad when he was only twelve. But Skipper mentioned situations with his deadbeat father so casually, just like this one, and always seemed amused when Jack was appalled. Maria was difficult to manage some-times for sure, but she would never make them steal or lie or deliber-ately put them in harm's way like Skipper's father seemed to do regularly.

'All part of the fun of being in the Malone gang.'

'Did he behave better when your mother was alive?' They rarely discussed Skipper's early life; it seemed to make him sad, so Jack usually avoided it.

Skipper shrugged. 'I guess. I was only eight when she died – Wyatt was eleven – so I don't much recall. She was nice, my mama, sweet and so pretty, but ole Earl Malone was always cheatin' and lyin' as far as I remember. Best thing he ever done was take off with Gina from the Orpheum Theatre. He was in Butte, and he went to see the dancin' girls. God only knows why, but one of 'em took a shine to Earl. I guess she didn't spend too much time with him, but anyways they took off. Never heard from him again after that.'

'Do you think he's still alive?'

Skipper smiled and stood up from the couch, stretching. 'Don't know and don't care.'

'Well, I suppose if he wanted to get in touch, he could find Wyatt easily enough,' Jack mused. The Bucket of Guts was a well-known bar in Bozeman. Jack had visited there once or twice with Skipper when he was over there and had met Wyatt and Laurie Lee.

'That old jerk sets one foot inside the Bucket, and bad foot or not, Wyatt would make sure it was the last move he ever made. Laurie Lee too. She and Wyatt have been together since school, and one night Earl made a grab for her. Her brother Jessie heard about it, and he was a wrestling champion, so he went and found Earl and damn near killed him. I think that's what made him move on to Butte.'

Jack shook his head. It was strange the way Skipper could laugh off such terrible events. 'And you still want to go back to the States?'

'Just for a vacation.' He grinned, then tousled Jack's hair affection- ately. 'Hey, don't look so glum for me. I'm fine. I got you, and I'm gonna see Wyatt and Laurie Lee real soon if you'll come, and maybe let's take us a trip to California.'

Jack considered the idea. 'I suppose we can afford it. When Mam and Klaus get married, she'll be living with him in Blarney so we won't have to mind her any more. And Molly and May can run the place fine when we're gone.' Although he still felt uneasy about going to San Francisco. What if they visited and Skipper wanted to stay where life was freer?

The 'sneakin' around' in Ireland, as Skipper called it, didn't bother Jack. He'd kept himself to himself all his life, and so keeping Skipper to himself felt like second nature. Sometimes he wondered if his family guessed. It was nice the way they included Skipper in every- thing, and he wondered if his father hadn't died, if he would have been able to tell Paudie the kind of man he was. He liked to think he could have, but he wasn't sure.

He'd often thought as a boy that he was the only person like this in the world. It was never mentioned, ever, and the only reference he'd ever heard was on the radio when they interviewed the actor Micheál MacLiammóir and he referred to his friend Hilton Edwards. Jack remembered listening to the programme in Deirdre and Bill Madden's house when he was about fifteen. Bill said ''Tis a quare friendship that pair have right enough,' and Deirdre laughed. The subject was shut down then, but Jack remembered walking home through the fields that evening feeling such relief that maybe he wasn't the only one after all.

CHAPTER 6

*L*ena was worried about Mrs Moriarty. She hadn't turned up to work, and it wasn't like her at all. The new housekeeper had fit right into the household over the last few weeks. She had no children of her own and had taken the Kogans straight to her heart. She cooked the children their favourite meals, she was already knitting them scarves and gloves for the winter, and she listened to their complaints about life without ever once pointing out how blessed they were compared to her.

The odd thing was, Frances Moriarty did think herself blessed. Over a cup of tea in the kitchen she told Lena how she couldn't believe the doctor's wife had plucked her out of poverty and domestic misery into this safe haven, where she was treated like a proper person with opinions and feelings of her own worth listening to and allowed to eat delicious food with the family and share their lives.

She filled her life with others, looking after people's children for them, helping all her elderly neighbours and never taking a penny for her selflessness. She'd been worried the Mouse would say no, just to spite her, but instead he had been happy to let his wife work for Lena in return for her handing over her wages, so she was blessed that way as well. Lena had insisted on giving her lots of dresses that she

claimed not to want any more, lovely bright colours, and nylon stockings and pretty shoes, the opposite of Frances's usual dark clothes and
thick woollen stockings pushed into old-fashioned boots. Mrs Moriarty's was a face that had never seen a face cream or a lipstick; she'd
never even been to the hairdresser's. But Lena Kogan had changed all
that with a wave of her magic wand, giving her bags of 'used' make-up
and a voucher for the hairdresser in Kilteegan Bridge, which Lena
told her she'd 'won in a church raffle and didn't want'. And Dr Kogan
gave her a free ointment for the skin on her hands, which had always
been red and sore, and now her hands were as smooth and nice as
could be.

There was only one thing she had said a flat no to. When Lena
tried to pay her twice her agreed wages, telling her to keep the other
amount for herself, she had refused. She was a very religious woman
and said it felt to her like stealing from her husband. After hours of
persuading, she'd finally agreed to let Lena set up a post office account
in her name and pay the extra money into that, but she wouldn't
touch it. Geraldine Cronin, the postmistress, had promised never to
let the Mouse know about his wife's secret account, and the money
would sit there unused until perhaps she had a sign from God
whether it was all right to spend it, or not, or maybe give it to
someone who really needed it.

Lena set off down the town on foot. It was a lovely morning in
early May, and all the children were out with Jack and Skipper,
cutting grass to make silage. The Moriartys lived in a row of one-up,
one-down cottages on the far side of town, with no running water or
electricity, and when Lena got there, it broke her heart to see the little
attempts Mrs Moriarty had made to make her own place nice: a
clump of daisies in a pot on the windowsill, a thin layer of whitewash
on the walls, bright patchwork curtains in the window made from old
scraps of material. The gate wasn't set right on its hinges, and Lena
had to lift it to go in. The front door was almost as bad and squealed
across the uneven flagstones as she pushed it open. 'Mrs Moriarty?
Frances?'

At first she thought no one was in, but she saw the back door was open and went to look out into the yard, thinking Frances might be hanging up washing. 'Mrs Moriarty?'

There was no one there.

As she turned to go back inside, her foot slid in something slippery on the back doorstep, and as she recovered her balance, she realised it was a huge splash of blood. There were more splashes of red on the stone path leading to a narrow ramshackle wooden hut.

'Mrs Moriarty? Frances?'

She hurried to the outside toilet. It was bolted from inside but had a cracked panel, and when she put her eye to it, she could just make out Frances inside in the dark, slumped over the toilet.

'Frances? Can you hear me?'

A very faint groan answered her.

'Frances? Are you hurt? Can I come in?'

Another groan.

Lena made her decision. She pushed her hand through the flimsy broken panel, widening the gap, and felt for the bolt. She drew it back and threw open the door, letting in the summer sunshine. Frances Moriarty was collapsed over the cracked toilet bowl, her head leant back against the flimsy wooden wall behind, her eyes closed and her knees apart. She was wearing one of Lena's summer dresses, the skirt pulled up to her waist, and the blue and white cotton was drenched with red, like someone had thrown a can of vermillion paint at her.

'Oh my God!' Lena rushed to kneel at her housekeeper's side. 'What happened, Frances? Who did this to you?'

'Nobody,' whispered Frances without opening her eyes. 'I'm losing the baby, and your dress is so lovely and I've ruined it, Mrs Kogan. I can't believe I was so stupid, but it came on me so suddenly...'

'There are plenty more dresses where that came from, Frances, but there are not plenty more of you. I'm going to get Eli right now. Don't move. I'll be right back.'

Instead of running to Kilteegan House, as it would take too long, Lena burst into Doc's old surgery, which now housed a physiotherapist, a dentist, an optician and a chiropodist. Without even asking the receptionist, she grabbed the phone at the desk to call her husband.

'Eli, quick. Frances is having another miscarriage, and she's bleeding very heavily. I'll call the ambulance from here while you're on your way.'

After she'd told the ambulance exactly where to come and arranged to meet it at the house, she handed the phone back to the rather po-faced new receptionist who had taken over when Eli relocated to the lodge of Kilteegan House, bringing his old receptionist, Margaret, with him.

To her surprise, the receptionist pursed her lips and said nothing, and when Lena turned, the whole waiting room was looking uncomfortable. If she hadn't been in such a hurry, Lena might have said something sharp about how miscarriage shouldn't be an unmentionable term in Kilteegan Bridge. Lots of women had them. It wasn't their fault, and it wasn't God's judgment on their sinful ways; it was just the way of nature. But she didn't have the time, so she bottled up her irritation and fled back up the street to where poor Mrs Moriarty still lay in the pool of her own blood, her lips and fingertips turning blue.

Five minutes later Eli was there with his bag. He worked to make the woman comfortable and staunch the bleeding. And then the ambulance arrived from Bandon and the men lifted Mrs Moriarty into the back of it on a stretcher. Lena climbed in to hold her housekeeper's hand while the paramedics took her vital signs.

Eli cast her a glance that said, 'I can't believe she's got pregnant again,' but mercifully he never voiced it.

She knew he wasn't blaming Frances, but she knew he thought she was at least partly at fault, when clearly the Mouse had forced himself upon his wife.

Mrs Moriarty groaned but tried to speak, a tear sliding down the side of her face. 'I'm sorry for causing all this fuss, and I know you told me, Dr Kogan, not to,' she whispered through lips still tinged with blue. 'You see, the Monsignor said it was wrong to refuse Joseph. It's God's will that married women have babies, that that's what marriage is for and there's no point in it otherwise, and he said he would pray for me. I am a God-fearing woman, and he said the Lord would protect me...'

For a moment, Lena didn't even know who Frances Moriarty meant by Joseph – she was so used to him being called the Mouse – but when she realised, her rage against the two men, the priest and the husband, for colluding to put this poor woman's life at such terrible risk threatened to explode out of her. She had to get out of the ambulance and walk up and down, taking deep breaths, while she waited for Eli to finish handing Frances over to the paramedics.

He was looking very serious when he finally climbed down out of the back of the ambulance, and he took Lena's arm as they walked slowly towards the pale-blue Rover he drove these days. The ambulance passed them a moment later with its bell ringing, heading for the cottage hospital in Bandon. 'I think she'll make it, but it was touch and go. Thank God you went to find her, Lena – you saved her life. It was placenta previa. It happens to her every time, and if you hadn't found her, she'd be dead.'

'Did you hear what she said about the Monsignor and the Mouse?' raged Lena as they got into the car. 'We have to do something! We have to talk to them, because next time she might not survive.'

He said nothing as he drove the Rover along the main street, and they were out again into the green lanes before he answered her. 'There's no point talking to that pair of men,' he said, pulling into a gateway to let a horse and cart go past, carrying a load of turf from the bog. 'But I did talk to Frances, and I hope it makes a difference.'

'Eli, what's the point of that? She can't help what's being done to her.'

'In some ways, she can. I told her as soon as she was out of hospital, she was to come to me and I would prescribe something to stop her getting pregnant again.'

He meant the contraceptive pill, of course. Eli was one of the few doctors in the region who would prescribe the pill. It was legal, and it was totally ethical in his book. But the Church was vehemently opposed to any interference in the production of new recruits for the fold, and their attitude made her husband so angry. The Church wasn't offering to carry these babies, or deliver them, or feed, clothe and educate them, but they felt they had the right to interfere in private family matters. It really annoyed and upset Eli how women were willing to risk their own lives with too many pregnancies rather than defy the Church.

'I do hope Frances listens to you.' Lena sighed. 'But she's very devout, so you'll be lucky if she agrees to go along with it.'

The horse and cart had passed, and Eli pulled out of the gateway. 'Well, I told her if she didn't do something to stop herself getting pregnant, then she was essentially dicing with death, and that was not what God wanted, ever, for anyone. She isn't a saint or a martyr. She is plain ordinary Frances Moriarty from Kilteegan Bridge, and the Good Lord has made it abundantly clear she isn't ever going to have babies, however hard she tries. So He must have a different plan for her, and that plan will become clear to her one day. And in the meantime, if she comes to me, I can keep her safe and nobody need know. I must have got through to her, because she promised she'd think about it.'

Lena immediately started worrying about what might happen to Eli if the priest found out he was prescribing the pill for contraceptive purposes. 'I hope she doesn't have a change of heart and blurt it out in confession. You'll bring the Monsignor down on you like a ton of bricks.'

Eli drummed his fingers irritably on the steering wheel as he drove. 'For a bunch of men who are celibate, your priests have a lot of opinions about sex. Maybe if they were allowed to marry, the mystery would be taken out of it and people like Collins would stop being so obsessed with it and keep his beak out of things that don't concern him.' He didn't usually criticise his wife's religion, but he was clearly upset by what he'd just seen and heard.

Deep down, Lena agreed with her husband, but she still found his dismissal of her faith and that of her whole family insulting. 'Well, to be fair, I'm sure the rabbis aren't too keen on artificial contraception either. Isn't it all about "go forth and multiply" in the Jewish books too?'

'At least we value the mother's life as well,' said Eli simply.

'Above the baby?'

'Yes, of course. I remember when I was a boy, my mother telling me about her sister Rachel, Rosa's mother. She kept having miscarriages after she had Rosa, and the rabbi said to her...' His voice trailed off. Although he'd got much better at talking about the past, the idyllic childhood he'd had before having to flee Nazi Germany, he still didn't like to confront it too often.

Lena didn't press him to continue. It was wonderful that Klaus had found her husband's cousin Rosa. She was a psychiatrist living in New York, and they'd been in touch now for a while. But her husband had lost too many other beloved relatives to the Holocaust to ever be able to look back on his early life with equanimity.

CHAPTER 7

hree weeks later, Eli strolled down the avenue of Kilteegan House towards the former gatehouse, where his surgery was located. He loved that his work was so near home, and that Lena could pop down with his lunch if he was very busy or he could stroll up and have a bowl of soup or a sandwich with her if he had a quiet day. Not that a quiet day came often, but knowing his family were close by was lovely.

He could see Sarah circling the corner field on Molly. It was a toss-up who his daughter loved more, the horses or her family. Emmet was usually with her, teaching her to jump, but today he was nowhere to be seen.

Eli sighed, thinking of his eldest son. The whole family had just been in Cardiff for a week for his mother's sixtieth birthday. Charlie, Eli's step-father, had organised a surprise party, and everything had gone off really well. But yesterday evening, he and Emmet had had a terrible row.

It all started when Eli mentioned that Charlie thought Emmet should follow the family tradition of going into medicine. Eli thought it was a great idea. The boy was highly intelligent, and his teachers were sure he would get the marks to do whatever he wanted in university. 'There's an excellent medical degree at University College Cork, Emmet, the best professors in the country. And you could come home for weekends.'

Instead of being interested, Emmet had been very disparaging, asking why on earth he'd want to spend his days 'listening to moaning and sticking things into people'. In the end, even Lena had reprimanded him, which sent him into a teenage sulk. Then when Eli tried to smooth things over by asking what he wanted to do instead, the boy announced that he intended to go to Stanford University, in California, to study engineering.

Lena had gasped in horror, and Eli nearly choked on his evening glass of whiskey. 'In America? Emmet, we just don't have that sort of money. And to pay for your board and lodging as well as fees? That's just not going to happen, so let's get a bit of reality going here. California indeed.'

The boy's green eyes had flashed in temper. 'Just because the furthest you ever went was across the Irish Sea. You don't need to worry – my real father will pay for it because he *has* got that sort of money. I'm going to study engineering like him – that's *my* family's tradition – and he's going to give me a sports car of my own for my seventeenth birthday.'

Eli had been so hurt, he couldn't respond. He stood and slammed out of the room before he did Emmet an injury, leaving Lena to sort it out. He'd never hit the boy, or come anywhere close to it, but to hear the words 'my real father' and 'my family' coming out of Emmet's mouth like that, and to hear the boy he'd adopted and raised as his own boast about how rich his biological father was, and then all that talk about a sports car when he knew perfectly well Eli didn't want him to drive until he was eighteen because of the number of accidents young men had on the roads... Well, it was as deeply cruel as it was infuriating.

Emmet had been to the States twice since he was seven, for a month each time, and each time it took him an age to settle back into the routine of Kilteegan Bridge after the excitement of California. Nellie was good at cutting her cousin down to size, reminding him he was no better than anyone else, but it was hard when an envelope containing two ten-dollar notes arrived each month from San Francisco.

Lena had forbidden their oldest son from splashing Malachy's money around the town, rubbing it in people's faces. She'd told him he had to save it for college, and they'd assumed that meant Cork, or Dublin at the most. But if Emmet insisted on going to Stanford, at Malachy's expense, Eli feared they could lose their son to America and Malachy for good. And then how would Eli ever get him back? It was heartbreaking.

Still, he comforted himself, that possibility was a year away, and a lot could happen in twelve months. One thing about being Jewish, as his mother, Sarah, always said, it taught you anything could change overnight at any time.

When Eli opened the door of the lodge, he found the waiting room full to bursting and Margaret, his receptionist, looking red and flustered. This was his first day back in the surgery after his holiday in Wales, and now he was paying the price.

He'd employed a locum, but only the absolutely desperate would agree to see him. They all said they'd rather wait for Dr Kogan. It was flattering, of course, but also exhausting.

'Good morning, everyone.' He smiled as Margaret handed him a bundle of letters – reports from specialists, results of blood tests and so on. 'It's nice to be home, but as you can see, there are lots of people here this morning. I'll do my best to get to see everyone as quickly as I can, so I appreciate your patience, patients!'

There was a ripple of laughter.

'How did you all get on with Dr Livesey while I was gone?'

'He had very cold hands, Dr Kogan,' Mary O'Connell complained.

'And he had to stick my Donal five times before he got blood. The poor child was like a pincushion,' Angela McSweeney added.

Sensing they were gearing up to issue a long list of complaints, Eli decided to beat a retreat. 'Right. Well, I'll warm my hands up and put my glasses on and hopefully have everyone right as rain in no time.'

Margaret handed him a cup of tea, and before anyone had a chance to complain further, he retreated to his consulting room and waited until Margaret rang the internal telephone he'd had fitted.

'Austin Campion is first, Eli.'

'Righty-ho, send him in.' Eli sat at his desk, which he kept pushed against a wall with another chair to the side of it; he hated sitting with a barrier between him and his patients.

The morning went by in a blur, and he could see from the long list that a lunch break wasn't in the cards. Lena must have realised it too, because soon he caught sight of her walking down the avenue with his lunch in a covered basket.

He only had a moment with her between patients.

'So how is Emmet?' he asked, wolfing the cheese and tomato sandwich.

She sighed. 'I think the poor boy is feeling very bad about what he said, but he's too proud to apologise right now. You know what he's like.'

'Mmm.' It was the only sticking point in their marriage. Lena thought Eli was too demanding of Emmet, and Eli thought Lena was too forgiving, always excusing their son's bursts of haughtiness and rudeness and saying 'poor boy', as if somehow Emmet had a hard life when in fact he had anything but.

'And I don't really think he wants to leave us to go to America. It's Malachy's fault, talking about giving him a car when we won't even let him drive one.' She came closer to him, in the way she did when she wanted to ask him a favour. 'Eli, do you think we could let Emmet drive ours the odd time? I don't mind showing him how.'

He sighed, exasperated. 'Lena, for goodness' sake, will you stop rewarding the boy for his bad behaviour!'

'But, Eli...'

He knew where this was coming from. When Emmet was born, she'd been forced to give him away, until Eli married her and adopted the boy himself, and ever since then, she had lived in terror of another enforced separation. It made her too blind to Emmet's faults, he thought, but he couldn't blame her. 'Look, if it will make you really happy, I'll give him a few lessons.' He'd bought his light-blue Rover

P6B 3500 last year in Cardiff, and ever since then, Emmet had been at him to let him drive it.

'Oh, thank you, Eli.' She threw her arms around him, and for several long seconds, they kissed each other until she pulled back, straightening her hair and frock. 'Well, Dr Kogan, they're getting restless out there, so I'd best let you to it. I've told Margaret to let in no more patients after four thirty, or it will be midnight before you're home.'

'Ah, my two Rottweilers, where would I be without you?' He kissed her again quickly, and she was gone.

He settled back into his seat after his speedy lunch and rang Margaret. 'I'm ready for my next patient please, Margaret.'

To his surprise, when the door opened, it was Mrs Moriarty. He knew she'd been kept two weeks in hospital, and then the Kogans had been in Wales for the last week, so he hadn't seen her since she was whisked off in the ambulance. He hadn't noticed her in the waiting room, and he guessed neither had Lena or she'd have said something. Maybe it was because the woman was so unassuming, always sitting with her head down.

'How are you today, Mrs Moriarty?' he asked with a smile. He was pleased to see she seemed a lot healthier than the last time, her hair neat and pinned back and skin clear. 'I'm glad you've recovered, and we're looking forward to you coming back to us as soon as you're ready.'

'Thank you, Doctor,' she said quietly. 'I'm sorry I was away from work for so long.'

'Not at all, not at all. And how can I help you today?' he asked gently. He hoped she was there as a result of their last discussion, when he'd promised her a medicine to keep her safe from pregnancy, but he didn't want to push her before she was ready.

She sat down and kept her head lowered, wringing her hands on her lap. Silence fell. His heart went out to her. He was used to this. Women were very shy about discussing anything bodily with him, especially anything gynaecological – the Catholic Church teaching them that their bodies were occasions of sin didn't help – but he tried to put them at their ease.

'Mrs Moriarty?'

He started to worry that she might be pregnant again already. He'd had a very frank discussion with the Mouse after the miscarriage, collaring him outside the Donkey's Ears and telling him that his wife's health could not withstand another pregnancy and that to insist on getting her that way again would be murder. The ratty little man had passed it off with a silly joke about trying to 'keep the mouse in his cage', which was the first time Eli realised where the nickname came from in the first place.

'Mrs Moriarty? I need to know how I can help.'

She flinched. 'I...I was thinking...' She stopped and swallowed. 'I might try...'

He used the coded language known by all. 'Something to regulate your cycle?'

The pill was never referred to by its name in Ireland, but women and their husbands could sometimes reconcile it with their faith if it was prescribed to manage heavy or irregular periods. Very few of the women who walked out with a prescription, which they would have to get in Cork for fear of anyone seeing them, did have irregular cycles. But it was an Irish answer to an Irish problem. Eli had learnt they were good at that over here.

'Yes, please.' Her eyes never met his.

He wrote the prescription, and then wondered how she would get to the chemist in Cork without her husband noticing. 'Do you know, Mrs Moriarty, Lena is going to Cork this afternoon. The young lad needs new shoes – he kicks the toes out of all of his with the football. So she could pop in to the chemist there for your prescription and you can get it from her when you come back to work tomorrow?'

She swallowed again. 'I'd be very grateful for that, Doctor.'

'Good. Now, I've given you six months of the regulator. You need to take it every day at the same time – don't forget now – and you start on the first day of your period. You'll have to be careful for the first week, but after that, once you take it every day, you'll be fine.'

She looked up at him then, and the expression in her eyes broke his heart. She was so grateful, so relieved that finally she was in control of her own body.

'And you won't tell my husband.' The words were barely audible.

'Of course I won't. Mrs Moriarty, what happens in here between me and my patients is not the business of another living soul. My wife will pick that up for you, and apart from that, this is between you and me and nobody else. Is that all right?'

'God bless you, Doctor. I'll say a prayer for you.' She smiled then, a ghost of a thing, but it was there. Frances Moriarty was feeling blessed again.

CHAPTER 8

'Mam, you did not need to invite Jingo to the reception, for goodness' sake.' Emily was struggling to control her frustration.

'But Peggy says he's a different man since he came back. He's so charming and kind to her, and she says we're to call him by his real name, John, instead of Jingo, because he wants to leave his bad old self behind him. He made a fortune working in England, and he only came home to mind her. He thought she must be lonely living all by herself with no one to take care of her.' Maria was getting upset now.

Emily sat her down. They were in Emily's kitchen upstairs over the shop. Maria had called in to the shop to get some lace for her veil and had mentioned that she'd agreed to let Blackie's mother bring her youngest son to the wedding. Emily had been horrified and brought her mother upstairs rather than have it out in front of the whole parish. A bit of juicy gossip regarding the Creans was too titillating for people to resist. Dick and Jingo's antics had been the subject of much discussion and debate over the years, and once they had gone, Blackie and Emily and Mrs Crean were very boring; Emily was determined to keep it that way.

'I'm sorry, Mam. It's not anything you've done wrong – it was very kind of you to let her bring him. It's just the very last thing we need at your wedding is that eejit.'

'Oh.' Maria looked dejected. 'I'm sorry, Em. I was just trying to please Peggy, and she says John has offered to drive her...'

Emily relented and hugged her mother. 'No, 'tis I should be apologising. He's just got us all on edge. He's trouble, you know he is, and I hate the thought of him being back disgracing us again. Blackie's given him the usual quiet warnings and all the rest of it, but that fella is a law unto himself. The only thing is he's still under the eye of Sergeant Flannery, so if he breaks the law, he'll be picked up again. But even if he doesn't, the thought of him hanging around, drinking, gambling, bumming money, being his smart, smarmy self...' She shuddered.

'But maybe Peggy's right and he's a reformed character?' Maria suggested hopefully.

'He isn't, Mam. He might be acting that way for now – and I know he looks very handsome and well dressed and clean-shaven and all that, and he seems to have money in his pocket – but I know in my bones there's no change in him from the old Jingo, when he had dirty long hair and drainpipe jeans and that tattoo of a swallow on his arm, which I notice he covers up these days. It's just poor Mrs Crean is powerless where he's concerned. She always wants to believe the best of him. Can you believe she even suggested we let Jingo manage the Cork shop for us when Lavinia Horan leaves us to be married? I'd have the Monsignor running the shop before I'd have Jingo, and no one in Kilteegan Bridge can stand that horrible man. He's cruel to everyone. I don't think he's a man of God at all.'

Maria looked frightened. 'Don't be talking about the priest like that, Em. The next thing he'll put a ban on people coming to the shop.'

'Oh, don't worry, Mam. I wouldn't say it to anyone but you.'

Things were changing in Ireland, slowly, but the Church still held massive sway with people, and Emily knew no one would defy the priest if he took against her and Blackie. It was another reason she was horrified at the thought of Jingo being back in town. At least the wedding was in Cork, so they wouldn't have to put up with

Monsignor Collins airing his views on women, marriage and babies from the pulpit. Klaus had booked the Honan Chapel in the university for the ceremony and the Imperial Hotel for the reception. There was going to be a buffet and a free bar, so she wasn't surprised Jingo was keen to tag along.

'I can't uninvite him, Em. Peggy would take it up all wrong.' Maria looked panicky. Emily knew things that wouldn't upset an average person could really send her mother into a spin, so she was already regretting her cross reaction. The wedding was originally going to be a very quiet thing, but Maria was getting into it now, and Emily and Lena feared it was the beginning of one of her manic phases that usually ended with a collapse and a stay in St Catherine's. Over and over and over it had happened, and while it was so much better with the lithium, they couldn't forget how things like this had affected their mother in the past, and it made them nervous.

'Of course you can't, Mam, and we'll have a lovely day,' she said soothingly. 'It was very kind of you to let Peggy bring him. And Blackie will tell your man not to come next, nigh nor near me on pain of death.' She gave a small laugh, and her mother relaxed.

'I can't imagine Blackie saying anything so cross to anyone, even Jingo,' Maria said, smiling.

'Oh, he wouldn't normally. Sure, look at the way his own daughter has a fool made of him, spending his money on make-up and clothes. I'm beginning to think it's something to do with a boy from school, her taking such an interest in the way she looks, but she's like the tomb, that one, tells me nothing.'

'Sure, which of us did at that age? I know I would never say anything to my parents, though that was different – they were like a pair of cadavers. But yourself and Blackie were knocking around together since you were children without a whisper of a romance till it was all settled, so 'tisn't from a stone she licked it.'

Emily laughed. 'I suppose so. And to be fair, she has got that weekend job pot-scrubbing at the hotel in Bandon, so she doesn't take as much of Blackie's money as she used to.'

'Good for her. Pot-scrubbing is hard work.'

'I know. She wanted to be a waitress or a receptionist, but they turned her down for that on account of the mad way she dresses and does her make-up.' Emily rolled her eyes.

Nellie was to be a bridesmaid at the wedding, along with her more conventional cousin Sarah, and when it came to their dresses, Emily had had to veto every suggestion by her daughter so far. Luckily Lena had found a pair of Laura Ashley maxidresses in a shop in Clonakilty, which Sarah loved and Nellie pulled faces about but was at least grudgingly prepared to wear, so at least that was done.

'Now, Mam' – she changed the subject – 'which type of lace did you want for your veil?'

Back downstairs in the shop, they spent a happy half hour looking over different types of Cork lace before they finally settled on Irish point from Youghal.

'Does Klaus have many coming?' Emily asked as she wrapped the lace in brown paper.

'Just some colleagues from the university, and his landlady and her husband. I'm glad he's happy to leave his city lodgings and live a bit further out. I've got used to the country now. I was a real city girl when I came here first. Your father thought it was hilarious I didn't know one end of a cow from the other.' She giggled at the memory.

'Are you excited to be living with Klaus?' Emily asked gently. Maria and Klaus had signed the contracts on the house near Blarney, a lovely red-bricked bungalow with straight walls and floors that hadn't buckled with age. Maria had taken Lena and Emily to see it, and they could understand why she loved it. It represented a clean start. Klaus too had nothing of his parents, no photos, no mementos, and the sisters had joked how they suspected the house would be really sparsely decorated, like a laboratory, but it would suit the newlyweds perfectly.

Klaus had bought a vintage dove-grey Humber that he would use to drive into the university every day, and there was a bus service from outside the door that went into Cork. If she wanted to, Maria could catch another bus from there to Kilteegan Bridge.

Maria took the parcel of lace from her daughter. 'Excited? I don't know if that's the right word. I'm nervous, I suppose. Not about marrying him – he's really lovely, Em. He's really very sensitive and emotional. We talk for hours, and he doesn't think I'm daft or away with the fairies like most people do.'

'We don't think that.'

Maria smiled. 'You know what I mean. I understand now about my mind, you know? Why it happens. And I feel much better in myself because I understand it. And Klaus makes me feel so safe, safe in a way I haven't felt since Paudie died, though they are nothing alike really. But I'm a bit peculiar, I know I am. Don't worry – I accept it about myself.'

'You're unique, that's what you are.'

'That's one word for it,' Maria said ruefully. 'I wish my parents had felt the same way.'

Emily was surprised; it was the second time her mother had mentioned her parents today when normally she never spoke of them at all. Not one of the O'Sullivan children had ever met their maternal grandparents. As far as they were concerned, they didn't have any. Maria was alone in the world, except for the ghost of her brother, Ted.

'Do you think your parents are still alive, Mam?' she asked tentatively.

Maria shook her head and sighed. 'I've no idea.'

'But they're only in Cork?'

'They might as well be on the other side of the world, as far as I'm concerned. My parents were afraid of me, of my illness, and I was a huge embarrassment to them. More than once they tried to lock me in an asylum for good, but my brother, Ted, wouldn't allow it.' Her eyes welled at the memory. 'I would so love to see him again, Em. He stood up to them, my cold and heartless parents. They barely endured each other and had no time for me, but they were a bit afraid of him, afraid he would put it around about the kind of people they really were. Their image was important to them. Having a lunatic for a daughter was bad enough, but to have everyone know, and then to have them judge how they dealt with it would have been a shame they were not willing to endure.'

Emily's heart broke for her poor mother. Being raised by Maria had been very hard on Emily and her brother and sisters, as she was so unpredictable, swinging from being absurdly full of energy and happiness to being in the depths of despair. But at least their mother hadn't made any of them feel unloved. 'That must have been terrible for you, being raised by people like that?'

Marie wiped her eyes and smiled bravely. 'It was, but I had Ted to care for me. And then I met Paudie, and well, after that, everything changed. I couldn't believe someone like your dad, who could have had anyone, picked me.'

'He adored you, Mam. Everyone knew it.'

Maria nodded. 'I'm so glad you and Lena told me what happened to Paudie. For all those years, I could never make sense of the way he died. He was never careless with his gun, so how he could have let it get in bad enough condition to backfire would go around and around in my brain. Knowing the truth gave me a sort of closure on his death. I didn't feel so abandoned, and I started to feel able to love again. And then Klaus was so kind to me.'

Emily hugged her mother again tightly. 'I wish Daddy were still here – we all do – but he would be so happy for you now, Mam. I know he would.'

'He would be, I know. He was always so generous, just wanting to take away my pain, to make me feel safe.'

'And now Klaus will do that for you in the future.'

'He does it already, Em. He really does.'

CHAPTER 9

he wedding Mass was lovely, celebrated in the university chapel by Father Tom Corrigan, who was the chaplain and a friend of Klaus. Maria looked hardly older than Emily in a dress she had made for herself, a simple shift of cream satin with a hint of a train that barely brushed the floor. Her long pale hair hung loose down her back, capped by a delicate veil made of the lace she'd picked out in the shop, with a few white flowers entwined in it.

Blond Nellie and dark-haired Sarah made gorgeous bridesmaids in their white dresses sprigged with tiny pale-blue flowers, and Molly and May were maids of honour, both truly beautiful in long pale-blue silk slip dresses with their scraggy fair hair cut into lovely short bobs. Neither of the twins had even the slightest interest in fashion or dresses – they were only happy when up to their ears in cow dung and manure – and it had taken all Lena and Emily could do to drag them to the hairdresser's in Kilteegan Bridge and make them put on a dash of lipstick.

Klaus looked even smarter and neater than usual, in a light-grey suit and top hat, a crimson carnation in his buttonhole to go with his bright-crimson tie. Jack, as best man, was in the good tailor-made black suit he'd worn to Mass every Sunday for years. There'd been a discussion about who should walk Maria up the aisle, and Maria had decided on Skipper, who seemed quite overcome by the honour. When the Montana cowboy led Maria into the church, Lena hardly recognised him. He looked so completely different in a dark suit and a tie, his long blond hair brushed and tied back in a ponytail, and she realised she'd never seen him in anything before but jeans and a plaid shirt.

The university campus was empty, as the students were all gone home for the summer, and the wedding party were able to have their photographs taken in the Quadrangle, surrounded by handsome Victorian limestone buildings with leaded windows.

Klaus joked that only people who had graduated were allowed to walk across the Quadrangle's perfectly manicured lawns; the old myth was if you walked on the grass before conferring, you'd never graduate. Maria laughed and said her days of education had ended when her parents took her out of school when she was fourteen, so she ran boldly across the grass and posed again for the photographer right in the centre of the Quad. Lena and Emily glanced at each other, sharing that age-old worry that Maria's high spirits were the portent of a crashing low to come, but Eli saw the look and leant in to reassure them.

'She's just happy. She'll be fine,' he murmured. 'The new treatment has made all the difference. It could be years before her next episode.'

Lena relaxed and exhaled. She trusted her husband completely with everything, including her mother's care.

The wedding photographer was concentrating on Maria, and he beckoned Klaus to join his bride in the centre of the Quad. Lena sat down on a stone bench to watch the guests mingle. Blackie and his mother were strolling the paths; Peggy Crean looked lovely in a lilac skirt and jacket. Eli was chatting to Klaus's academic friends, one of whom kept looking over his shoulder at Peggy as if he was rather taken by her. And the twins were showing Pádraig and Sarah some unusual flowers in the President's Garden.

Emmet and Nellie had drifted off together, clearly finding all the grown-ups boring and ridiculous. Nellie had decided to be annoyed all over again with Emily for not letting her wear a white minidress instead of the demure Laura Ashley maxidress, and Emmet still hadn't apologised to Eli for his outburst about Stanford University and the car. The usual warmth between Emmet and Eli seemed to be gone for now, and Lena longed for it to return.

Emmet was showing his cousin the large standing stones in the north wing of the Quadrangle. He was so handsome, his dark-red hair gleaming with copper streaks in the sunlight, taller than his father, Malachy, perhaps because the men in Lena's family were all over six foot. She could hear him explaining to Nellie how the crosshatched rows of lines carved into the stones were words in ogham, the ancient Irish alphabet, and dated from the Bronze Age to the Middle Ages. Nellie didn't look that interested; she was filing an errant fingernail that had been caught on the zip of her dress moments before the ceremony.

'They're like chalk and cheese, our pair.' Emily smiled, sitting down beside Lena and following her sister's eyes. 'I wish some of Emmet's studious nature would rub off on Nellie. She doesn't give a hoot about school, only dresses and hair and make-up. She thinks she's the epitome of all things cool.'

'There are no flies on our Nellie, Em, don't you worry about her. She'll buy and sell us all yet.'

'Oh, don't I know it. And she has Blackie running after her like a butler.' Emily gave a resigned sigh. 'Well, she's a good girl and she'll be fine. A couple of weeks ago, I was wondering if she might have some poor innocent boy on the go, but there doesn't seem to be any lad on the horizon, as far as I can see. The farmers' sons coming into the shop are always making eyes at her, but she doesn't even notice them. I suppose she's not sixteen yet so probably doesn't think of boys that way just yet.'

'Ah, I'd say she has her sights set on something a bit more exciting than a farmer's boy from Kilteegan Bridge, Em.'

'No more than you did yourself then.' Emily gave her a wink.

It was true. Lena had no interest in the local boys when she was young; she wanted more than the little rural village had to offer. But having seen the harsh reality of life, the lure of home and family had brought her back, though with a foreign husband. She and Eli always laughed at how Kilteegan Bridge had seen Eli as such an exotic specimen, when he was only from Cardiff, the other side of the Irish Sea. Of course he was German and Jewish as well, but because of his strong Welsh accent, people usually assumed he was British born and bred.

The photographer began packing up his camera and tripod, and Klaus called everyone to follow him and his bride to the beautiful Aula Maxima, a book-lined room, ornately decorated, where a sherry reception had been laid on by the university. The president popped in to wish the newlyweds well, and young waitresses circled the room with tiny snacks as glasses were refreshed.

Lena popped out to the ladies, and on her way back, she saw Skipper leaning against a wall, smoking a cigarette, and walked over to him. 'Hi, Skipper. You look very handsome today.'

'Hey, Lena, how're you doin'? It sure is a nice weddin', right? Your mama looks happier than I've ever seen her.'

Lena smiled. 'Well, if a woman can't be happy on her wedding day, I suppose there isn't much hope. It was lovely of you to give her away.'

He gave her his slow smile, one that animated his whole handsome face. 'Well, it was a special experience for me as well. That'll be my first and last time walking up the aisle, I'm guessing.'

'Sure, you might be married yourself one day…' Her voice trailed off as she realised she'd spoken without thinking.

Skipper took a drag of his cigarette and gave her a sidelong glance, his sapphire-blue eyes thoughtful.

She changed the subject. 'Jack tells me you are going to America for a visit.'

He pushed himself off the wall, and they strolled back together towards the sherry reception. 'We sure are. I ain't been back in seventeen years, and a lot's happened. We're gonna visit my brother and his wife. They got kids now, and I ain't never met my nieces, so that's gonna be nice, and then we're going to San Francisco to meet up with some friends.'

'Do you ever think of going back for good?' she asked, dreading the answer. She couldn't imagine being away from Ireland for seventeen years, so why wouldn't Skipper be homesick for America? To her relief, he shook his head.

'Nah, I love the farm here, and it's a good life. I ain't never had roots before I came here. We moved around all the time when I was a kid, and then my mama died and my old man took off not long after that, so I never really had a home. I feel like I got that now, so...' He shrugged.

'I'm glad. We'd hate to lose you.' Lena stopped and turned to him, standing on tiptoe to give him a kiss on the cheek. She and Skipper had always got along but had never been demonstrative, and she wanted him to know how much he meant to her. 'I'm glad you see Ireland as your home, and us as your family too, I hope?'

He smiled. 'I only ever had Wyatt. He's just a few years older than me, so he weren't no father figure or nothin'. I bummed around for a few years and got known round about for being good with horses, so I always had work, but I never settled nowhere. Then I met Jack and came to Ireland with him, and finally found a place to stop.'

Lena nodded, pleased. 'You know, back then Jack was so quiet. We were stunned when he said he was going to go to Montana to study farming techniques and things like that – we'd never known anyone to go there. There would have been families in the parish who'd had people in New York or Boston, but never out there. But off he went, and when he arrived home with you in tow, well, you were the most exotic thing to ever hit Kilteegan Bridge, more so even than Eli and Father Otawe, and I think you might still be actually. I remember Bina Kingston was very anxious to show off her second cousin, a nun from Philadelphia, but it still didn't beat a real live cowboy – we only saw them in the pictures.'

Skipper laughed. 'Exotic in one place is plain ordinary someplace else,' he said as they reached the Aula Maxima.

Before they could enter, Jack stumbled out of the party, looking more animated than usual. 'There you are, my two favourite people in all the world.' He grinned, holding out his arms, and Lena realised he was a little drunk. He looked gorgeous in his suit. He was fair-haired like Maria and Emily and the twins, though his hair had darkened to a sandy-brown as he aged, and his pale skin was freckled from all the time he spent outdoors.

Beaming, her brother moved towards Skipper. Skipper laughed at seeing the normally quiet Jack acting so exuberantly. 'OK, Jackie-boy, time for some fresh air for you, I think. We got a meal and speeches to get through yet.'

'There's a nice walk down by the river, just beyond that belt of trees,' suggested Lena. She remembered walking there with Malachy years ago when he was a young student at this very university.

'Thank you, ma'am,' Skipper said, still laughing. 'I think he needs that.'

Lena stood and watched, smiling as the two young men crossed the grounds of the university towards the river.

* * *

THE WEDDING MEAL at the Imperial Hotel was delicious and the speeches short but poignant. Klaus had insisted on paying for everything, including for everyone from Kilteegan Bridge to stay over in the hotel; no expense was spared. Blackie had at first offered to drive his mother and Jingo home early, but Peggy had looked so sad. She had never stayed in a hotel before, and it seemed cruel to do her out of the opportunity.

Emily's evening was a bit spoilt as a result, because although Jingo Crean had stayed away from the ceremony, he'd turned up at the reception, clearly keener on the free food and drinks than he was on the religious side of things.

His mother, who was sitting with Emily and Blackie, kept beaming at the sight of her son. He was down at the far end of the table next to Jack and Skipper, who had been told to keep an eye on him. 'Dear Jing… I mean, John. It's so wonderful he's left his bad past behind him – he's a new man altogether. He takes such good care of me. He bought me a beautiful flower the other day, a gorgeous purple and white orchid in a ceramic pot.'

Emily met Lena's eyes across the table; Lena went pink and looked like she didn't know whether to laugh or explode. Every year around this time, Anthea O'Halloran, the mother of Doc's godson, Mike, came from Dublin to leave a potted purple and white orchid on Doc's grave in the Kilteegan cemetery, explaining that the colours symbolised Doc's honour and integrity. It could be a coincidence that Jingo had given his mother the exact same expensive flower, but…

At least Jingo was in a smart suit, his black hair greased with pomade and curling slightly around his ears. Emily watched surreptitiously as he flirted with the waitress, who was giggling and blushing. Why did women go for Jingo? To her he looked like nothing so much as a ferret, with his high cheekbones, hollow cheeks and very narrow dark eyes, but maybe he was better looking than she imagined and her hatred of him clouded her judgement.

She tried not to keep glancing in his direction, but each time she did, he caught her eye, a self-satisfied look on his horrible face. Emily wasn't naturally a person who took a set against people, but Jingo was a penance.

Blackie and his mother had worked so hard – not just in the shop, there too – to rebuild their reputations as respectable people, trustworthy business owners, against all the odds, and Emily loved them for it. If this upstart thought he could come back and plunge the Crean family name back into the gutter, then he would have her to answer to.

She wished she could relax and enjoy the night, but she felt afraid to let him out of her sight. She tensed as he winked at the waitress and indicated for her to top up his already half-full wine glass. He'd already ordered a T-bone steak, and now he had two desserts in front of him. She was certain she'd seen him pocket a silver teaspoon; at least she was sure it had been there one minute and gone the next.

'Ignore him,' Blackie murmured in her ear. 'He's enjoying watching you get annoyed.'

'I know,' she whispered back, 'but he's just being so greedy.'

'John's having such a lovely time. It's a pity the seating plan didn't put him with us, the whole family together,' said Peggy. 'Blackie, I wonder if you wouldn't think again about letting John manage the shop in Cork. I know you say he has no experience of retail, but do you know he told me only yesterday that when he was in England, he spent two years managing this huge wholesale business? I can't remember the name of it now. He says retail is in his blood. Both you boys got it from me, he says.'

'Well, it wasn't from our father,' said Blackie lightly. Dick Crean had never lifted a finger around the business in his life. He and Peggy had inherited it off his wife's parents, and the only thing Dick Crean had contributed was the name, back when it was still called Crean's Hardware.

'So you'll think about it?'

Blackie hesitated; he hated upsetting his mother.

'I'm sorry, Peggy, no, we won't,' said Emily sharply. 'I know you're Jingo's mother and want to believe he is all reformed and everything – I'd be the same about Nellie if she went off the rails, God forbid – but he's only been home for a couple of weeks and that's simply not long enough to tell whether a leopard has changed his spots. I'm sorry.'

Peggy looked downcast and sighed. 'I know, but John says look how Blackie turned his life around after you came on the scene, Emily, and he thinks his brother should be glad for him for doing the same.'

Emily was a less fiery character than Lena, but she still had her moments, and she wasn't going to let her lovely husband be compared to his wastrel brother. 'Peggy, Blackie was never like Jingo. He's always been as honest as the day is long. Everything good about him, he got from you, while Jingo is his father all over again. I could never have loved Blackie at all if he was remotely like Jingo. And it wasn't Blackie's character that was holding him back when I married him, it was that father and brother of his. As soon as they were out of the picture, the business flourished, and so did you, Peggy. Don't forget that, and don't let that son of yours pull you down again. The next thing, we'll have Dick moving back in after him, and then where will we be?'

Peggy's shoulders slumped. The threat of Dick coming back to Kilteegan Bridge was an awful one, and Emily hated making it, but there was a truth to it all the same. If Jingo got his feet under the table and started leeching off the business, then whether he had another family in England or not, Dick Crean would not be far behind.

'Well, Emily, at least can you call him John instead of Jingo?' Mrs Crean asked plaintively.

Emily stiffened, and Blackie put his hand on hers and murmured, 'Well, well,' which was his way of saying to move on.

'Maybe we will call him John, Mam,' Blackie said. 'Sure, it is the name he was christened by. Now how about a dance? The music has started up in the ballroom.' And he took Peggy off and then arrived back for Emily only a few minutes later, saying Peggy had been swept away by one of Klaus's grizzled academics who seemed to have taken quite a shine to the diminutive woman.

Emily felt a wave of love for her husband. He was trying his best to manage an impossible situation between his mother and brother and her as well. She knew he'd rather she was kinder about Jingo in front of Peggy, but she simply couldn't afford to let down her guard. And there was no way she was going to call Jingo 'John'; that was just him trying to manipulate Peggy and Blackie into agreeing he'd changed. She suspected Blackie of weakening recently in regards to his brother; they'd been out for a drink together, and Jingo had paid, and Blackie had commented on it favourably.

'He's just trying to soften you up,' she'd told Blackie firmly, 'and don't you dare fall for it.' Sometimes she felt like she was the only thing standing between him and his mother and their total destruction.

* * *

'Hi, Emmet.'

Emmet blinked and looked up to see his Uncle Blackie's elegant, good-looking brother, John Crean, standing over him, two glasses of whiskey in his hands. He brightened. 'Hello, John, good to see you.'

'Do you mind if I join you?'

'Of course not.' Emmet indicated the empty chair at his table, on the edge of the dance floor. Nellie had gone off dancing with Sarah. Everyone was making fools of themselves doing the twist; he was embarrassed for them even if they weren't embarrassed for themselves. Sometimes even Nellie sunk to the level of Kilteegan Bridge.

'They'd mortify us, our families sometimes, wouldn't they?' John grinned, nodding towards the dance floor as he sat down, and Emmet laughed, glad to find a kindred spirit.

'God, yes, they're such hicks sometimes, it makes my toes curl. They don't understand that in other places, people don't go on like this.'

'Seen a bit of the world, have you?' John asked.

Emmet nodded. 'I go to San Francisco now and again. California.'

John Crean nodded gravely. He didn't seem at all surprised to hear Emmet had spent time abroad. 'I know, it's the same in London. It's very hard to come back to the old country when you've been abroad and seen what's out there, isn't it? You come back different, and then it's hard to fit in. It's only my poor mother is so lonely now that she's not in her own place over the shop any more – my brother moved her out – or I wouldn't have come back here at all. But someone has to mind her. Drink?' John pushed one of the two glasses towards Emmet and held up his own. 'Or are you too young?'

In reply, Emmet threw the whiskey back in one like he'd seen men doing in the films. It took every fibre of his being not to choke. His eyes watered, and the whiskey scalded his throat like paint stripper on its way down. He'd never had anything so horrible in his whole life, but he hoped he'd managed to hide it well enough for this sophisticated man not to guess at his inexperience.

With a slight smile, Blackie's brother downed his own drink and immediately went to the bar, replacing the empties with two more. This time Emmet cradled the amber liquid in his hands and sipped cautiously, and he was relieved to see the other man do the same.

Once he got used to the taste, it wasn't too bad after all. A warm glow spread through his midsection, and he wondered why nobody in the family had ever spoken to him about John Crean. He knew Blackie's brother had gone to England when he was twenty-eight, nine or ten years ago, but hadn't realised he was back until they met up in Kilteegan Bridge yesterday. Emmet hadn't recognised John, of course, but somehow John had recognised him.

'Emmet Kogan!' he'd called, running after Emmet up the street. He was holding up Emmet's post office book, with the letter from Malachy and two ten-dollar bills still inside it. 'You dropped this.'

Emmet was very grateful for John's honesty. He'd had the book in the back pocket of his jeans, but it must have slipped out. It would have been upsetting to lose that twenty dollars, which brought the amount he had in his account to just over one thousand pounds, a huge exciting sum that had accumulated since Malachy had started sending him money when he was thirteen.

He'd been thinking about that money while he sat here, ignoring Nellie, who was waving wildly for him to join her on the dance floor. He'd never spent any of it. His mother had insisted he save it all for college, probably because she didn't want him having lots of cash to flash around while his brother and sister just had the normal amount of pocket money, the same as they gave to Emmet.

Things had changed now, he thought. He had turned sixteen, and Malachy had said he would pay for Stanford, and maybe it was about time his parents stopped treating him like a child and allowed him to spend his own money on what he liked.

Besides, if he was going to impress Isobel Lamkin at the Carbery Hunt, he needed a big, fast, powerful horse, far better than the one his parents were likely to buy for him. He'd practically given Molly to Sarah now, so his mother could hardly accuse him of putting himself first over his little brother and sister if he bought himself a replacement.

Speaking of which, he could see Lena bearing down on him, a stern look on her face.

'Emmet, please go and check on Pádraig – Dad sent him up to the room. It's quite late enough for you all to be up actually. Take Sarah and Nellie too, and off to bed. We won't be long, and I'll check on you all in a few minutes.'

Emmet felt his cheeks burn with shame. How could his mother speak to him like he was five years old in front of the sophisticated John Crean?

'Good evening, Mrs Kogan. It's a lovely wedding, and your mother is looking so well,' said John courteously.

Lena nodded and said coldly, 'Thank you.' Then she turned to her son. 'Emmet, go.'

Emmet got furiously to his feet.

'Night, Emmet,' said John, raising his glass in a salute.

'Goodnight, John,' said Emmet, then he stalked past his mother without even acknowledging her.

CHAPTER 10

*E*mmet's heart sank as Molly and May waved enthusiastically to him across the yard. He was only here to find Skipper and work on the new horse with him, but his aunts seemed to have other plans. They were hard to stand up to because there were two of them for the price of one. They sometimes seemed like a single person, always dressed the same in dungarees and wellingtons and finishing each other's sentences.

'Hi, Emmet!' they called.

He hung back cautiously. 'I'm just here to see Skipper and the bay mare.'

'Sorry, Jack and Skipper had to go to the creamery this morning, some kind of a meeting about getting a bulk tank to collect the milk instead of us having to take it in churns every day. It would be a godsend if it can be done.'

Emmet felt he couldn't care less if the milk was collected by reindeers. 'Fine, I'll come back later.'

But they weren't going to let him get away with that. 'Don't go running off, you lazy article. There's lots to be done, and it's your school summer holidays now so you've all the time in the world.'

He groaned. There was no getting out of it. If they told on him to his mother, she wouldn't back him on the horse idea, so it was best to go along with them. 'Oh all right, just till Skipper gets back. What needs doing?'

'We have to do the pen for the hens. We need to take out the posts and move the chicken wire to a different patch of grass – they have that bit pecked to nothing. But we need to dig a trench around the perimeter and bury the wire about a foot horizontally to the ground to confuse the fox. He's around there a lot, so it's a game of wits, us against him.'

The two of them roared with laughter. They seemed to think going head-to-head in a battle of wits with a fox was the most enter-taining thing in the world, and they looked at Emmet as if expecting him to find it hilarious too. When he didn't laugh with them, they looked puzzled. He sighed to himself.

His twin aunts, who were only three years older than him, had barely made it out of primary school, and he doubted either of them had ever read anything more than the *Farmers Journal* in their lives, yet they looked down on him like he was the strange one. Well, he had bigger dreams than being up to his eyes in cow dung for the rest of his life, and if they didn't like it, bad luck to them.

'Fine,' he said heavily. 'What do you want me to do?'

'Right, well, if you get a couple of shovels from the barn, we'll get started. And we'll need the pickaxe too to pry the stakes out.'

Emmet arrived back from the barn with the tools and began to swing the pickaxe at the well-grounded stakes supporting the hen run. He was strong for sixteen – riding horses had given him a lot of muscle – but he kept on missing, and after he split one stake in half, May, in poorly concealed frustration, took the pick and swung it expertly, pulling out the next stake after three well-placed blows.

'Can you get the hens into the coop while we do this?' she asked Emmet.

He had picked up a shovel to help Molly dig the trenches, but he threw it down willingly and began to shoo the hens towards the door of the coop. The fat poultry were unhappy to be taken from their sunny patch and refused to cooperate.

'They won't go in,' he said in frustration as the hens clucked and flapped around.

'That's because it's daytime. They only go in at night usually,' explained Molly patronisingly as she shovelled away.

'So what am I supposed to do?'

'Try luring them in with a bucket of scraps?'

'They're not even looking at me.'

May pulled another stake out. 'Don't worry, they have great eyesight, better than humans actually, and they've three eyelids. They can move each eye independently and a full 360 degrees, so if you just crawl inside the coop and bring the bucket with you, they'll see you and follow. Won't you, girls?' she added, as if the flock could understand her better than her nephew could.

Emmet was horrified. He was not a fan of manure at the best of times, and today he had a good pair of trousers on. 'You want me to crawl into the coop?'

'Yes, the actual coop. Honest to God, Emmet, sometimes you're as useful as an ashtray on a motorbike.'

'Into the actual coop?'

'Yes!' May looked like she was trying not to laugh, and then she did, and then Molly started giggling as well, and within seconds the two of them were doubled over laughing. Emmet could feel his face getting redder by the second. He didn't know if they were winding him up by telling him to climb into the coop, or if they meant it and thought it was funny he was so reluctant to do it. Either way, they were intolerable.

Sick of his aunts' nonsense, he stormed off and would have left and gone home, but Jack and Skipper came trundling up the lane in Jack's ancient car and piled out to greet him, followed by the two young sheepdogs who worked the flock now that old Thirteen had died happily in her sleep after seventeen long years. The entire family was so sad after her, she'd been Paudie's dog, but in her honour the next two were called Fourteen and Fifteen.

Emmet was very fond of his uncle and Skipper. They were completely different from the twins; in fact they were the most interesting members of his family as far as he was concerned. They had lived on both sides of the Atlantic, and they even knew all about San Francisco where Malachy lived and were talking about going there for a holiday. He wondered if they might let him join them on their trip. They could stop off at Malachy's place and maybe they could all go out together.

'Emmet, come and see the bay mare. She's about ready for riding now, I reckon,' said Skipper, and Emmet eagerly fell in step beside him. Jack turned off to see to his Tamworth pigs, with Skipper shouting after him to be careful around the new boar, who was a vicious animal.

Jack was experimenting with breeding pigs these days, which was apparently a very exact science, but the animals were half savage in Skipper's opinion, and he confided in Emmet that the only possible outcome that would please him was to see them as sausages. He was especially not keen on the new boar, he said. He was worried Jack would get trampled to death by him, which was ironic given the crazy animals Skipper worked with.

Emmet was fascinated when he watched Skipper with the horses. People from all over Ireland brought their unmanageable animals to the Montana cowboy, and he charged them to keep the horse for a few weeks. By the time the owner came back, stallions that were deadly dangerous were happily trotting along behind him, docile as anything. Skipper insisted that the owner stick around to learn how to communicate with the horse once he'd calmed the animal down, and it was intriguing to see him teach the humans too.

Just last week a man from County Waterford had arrived with a bay mare that had almost kicked the horsebox out on the way. The man had a massive bruise on his neck where she'd charged him. She clearly had the makings of a fantastic racehorse, long clean legs and powerful haunches, but not one of the grooms in his yard would go near her, he said. Skipper was his only hope.

Emmet had hung around listening to Skipper talking with the man once they'd got the mare into a stable, and Skipper had drawn Emmet into the conversation, introducing him as another expert on horses, which made him feel good, like he belonged.

'The thing y'all gotta understand is horses are pack animals,' Skipper explained to the mare's owner. 'They respond like pack animals, and they need a leader, someone to follow. That's what they want to do instinctively. So if you can make yourself the leader, then that animal will do as you want him or her to do. You ain't never gonna get the best from an animal you break by force.' He tipped his cowboy hat back on his head, wiping his forehead with a handkerchief he had stuffed in his pocket. The exertion of trying to manoeuvre the half-crazed animal out of its box and into its stall had them all sweating, Jack, Emmet, Skipper and the man himself. She'd bitten Jack on the shoulder and kicked the man a glancing blow on the shin.

The twins had refused to help or go within fifty yards of her, which rather pleased Emmet, because it was nice to be better at something around the farm than his aunts for once.

'Now she could be broken that way,' continued Skipper, 'but I'm not your guy if that's what you want. A broken animal is just that, broken. You can break a spirit of a horse by force, for sure, sticks and pain. And if y'all hurt 'em enough, they'll do what you want them to 'cause they're scared. But jus' like me and you, we're not going to give our best performance if we're scared half to death now, are we?'

The Waterford man looked sceptical but nodded.

'Mister, I can get your horse to do what you want her to because she wants to, because it's her nature to follow instruction from the pack leader, but that's one scared animal you got there, and it's gonna take some time and a whole lot of patience.'

'That mare is out of Medusa and by Hoopers Fancy. The blood is there, she's strong and fast as lightning, she runs like the wind and can jump too, but she's totally out of control, as you can see.' The man lit a cigarette. 'She could win the Grand National, but at the moment, she'd kill the grooms and the jockey before she got to the starting line.'

'Well, give her a month with me and then we'll see. If it doesn't work, you can have half your money back, but that ain't never never happened yet.'

Still looking doubtful, the man handed over a wad of cash and departed.

Emmet had leant on the fence of the sand arena watching intently as Skipper brought the mare from her stall and walked her around. He kept his head down, never making eye contact and never showing any fear, though the horse bucked and reared up, her terrifying hooves lashing out. After maybe an hour of patient walking, with Skipper not reacting at all to whatever she did, the horse slowly started to behave differently. She was still skittish, but she stopped trembling and rolling her eyes, and she lowered her head.

'That's the easy bit,' Skipper said, coming over to Emmet with the horse walking nervously behind him. 'She trusts me a little now, but she still hates the rest of the world. Someone done somethin' pretty bad to her to make her so scared. Horses, just like people, aren't born mean – they gotta learn it, and it's hard to unlearn. Do you want to soothe her a while?'

Emmet was delighted that Skipper thought he could do this, but at the same time, he was alarmed. All the horses he'd owned had come to him well ridden; he'd never had to handle a wild one for himself. He took a deep breath. He could do this; he could prove himself to Skipper. He climbed over the fence into the arena.

As soon as the cowboy handed him the halter, the mare started quivering again, sweating and snorting and showing the whites of her eyes.

'Now keep your head down, just plod along quietly. The idea is she starts to mirror you,' Skipper said in a confident voice. 'And don't wind the halter around your hand – she'll pull your arm out of your shoulder if she takes off on you.'

Emmet set off around the sand, his eyes on the ground, trying not to show his fear and hoping the horse couldn't smell it off him; he was sweating like a horse himself. He kept his touch on the halter as light as he could and just went on walking and walking, ignoring the mare's bucking and rearing. Gradually, he felt her settle down, and amazingly, on the fifth circuit of the arena, she fell into step just behind him and nudged him between the shoulder blades with her nose.

'Now turn and blow into her nostrils,' said Skipper. He was leaning against the fence nearby, his thumbs hooked into his belt. 'That's the way horses say hello to each other.'

Very cautiously, Emmet turned, still not making eye contact, and blew up the horse's quivering nostrils. The horse snorted back and laid her heavy head on his shoulder, and when Emmet gently patted the side of her neck, she shuddered and sighed as if with pleasure.

'Now lead her back to the stables and let her take a good drink of water from the trough. Give her a few pony nuts out of your hand and a feed of hay in the stall,' instructed Skipper, and Emmet did as he was told. The mare flatly refused to go into the stall at first, but he stood still and patient while she had a good look around and snorted hello to the black stallion, who had his head poking out over the half-door of his own stall. She finally agreed to go in and stood munching hay while he removed her halter.

'Good work.' Skipper was waiting for him out in the yard, sitting on a bale of hay and smoking a cigarette. 'Want to come back and do the same thing all over again tomorrow?'

'Yes, I do.' Emmet was surprised how keen he felt. Nothing in Kilteegan Bridge had enthused him like this for a long time; his mind had been fixed on the future and Stanford and San Francisco. But the mare was a challenge, and she was gorgeous, clear-eyed with a glossy bay coat and a flash of white between her eyes. 'I'll come up every morning if you like.'

Skipper nodded and took another deep draw on his cigarette, and Emmet decided then was the time to ask whether Skipper thought the black stallion's owner would sell him the horse for the thousand he had saved in his post office account. He explained he'd been keeping it for his college fund, but now Malachy had announced he was going to pay his way through college, so he was hoping his mother would let him spend it any way he wanted.

The cowboy pushed his Stetson back on his head and smiled slowly. 'Well, now, I'm 'fraid that buck is worth upwards of twenty thousand now, Emmet. You coulda bought him I guess when the guy brought him – remember how nuts he was? But now he's sweet and willing and still fast, I think, so he'll be takin' him back and makin' a fortune with him.'

Emmet's eyes widened; he'd never known a horse could be that expensive. It looked like his dream of owning the stallion was just that – a dream.

'Don't you worry, Emmet,' said Skipper, stretching and getting to his feet. 'When a horse is meant for you, it'll find you. It's more like love than ownin' someone. It's a match or it ain't. Now I'm going to check on Jackie-boy to make sure that there pig ain't torn him limb from limb.'

Ever since that day, Emmet had been coming up to the farm every morning during the week to work with the bay mare.

* * *

AFTER AN HOUR of riding the mare for the first time, very carefully and with a light touch, not letting her go faster than a walk and with Skipper's hand on the halter, Emmet headed down to the village, thinking he might buy a new noseband for her, a nice soft red leather one from Jimmy Piper, the leather worker.

A couple of boys in his year were sitting on the wall outside the new little garage just at the start of the town, smoking and commenting on people. They shouted at him as he went past.

'Oi, Professor! Come and join us!'

It was Benny McLoughlin and his moronic sidekick, Rob McGrath, the boys Nellie had said he should be sympathetic to because they hadn't his advantages. Emmet didn't agree with her. He was damned if he was going to hang out with two idiots who could barely spell their own names and thought it hilarious he got straight As when they could barely scrape an E between them.

He'd always thought his parents should have sent him to Larksbridge in Dublin; they would have taken him without question because Malachy had been a student there. At least this next year would be his last at his crappy little country secondary school, then he could head out to the States and mingle with the brains of Stanford, whether his parents wanted him to or not. He was sick of being kept down and treated like a useless kid by everyone except Skipper.

Something hit him between his shoulder blades and stuck briefly before it fell. He spun around to see a dog turd lying on the pavement, and with a shout of fury, he grabbed it up and flung it straight back at the boys on the wall, where it hit Benny right in the face. It wasn't the wisest move. Benny and his friend weren't the sharpest knives in the drawer, but they were big strapping lads, and while Emmet was strong and tall, he was slender, and it was two against one.

He braced himself for a beating, but before anything could happen, Benny was lying flat on his back, clutching his groin and groaning, and Rob was racing off down the main street in a panic.

'Don't mind the lowlifes of Kilteegan Bridge, Emmet.' John Crean smiled, giving Benny one last gentle kick in the side. He was dressed as well as he'd been at the wedding, and his silk shirt wasn't even ruffled by what had just happened. 'This one won't be singing bass for a while.'

'Oh…um…thanks…' Emmet was reeling; the whole thing had been so quick.

'Era, a swift kick where it hurts is all it takes most times.' John winked at him and wrinkled his nose. 'C'mere, boy, that shirt stinks, though. Come up to my place, and you can get washed and I'll give you one of mine. Mam's gone to Cork with your Auntie Emily, so we've the place to ourselves.'

Still in shock, Emmet followed the young man up the street to Mrs Crean's house. The bright cottage was lovely, sunny and spotless, and John let him through into the beautifully tended back garden bright with summer flowers, where he washed his hands with carbolic soap under the outside tap and took off his shirt to rinse it through and hang it on the line.

Back inside, he found John rooting in a pile of ironing in the kitchen, upending neatly folded clothes all over the scrubbed pine counter. He extracted a very good–quality shirt with a grandfather collar and handed it to Emmet. 'That's for you.'

Impressed by the style of it, Emmet pulled it on; it smelled of soap and starch. 'Thanks. I'll get it washed and back to you tomorrow.'

'Not a bit of it. I've plenty of newer ones, and that one's at least a year old. I was going to give it to the charity shop, but you keep it. It's a Harrods shirt. They wear well, and the fashion is good enough for around here. Sure, it's ahead of the times for Kilteegan Bridge. Cuppa? Or a glass of something stronger?'

Emmet had a feeling he was being old-fashioned himself when he asked for tea, and sure enough John laughed and said something about the sun being over the yardarm. But he took down a willow-patterned teapot and set about making the tea, then brought it with some matching china cups and biscuits on a tray into the living room.

'In London, I'd have my housekeeper do this for me, but here in Kilteegan Bridge, you'll have to take me as you find me.' He smiled at Emmet. He had a pleasant baritone voice, and his accent was a sort of meld of Irish and English, very different from the musical sing-song Cork voices Emmet heard around him every day. Emmet had the Cork accent himself, of course, but he'd done his best to flatten it since his holidays in San Francisco, where no one had understood him.

Suddenly he felt an urge to impress Blackie's brother. 'Our house-keeper is Mrs Moriarty from the village. She's very good.'

'Ah yes, poor Frances. I'm surprised your parents took her on, but it's hard to get staff in a small town.' John gave him a sympathetic look.

Slightly crushed, Emmet looked around for something intelligent to say. He pointed to a large oil painting of the village with the azure ocean glinting in the distance. 'That's a lovely painting.'

'My mother did that. It's fine for a local landscape. I like to encourage her, although she's no van Gogh or Michelangelo.'

Again, Emmet felt like a bit of a hick. He had thought there was genuine talent in Peggy's painting, but maybe he was wrong; it was just his horizons were so narrow.

'Well, I meant it was good for an amateur,' he said apologetically. Then he felt he was being disrespectful towards Peggy and added, 'Professor Lamkin commissioned her to paint a picture of his new greyhound for fifty pounds.'

'Fifty pounds for one of Mam's paintings?' John laughed in amazement, but not as if he were impressed, just as if this were more proof of the backwardness of Kilteegan Bridge. 'God, I love this place.' He stood up, put a shot of whiskey in his tea from a bottle of Powers on the sideboard, drained his cup and fixed Emmet with his narrow eyes, so narrow they seemed like black slits with none of the whites showing. 'So where were you off to when those gobshites were jeering you?'

'To buy a leather noseband off Jimmy Piper for a horse I'm... breaking in.' He would have said 'soothing' instead of 'breaking', like Skipper did, but somehow he thought John Crean would think that sounded silly, even a bit girly.

'Not some old hack got from the Travellers, I trust?'

Emmet laughed. 'God no, a proper racehorse.'

'Oh, a racehorse?' John looked interested.

'Yes, she's out of Medusa and by Hoopers Fancy, and she's totally out of control, so I'm helping to...break her.' Emmet was pleased to find a subject that appealed to this man. He should have thought of it before; racing and hunting were gentlemen's sports. 'Do you like horses yourself?'

'I do indeed. I've a great tip for the three thirty at Cork Racecourse Mallow, Dolly's Fancy on the flat, a cast-iron guarantee, eleven to one. But I've no one who can talk sense about horseflesh to go with, and it's dull drinking champagne and smoking cigars by myself. I don't suppose you have the afternoon free?'

Emmet thought for a moment. It wasn't quite what he'd meant; he'd been asking if John liked to ride. Still, betting on horses was a gentleman's game too, and it was flattering that this sophisticated man thought Emmet knew what he was talking about. He made his decision. This was turning out to be some day, first Skipper letting him ride the mare and then John wanting him to come and drink champagne and smoke cigars, whatever that was like, at the Mallow races. He'd been thinking of buying the leather noseband and going back up to the farm, but tomorrow morning would do for that.

'I do have a couple of hours free.' He hoped he sounded casual enough, one gentleman to another.

'Good, we'll take my motor. And if I was you, I'd throw a few bob on Dolly's Fancy. Can't lose.'

'I haven't got...' He stopped. The black stallion was so far out of his reach, he'd have to lower his sights anyway, so maybe it wouldn't matter to have a few pounds less in his account. 'I haven't got many notes in my wallet. I'll have to stop by the post office.'

He suspected his parents would be appalled. They'd never put a bet on a horse in their whole lives, he was sure of it, but it was his own money and his parents need never know anyway.

And what if they did find out? He had to stop thinking like a child, feeling he wasn't allowed to spend his own money on anything he wanted. If he was going to go to the races with smart, elegant John Crean, he wanted to go as Crean's equal. Two champagne-quaffing, cigar-smoking gentlemen with independent means, enjoying the sport of kings.

CHAPTER 11

*E*li often thought being a country GP was more to do with being a listening ear than anything medical, but listening to Jimmy Piper was hard work. The cheerful little man was on one of his stories, full of people Eli didn't know and events he neither knew nor cared about, but it had to be done. Poor old Jimmy lived alone, and his only chat in the week was his visit to the doctor.

Jimmy was a leather worker, and a good one, but there wasn't much call these days for things that were lovingly handcrafted when one could get the bus up to Cork and go to Roches Stores and buy something made in a factory for a quarter of the price. Skipper still had bridles and saddles made by Jimmy, insisting they were so much better than anything he could buy elsewhere, and Emmet had recently bought a soft noseband, dipping for the first time into his account for the money, but Eli thought the old man's products were very expensive.

Jimmy was explaining at great length, and with specifics relating to dates, times and people that were not central to the tale, something to do with the mart in Bandon, a yearling and a heifer, and how some confusion had led to an altercation in a pub in the town where some man inexplicably called Frogger hit Jimmy a punch.

Jimmy had a very cavalier attitude to washing or changing his clothes, and the stink off him would knock a donkey. He had big yellow teeth and a shock of grey and orange hair plastered to his head by grease.

'Now, Dr Kogan, I knew him and all belonging to him since I was seven years of age – actually, no...I tell you a lie, I was eight, because I was below with Sister Dymphna in the national school till I was eight and we were in Sister Dymphna's class, or was it Sister Gerard? Maybe it was Sister Gerard, now I come to think of it, because she came to Kilteegan Bridge from the missions because her brother was a brother, a Capuchin, I think, in Ghana. Or no, it was the Congo, he was? I don't remember exactly. Anyway, I knew Frogger since then, so when he said that I had made a smart remark about his heifer, I thought he was messing. But he wasn't, and this is the whole crux of it...'

On and on he droned, and Eli was still none the wiser as to what his medical problem was, if there even was one. He also knew that interrupting or trying to get Jimmy to the point was a complete waste of time. Normally Margaret gave Jimmy an appointment at the end of the day so he wasn't holding everyone else up, but this time it must not have been possible. He was conscious that the waiting room was full and people were beginning to murmur outside.

Eli's mind wandered. Emmet still hadn't apologised for that outburst about his 'real father', although Lena insisted it was because the boy was ashamed and said not to push him about it, to just let it go. It was hard to pretend it hadn't happened, though, and Eli felt there was still a distance between them. But at least his son was being polite to him again, especially since Eli had started giving him driving lessons. They'd had just the one small argument the other day when Emmet wanted to take the car off by himself and Eli flatly refused. He felt his son was too young and arrogant to be given free rein on the roads. Young lads like him had a tendency to think they were invincible, and Eli had seen too many of their bodies scraped off the road when he was a young registrar in the hospital in Cardiff. They never thought it was going to happen to them.

At least Emmet wasn't spending the summer holidays lounging and sulking around the house. He was spending most of his time up at the farm with Skipper, and that was good. The cowboy was a great role model for his son, always calm and kind and sensible.

He forced himself to tune back into Jimmy's tale.

'And the thing is, Doctor, I actually didn't need shoelaces because my mother, God be good to her, made sure we had at least fifteen spare pairs in the drawer. She had a terror of running out of them, the poor woman.'

How the conversation had gone to shoelaces, Eli had no idea. 'Jimmy, that's fascinating. I could listen to you all day, but I'll have to stop you there for now. What did you need to see me about? I've a waiting room full, and I do need to get on.'

'Sure, Dr Kogan, I'm after telling you, Frogger O'Riordan attacked me for no reason whatsoever. I met him in Kit's after the mart, because I said –'

'And he hurt you, did he?' Eli swung around in his chair, facing Jimmy, determined to get to whatever the man wanted him to look at and then out of the surgery till next week.

'Hurt me?' Jimmy looked perplexed. 'Him? Hurt me? Frogger O'Riordan?' He was deeply confused. 'And he only after getting a bronze medal in the tug-of-war in 1934 when Kilteegan Bridge were up against Orbenstown? And we had no carnival the two years before that because of the blight, and the fact that Francie Kelleher's threshing machine was out of action?'

Eli was wondering if there was anywhere in the Hippocratic Oath that allowed a doctor to use his medical skills to silence a patient who was the most irritating man on the face of the earth, when he heard the commotion outside.

Jimmy was still going on and on, something about his late mother and Francie Kelleher's sister being after the same man a hundred years ago and nothing ever being right again between the two families, but Eli listened instead to what was happening in the waiting room.

'Is he here?' a cold male voice demanded.

The loud authoritarian tone of whoever it was stopped even Jimmy in his ramblings, and now both he and Eli sat listening.

There was a muffled response from Margaret, and then the voice again, hard as flint.

'Woman, I do not care in the slightest who he's with.'

'It's the priest,' whispered Jimmy, his eyes widening.

'Tell him I want to see him this very second.'

This time, Eli recognised the voice of Monsignor Collins. Despite being Jewish, Eli did go to Mass on Sundays with Lena and the children. It was a nice hour, sitting there, thinking his thoughts, communing with God in his own way. He didn't feel like a liar or a hypocrite, nothing like that; to him it was just another of God's houses. The way Eli saw it, God had many rooms in his mansion: mosques, temples, synagogues, mud huts, sacred caves. Wherever people went to sit with their community and acknowledge that there was a higher power and that they didn't have all the answers was a good thing in his opinion. He had a friend from university, Ben Webbe, a gifted surgeon now, and when they were young, Eli used to sometimes go with him to the Baptist church, especially if they were out on Saturday night. His mother, a fantastic woman from Kingston, Jamaica, was a generous and welcoming hostess, but if you slept under her roof and ate her food, then on Sunday mornings, you went to worship. Ben used to apologise, but Eli had loved it. The singing, the dancing, the young Black preacher talking about dignity and compassion – he'd learnt a lot from that man. This Monsignor Collins was a very different kettle of fish.

For one thing, Eli had heard the new priest was not best pleased with his relocation to Kilteegan Bridge, feeling it beneath him. Mrs Timlin, who was very pregnant with her fifth baby, had told Eli she had gone up to ask him to say a special Mass for the repose of the soul of her late mother on her anniversary and was greeted with a disdainful stare. It didn't stop him taking the two shillings she offered, though. On the day of the anniversary, he'd called Mrs Timlin's mother 'Mrs Timlin' as well, when in fact her name was Abina Kiely.

Mrs Timlin had written it all out on a piece of paper for him, but he obviously hadn't bothered to read it.

'Fetch him out or I'll do it myself,' the priest roared at Margaret, who was obviously still trying to stand firm.

Eli stood up. 'Excuse me, Jimmy. I'll just see what's going on here.'

He stepped out to the waiting room, which was so silent one could hear a pin drop despite it being full of people. Babies that had been fractious moments earlier were staring at the tall, powerfully built priest with his head of iron-grey hair brushed back from his high forehead. He had a pronounced widow's peak, giving him an owlish look, which was exacerbated by heavy horn-rimmed glasses. He wore a black floor-length soutane with red buttons all down the front and a red sash around his waist.

'Good afternoon, Father,' Eli began pleasantly.

'You will address me as Monsignor Collins, Kogan!' boomed the priest. Lena had told Eli that Monsignor wasn't a rank as such; a priest could not be elevated to a Monsignor. More it was an honour bestowed upon a priest by the pope in recognition of a service. It made Father Collins an Honorary Prelate apparently, and it allowed him to dress differently and behave as if he were better than anyone else, like for instance dropping Eli's own title of 'Doctor'.

'Good afternoon, Monsignor.' He caught Margaret's eye. She was red in the face, and he gave her a slight encouraging smile. 'Can I help you?'

'You will not "help" me, Kogan. You will do precisely as I say and no more about it.' The priest was breathing heavily now, clearly furious. Eli could see a vein pulsating in his neck. He also noted the priest's huge hands; they were like shovels, and if he presented as a man of the land, doing hard labour all day long, one would believe it without question.

'Well, if you'd like to come into my surgery... Jimmy, if you could excuse us?'

Jimmy was very disappointed to be removed from what could potentially be an exciting juncture of the day, but he reluctantly did as Eli asked, slipping past him into the waiting room.

The Monsignor didn't take up Eli's offer of somewhere more private. 'What I have to say to you will be heard by everyone from the pulpit anyway this Sunday, two days from now, so they might as well hear it today,' he intoned darkly.

Eli leant on the reception desk and gestured that the priest had the floor. Stopping him was not an option anyway. His patients all had their heads down, staring at the lino.

'Pope Paul VI is very clear. And in his *Humanae Vitae* of 1968, he leaves no room for conjecture or interpretation. Marital relations are more than a union of two people, yes indeed.' The Monsignor glared at those in the waiting room as everyone kept their heads bowed.

'Marriage is to unite a couple with God and His purpose. The transmission of human life is a most serious role in which a married couple collaborate with God. No individual, and no medical person for that matter, has the right to interfere in a God-given covenant that might limit divine providence.'

Eli shoved his hands in his pockets to stop himself wanting to choke the man. Several of his patients glanced at him; they had no idea why the Monsignor was going on like this, he could tell from their confused faces. But Eli knew exactly what Collins was getting at. Somehow he'd found out about Mrs Moriarty and the pill. Had the woman felt so guilty, she'd confessed? Or had she been caught out by that awful husband of hers, the Mouse? Either way, this was not good news, and it was exactly what Lena had worried about.

'And you can take your Protestant ways, *Doctor* Kogan' – this time the priest emphasised Eli's title as if to infer he doubted the validity of his credentials – 'and use them over in the heathen lands of the British, but this is a *Catholic* country and we obey God's law, as ordained by His Holiness, the pope, nobody else's.'

'I'm not a Protestant,' he heard himself say mildly, refusing to match the loud booming tone of the Monsignor. 'So on that score, as well as many others, you're wrong.'

Collins puffed up like a bullfrog. 'How dare you! If you are indeed a Catholic as you claim, then let me suggest a rapid and involved trip to confession to beg forgiveness for your most heinous sins. Our parish doesn't need morally bankrupt, deviant men using their influence to corrupt –'

'I'm not a Catholic either. I'm a Jew actually.' Eli was enjoying watching the priest nearly explode. His face was puce now; he was clearly not used to being challenged.

'A Jew! How on earth did a Jew get to administer medicine to the people of this place?' he spluttered, his attitude suggesting that someone had made a donkey the local doctor.

'I took over the practice from my wife's godfather, Dr Emmet Dolan.' Eli outwardly remained calm as a breeze; he would not let this man see how much he'd annoyed him. 'Now, Monsignor, I need to get on, so if that's all…' He spread his hands in a herding gesture, indicating that the priest should move towards the door, and heard a few almost inaudible gasps at his audacity. To speak to any member of the clergy like that was bad enough, but to a Monsignor – it was unthinkable.

'You will not dismiss me, you young upstart.' The man was really furious now, spittle spraying from his lips. 'You will not break the laws of God and His Church and suffer no consequences! And let me tell you people something.' He turned to the full waiting room. 'Having anything whatsoever to do with this person is endangering your mortal souls. You are making a choice today, the path of sin or the path of salvation, so think carefully, each and every one of you.'

'I'll tell you what we'll do so, Father.' Eli deliberately demoted him. He was in the bad books now either way, so he might as well win this battle, though he knew enough about Irish rural life to know the inevitable war to come would be a very different prospect. It was a rare beast who took on the Catholic Church and won. 'You head back into the village there, and up to the church, and you take care of your business, and I'll stay here and take care of mine. I won't interfere with your work, and I'll thank you not to interfere with mine. Good day to you now.'

He marched the furious cleric to the door, then called, 'Next patient, please,' as he strode back into his surgery. He was under no illusion – he'd drawn the battle lines – but he had no idea how he could have handled the situation better. He couldn't have the Church telling him how to practise medicine. He remembered Lena telling him about a man accusing Doc of giving his wife 'a rubber yoke that is flying in the face of God', and that Doc had told him to go home and mind his own business. But that was before the days of Monsignor Collins.

Out in the waiting room, he could hear Margaret calling out, 'Janice Walshe, please,' so at least he wasn't getting Jimmy back again, at least not right away.

For a long, long minute, nobody entered. And then the door did open, and it was Jimmy Piper again. 'Well, Doctor, it's me again, and let me tell you –'

'Hang on a moment, Jimmy.' Eli stood up and went to talk to Margaret. He wanted to quietly beg her to knock on his door after five minutes and tell him the next patient was an emergency. But when he stepped out of his surgery, the waiting room was empty.

CHAPTER 12

'Are you sure you don't mind?' John asked. 'I thought fifty pounds would be enough for the day, but with the champagne hamper and Martin's Mistress throwing a shoe, I seem to be out of brass until I can get to the bank.'

'Not at all, happy to help.' Emmet passed over another ten-pound note, and John Crean took it and shook his hand. They had a gentleman's agreement that John would pay him back the five hundred Emmet had already lent him as soon as the cheque arrived from his solicitor in London. John had just sold a large property in London's Park Lane for 500,000 pounds. It was how he made his money, buying and selling property. He was talking about purchasing a couple of houses in Cork. He said they were going for rock-bottom prices and were bound to go up in the next couple of years. John had suggested Emmet reinvest the money John owed him into Crean Property, because that way he would be sure to more than double the amount in two years.

Emmet had explained to him about wanting to buy a horse.

'Well, why don't you get your parents to buy one for you?' asked John. 'Then you'll have your own money still free to invest in property.'

'They don't understand horses, John. Anything they buy me will be no good for the Carbery Hunt.'

'Sure, they should buy you any horse you want.' John got up from the tartan blanket Emmet had bought them to sit on at the races because John had insisted it was much nicer out on the grass than in the clubhouse, even though of course he had membership. 'Don't they owe you years of rent on that mansion of yours?'

'What?' Emmet was confused.

'Think about it, Emmet *Berger.*' And without waiting for a reply, the elegant young man sauntered off to lay the ten pounds on Sultan's Girl for both of them, Emmet being too young at sixteen to place his own bets, even though it was he who had picked out the horse, which looked a good bet to him despite being only at 15:1.

Emmet sat there, sipping the last of the champagne. He didn't really like John calling him Berger; it felt like a betrayal of the father who had brought him up. In fact, he really wished he'd never mentioned his biological father to John. It was just that on their very first day at the races, weeks ago, John had been curious about where Emmet's money came from. Emmet had drunk too much champagne, and one revelation had led to another, until somehow John wrangled the whole story out of him: that Emmet's natural father was an American millionaire who owned a successful engineering firm and had left Kilteegan House to Emmet because it had belonged to Malachy's mother, Hannah, and she would have wanted it to pass from Malachy to his oldest son.

Ever since then, John had kept insisting that Emmet's whole family were exploiting his birthright by using Kilteegan House as their own. For instance, he pointed out, Eli had converted the old gatehouse into his surgery without even asking Emmet's permission, Jack and Skipper farmed the fields on Lena's say-so, and Blackie and Emily were using the storage facilities for free without paying a penny.

Not long ago, Emmet would have been tempted to agree. He was so annoyed with both his parents for treating him like a child, telling him he was too young to have a car and ordering him to bed at his grandmother's wedding in front of his new friend, John Crean. But lately Eli had been teaching him to drive the Rover, and Skipper was patiently showing him how to school the bay mare every morning, and Blackie had been building proper jumps for himself and Sarah. So the thought of asking any of his family to pay rent just felt wrong. He'd always envisaged the house as belonging to all the O'Sullivans anyway, and he hadn't really thought about how that might change after he came into his inheritance at the age of eighteen.

Around where he was sitting, families strolled, clusters of old men in flat caps were exchanging hot tips, and well-dressed ladies in hats sat on chairs with champagne bottles in ice buckets beside them. The bookies were down at the trackside, and he could see John there, chatting away to a couple of other fellows in well-cut suits.

About fifty yards off, he thought he spotted Professor Lamkin with his wife and daughter, Isobel, sitting on a green blanket with a wicker hamper, and normally he would have strolled over to say hello, but John had told him how he didn't speak to the Lamkins; they'd tried to pin a robbery on him that had been carried out by their own housemaid. Emmet turned his back on the family, hoping not to be recognised at this distance. John had advised him to keep it quiet to everyone that they were 'knocking around' together, even his own parents.

'Thing is, Emmet, no one in this backwater seems to be able to forget the mad pranks I got up to as a teenager, and they can't get their heads around the fact I'm better and richer than them all now. I think they're envious, truth be told.'

Emmet liked the idea that someone of John's age was happy to 'knock around' with him like they were equals, and he sympathised with John about how hard it was to live down a bad name. Even kind-hearted Eli was still a bit frosty with Emmet after his outburst about Malachy and Stanford and the sports car, and sometimes it was hard to know how to put a mistake like that right. He wasn't even sure his adoptive father would accept an apology if he offered one, so he kept putting it off.

John came back and slumped on the rug, shooting a dirty glance in the Lamkins' direction. He had bought another bottle of champagne, and he topped up Emmet's glass and passed him a Cuban cigar. Emmet lit it cautiously. The first time he'd tried a cigar, it tasted disgusting and his world had descended into a blur of coughing, watering eyes and, most embarrassingly, a vomit into the grass beside the racetrack. His cheeks had blazed in shame, and he'd felt so young. But John had laughed, and not in a cruel way. 'Sure, it took me the same way the first time,' he'd said. 'But you'll get used to it, and then you'll wonder why you didn't take it up sooner.' Emmet was still waiting for this to happen.

'There's no flies on your mother anyway,' John announced now, rolling his own cigar between his fingers.

'I know there's not,' said Emmet cautiously. It made him a bit tense when John started talking about their shared extended family. He clearly looked down on his own brother, and although he never voiced it outright, Emmet suspected that contempt extended to Emily, and even to Lena.

'Yeah, it was a great move of hers to have a baby by Malachy, and get him to leave you the house, and get you to let them all live in it.'

Emmet inhaled too sharply on his cigar and nearly got sick again like he'd done the first time. He stubbed it out hurriedly on the grass and took a swallow of champagne to clear his throat. 'I really don't think she chose it. It was an accident and –'

'Ah, don't get up in a heap over it. I'm not criticising her. Women have to use the weapons they were born with to get along in life, and your mother had her sights set higher than the likes of my gobshite brother, that's for sure. And I'm not saying she had to go out of her way to trap Malachy Berger either – I'm sure he came to her. She's a cracker, always was, and not po-faced like a cat's arse the way her sister is.'

Emmet's cheeks felt hot with confusion. He knew how babies were made, but it shocked him that John found it so easy to talk about sexual things. Nobody in Kilteegan Bridge talked about sex, ever. Though Kilteegan Bridge was hardly the epitome of cool, so maybe he was being childish; maybe it was different in London, more forward-thinking.

'I was surprised when you told me who your father was,' added John, leaning on his elbow and blowing out a perfect smoke ring. 'Malachy Berger had such a pretty face, all us lads in Kilteegan Bridge thought he was a poof.'

'Well, I can tell you, he's not,' Emmet replied hotly. He knew what 'poof' meant and was horrified that anyone might have thought his father was that way. 'He's had a different girlfriend every time I go to see him.'

'Glad to hear it. Hate poofs myself. When I... When this man who works for me in London was in prison for a while – nothing serious, he didn't pay his TV licence or something – he told me the place was crawlin' with them, dirty scum. And other fellas, big shots, use it as a threat, y'know? If you don't do what they tell ya, someday you'll be in the showers and Daisy Davy would be sent in after you. Everyone else would scatter and keep sketch so the screw didn't come in, and if that happened, well... Like this fella told me, most of the poofs are weedy – you'd take 'em on fine. But Daisy now, he was a bruiser, and loved other fellas, but you'd never be the same after him.'

Emmet shuddered. 'God, that sounds awful.'

'Too right. Anyone like that came near me, I'd kill 'em.'

'Me too.'

'Good man yourself. Make sure you stay out of prison then.'

There was a thunder of hooves in the distance, and the two of them leapt to their feet, waving and roaring encouragement with the rest of the crowd as the frontrunners streamed by, Sultan's Girl leading the field.

It was great when a horse Emmet had picked out won, and they often did; John said he had a knack for it. Unfortunately the winnings turned out not to be much. John had spent part of the tenner on champagne and cigars, and the odds weren't that good at the bookies after all; in between Emmet picking out the horse and the race, apparently they'd dropped from 15:1 down to 2:1.

'Got another tenner?' asked John casually.

Emmet opened his wallet, but it was empty.

John looked vaguely annoyed. 'You should have brought more than fifty, Emmet. Those men I was talking to tipped me off to a dead cert in the next race.'

'I'm sorry, I thought I had enough...'

John relented. 'Tell you what. I'm friends with a bookie called Bunny Cotter. He'll allow us to bet "on tick", and he'll pay out if we back a winner, but if we don't, we owe him the money with a bit of interest. OK by you? I'll have that cheque next week, my solicitor says, and I'll cover any interest owed.'

'Of course it's OK by me,' said Emmet, and the two young gentlemen of independent means shook hands on their deal and celebrated with another glass of champagne.

CHAPTER 13

*E*mily sat at her mother-in-law's kitchen table, sipping a cup of tea. She knew something was wrong. Peggy was nervous and seemed to be regressing to the beaten-down woman Emily remembered from her childhood. Back then, Blackie's mother had always had a hunched back and seemed to never wear anything but a dirty overall. Drudgery and hard work in the shop was her lot in life, to fund her husband's drinking and cover all the debts he kept running up at the bookie's. But when Blackie grew up, and especially when he married Emily, that all changed. The two of them took over, insisted Mrs Crean retire and enjoy her life, and Emily had taken her shopping for a new wardrobe. Gone were the dun-grey housecoats and wellington boots, and now she wore smart blouses and tweed skirts and lovely jewellery.

The jewellery was what had brought Emily here.

At last Sunday's Mass, she'd noticed the lovely gold cross and chain she and Blackie had bought Peggy for her birthday a few years ago was no longer around her mother-in-law's neck. She didn't say anything at the time, not even to Blackie, but she suspected the hand of Jingo and decided she was going to get to the bottom of it. Peggy had never taken the chain off since they'd got it for her. It was not just twenty-four-carat gold; it had also been blessed at the Shrine to Our Lady in Knock, County Mayo, and she loved it.

Emily had bided her time, and having seen Jingo driving off towards Cork an hour earlier, she knew the coast was clear for her to pay a visit.

Blackie's mother and she had always got along really well. Emily was kind but firm in the rejuvenation of the shop, though Mrs Crean had been so nervous at the start, it was done more by stealth than by open intention. A light fitted here, a lick of paint there, until now the shop was by far the nicest in town, and its sister shops were doing just as well in Bandon and Cork. Emily had noticed other business owners emulating some of their ideas. Like having produce in baskets out in front to attract passers-by, or having a 'special discount of the week' so people were now in the habit of just popping in to see what the deal was that Monday.

Emily went regularly to trade fairs in Dublin and even in the north of Ireland to get unusual things for the shop, and it was really paying off. She'd had a few brides-to-be recently looking at her table settings, easily made centrepieces and napkin rings, all colour coordinated and so on. Girls nowadays wanted their weddings to be a bit more special than they used to be, and she was happy to supply those little touches.

'Those little lavender sachets for drawers are sold out. Can you believe it?' Peggy poured another cup of tea and sat down. She no longer slaved in the shop, but she was always in and out, helping and taking an interest.

'I know. It was Mam's idea. She has loads of lavender growing in her new garden, so we ordered some muslin and some purple ribbon and she ran up the little bags in no time. They're really popular.'

'Your mother is a genius with a needle, no doubt about it.'

'She is, and she's in such better form these days too. I was worried the wedding and all the hype would send her into a spin, but Klaus seems to be really good for her. She relies on him, and he's so patient and really adores her, so I'm relieved.'

'He's a lovely man,' agreed Peggy. 'I'm so happy they found each other. I remember the years after your father died, and she was like a lost soul, God love her. Though at that time, Dick was around, so I was a bit envious too. How could a fine decent man like your father be gone and Dick still alive and kicking, may God forgive me.'

Emily smiled. This was new as well. Dick Crean was awful, but it was a long time until Peggy Crean had been able to admit it out loud. When Blackie pointed out his father's many failings, Peggy was inclined to admonish him for doing it, but now she was in open agreement.

'Well, he's out of our lives now, Peggy, and if he turns up, then he'd better expect a frosty reception, so hopefully he won't follow his son back to Kilteegan Bridge. That is, if Jingo's staying here for any length of time, which I suppose he's not, is he?'

Emily glanced hopefully at Mrs Crean, but the old woman just sat, stirring her tea, avoiding eye contact. With a sinking heart, Emily leant forwards and touched the older woman's hand, making her start.

'Peggy, it's your own business who you have in your home, but while we're on the subject, I hope Jingo isn't taking advantage?'

'Ah, no.' Mrs Crean clattered her spoon in the saucer, flushing slightly. 'John's fine. Sure, hasn't he got his life back on the straight and narrow. He's been dealing in property in London these last nine years and made a fortune. He's expecting a cheque from his solicitor only next week from the sale of his house in Park Lane, which is the most expensive street in all of London.'

'Are you sure about that?' Emily asked gently.

Mrs Crean looked even more uncomfortable. 'Ah, Emily love, of course I'm sure.'

'You know, Peggy, I don't think you should go lending him any money on the strength of it.'

Peggy flushed. 'Emily, I wish you'd remember to call him John. And I know he was trouble as a teenager, but he's definitely changed for the better. And I'm very happy to give him a few bob for the pub if he has a cash flow problem, but that's all it is.'

'Is it?' Emily tried to keep the dread out of the question.

'Yes, it is. Emily, please don't ask me to speak badly of my son. He came home especially to look after me. He says it's lonely for me in the house by myself.'

'Oh, Peggy, I didn't realise you were lonely...' Emily felt a sharp pang of guilt. She and Blackie had moved Peggy out into her own place a few years after Nellie was born, and they hadn't thought for a moment.

A smile lit up the older woman's face. 'Ah, no, don't be thinking that. It's a beautiful little cottage you've bought me, so warm and cosy. I've been as happy as Larry here ever since I moved in. The peace and quiet is wonderful for getting on with my painting. And you know, John's showing such an interest in that. He's very impressed with me for earning so much from my commissions for painting people's houses and animals.'

Emily could just imagine what sort of interest Jingo was taking in Peggy's art, and she decided to get to the point of her visit. 'Peggy, where's your cross and chain?'

Peggy's eyes met Emily's for a guilty moment, then she glanced away, and there was no need for an explanation.

Emily felt her blood boil. How could Jingo repay his mother's loving kindness by stealing from her? Maybe it was time to let Blackie get rid of him anyway, without waiting for Peggy to say the word. His mother would be in a much better place if her precious son took off, never to be seen again, even if she could never admit it to them or herself.

'This can't go on,' she said quietly.

Peggy got flustered. 'Look, I know you and Blackie mean well, love, and I agree, I was disappointed when he asked to borrow it to pawn it. But it's only short term – he'll buy it back when his cheque comes in.'

Emily shook her head and said nothing. What was the point?

Her mother-in-law said defensively, 'And we have to remember, before we throw the first stone, that my John got dealt a very poor hand in life.'

'No worse than many others, including his own brother,' said Emily shortly.

'No, Emily, John's right. He says I should have been a better mother to him, and I should have. I let his father get away with too much. I let Dick bring him around with him to the pub, and he got him involved with all sorts of blackguarding when I should have protected him...'

'Stop that right now, Peggy.' Emily was furious to hear Jingo had been blaming his mother for his awful behaviour, and she stopped trying to be remotely diplomatic. 'Jingo is a crook and a liar and a thief, and that's the truth, and you owe him nothing. It's nobody's fault but his own the way his life turned out. We could all go on with that old claptrap. My mother had a mental illness, my father died, we had a difficult enough upbringing, but we all made something of ourselves, and at the end of the day, every person is responsible for themselves. Like I've said before, Blackie came out of the same house, and look how wonderful he is. You're a good mother, you worked so hard, and if anyone should be whining about being dealt a bad hand in life, it's you, and you never complain.'

Mrs Crean gave her a weak smile. 'I don't complain because God was good to me. Didn't he give me Blackie? And sent you to him? I've no complaints.'

'Right, well, what will we do about Jingo then?'

Mrs Crean shook her head. 'I won't have him on the streets, Emily. I couldn't.'

'Will you at least let Blackie get your chain back?'

A tear formed in Peggy's eye, and she wiped it with the back of her hand. 'Ah, that's gone. He would have sold that for booze money or put it on a horse. Either way, it's gone.'

'Oh, Peggy, it's so unfair...'

'Era, I loved it, you know I did, but I love him too. I promise I'll make sure anything else valuable you've given me is locked away, and I won't leave any money out, and I won't give in to him when he tries to cajole me or bully me into handing him anything else to pawn. But that's as far as I'm willing to go, Emily. I'm sorry if you think I'm weak.'

'I don't think you're weak, Peggy. Look at all you've survived. And it's your life, and you have to live it in the way you think best. But remember, just one word of agreement from you and Blackie will put the run on Jingo in no uncertain terms, and Jack and Skipper will help.'

'You're still calling him Jingo,' said Peggy dejectedly.

'I know. I'm sorry. He just doesn't feel like a John to me. Let's talk about something else.' Emily wished there was more she could do about the situation, but she knew there wasn't, not for now at least. She was furious on her mother-in-law's behalf but knew any further discussion at this time was pointless. Blackie was a lot like his mother in that regard; he was amenable to a fault and generally very easygoing, and she could convince him of almost anything. But once or twice in all the years, he'd made up his mind on something and then there was no budging him.

CHAPTER 14

'Because, as Dad and I have explained, we think you're too young,' Lena said wearily. Emmet was trying once more to take the car. She really didn't need this now; she'd hoped for a few hours to herself in peace. It was lovely and sunny in the library, and she'd been planning to go through the accounts for Eli's surgery.

The practice had nearly collapsed over the last few weeks, and she needed to figure out how much of a financial hole they were heading into, and what to do about it.

She knew what the problem was, of course. She'd been at Mass when the Monsignor basically repeated what he'd roared out in Eli's surgery, followed by a few choice remarks in the sermon about how people should be careful whose advice they follow, that the Church had the final say in people's lives and they would do right to listen to the teachings of the pope, that kind of thing.

Eli had blended into life in Ireland seamlessly and was universally adored, but facing down a Monsignor was not to be done lightly. People looked to the Church for how to live, and few people didn't conform. Eli had tried to laugh off the encounter, but even before that awful Mass, Lena had been seriously worried. The Monsignor was new to the parish, but she knew enough about clergy like him to know you didn't cross them and get away with it, and she was worried Eli didn't understand that.

The day before the sermon, Mrs Moriarty had crept up to the house in tears to hand in her notice. She'd told Lena that the Mouse had caught her taking the pill and had marched her up to the Monsignor to confess, and now he wasn't even allowing her to work for the Kogans any more, money or no money. The poor woman then tried to give Lena the money back from her post office account to make up for the income Eli would lose because of her stupidity, but Lena had flatly refused.

'That's your money, Frances. If you like, you can think of it as the pension that went with your job. All I ask is you don't go confessing to the Monsignor about it, or you'll be making a liar out of Geraldine Cronin, who assured your husband the other day that you hadn't kept any of your wages back for yourself.' It wasn't actually true that the Mouse had approached Geraldine, but Lena knew Mrs Moriarty well enough to know she would do things to protect other people that she would never do to protect herself, and sure enough, Frances promised faithfully to say nothing about the money.

Lena hadn't looked for a replacement housekeeper yet. Because the Kogan income had taken such a knock, she wasn't sure they could afford one. They had savings and the rent from Doc's old surgery, so they weren't about to go under, but the situation was not ideal.

That's why she wanted to go through the books. She wanted to have the facts and figures in front of her before discussing the problem with Eli. He hadn't a financial bone in his body. He was a doctor for the love of it, and sometimes she was frustrated with how little interest he took in the business side of things. He was nothing like the pompous medics she saw at the conferences she sometimes attended with him, with their Savile Row suits and flash Mercedes. His white shirt always had the cuffs rolled up, and the pockets of his charcoal-grey trousers bulged with keys and other things he stuffed in there. Just last week he'd been undressing for bed and casually took a urine sample from his pocket. 'Ah, Mrs Butler's sample. I wondered where I'd put that.'

He reminded her so much of Doc, caring nothing for the trappings. Her godfather had worn the same three suits for her entire life, all interchangeable and shiny with wear.

'But you never drive it, Mam,' complained Emmet, refusing to leave her alone. He was standing in the bay window overlooking the front of the house, where the light-blue Rover sat idly most days. 'It's just there, doing nothing.'

Lena exhaled. She would not lose her temper with her son no matter how hard he pushed. She didn't know what the matter was with him; he seemed so on edge all the time. She and Eli had thought spending so much of his time at the farm with Skipper and Jack would do him good, and it had at first. But recently he had become increasingly impatient with her, as if something about his life was seriously upsetting him, though every time she asked him what it was, he fiercely denied anything was wrong. She suspected a girl, but it was hard to know who. Nellie was no good for giving out information. She was loyal as a dog to Emmet and would give nothing away even if she knew anything. Whatever the matter was, she hoped it would soon pass and she could have her boy back. 'Emmet, can we discuss this later over dinner, with your father?'

'But he'll only take your side because he always does, and it's not fair. You walk everywhere and he's down at the surgery morning, noon and night, so it's just sitting there. And he taught me to drive, so I can do it, and the cycle up to the farm every morning takes so long, it's just a stupid waste of time.'

She put down her pen sharply. 'Firstly, Emmet, your father has a name. He's your dad, not "he". And secondly, I'd like you to show me a bit more respect. I'm your mother, who gave birth to you and raised you, and it would be nice to get something back in return.'

Emmet muttered something under his breath. She thought she caught it but wasn't sure.

'What did you say?'

'Nothing.' He looked both furtive and angry.

'Well, clearly it wasn't nothing, Emmet, so I'll ask you again. What did you say?'

He looked at her then, his green eyes fixed on hers. Sometimes he looked so like Malachy, she got a fright, even though he'd grown taller than his biological father in the past year. Malachy had been only a little older than Emmet was now when she and he were together. It felt like a lifetime ago.

'I said,' said Emmet, 'you've got enough back from me already.'

'I'm sorry?' She didn't understand him. 'What are you talking about?'

He lifted his chin, and she recognised that set of his jaw, the defiant stance she'd seen, not in his father but in his grandfather, August Berger. The memory of that murderer sent a shiver down her spine.

'I'm talking about my house,' he said with all his grandfather's cold authority. 'I let you all stay here, don't I?'

'Let us all stay...?' Her mind whirled in confusion. She felt like she must have misheard. Yes, Malachy had given Kilteegan House to Emmet, with Lena and Eli to keep it in trust for him until he was eighteen, and Emmet had known the truth about that since he was seven. But never before, not even when he was at his most bad-tempered and arrogant, had he ever tried to hold it over her. 'But, Emmet, we're your family, Sarah, Pádraig, your dad. Don't you want us to live here?'

'But you don't just live here, do you, Mam? Your family profits from my house. Your brother, Jack, has the fields, your sister has the sheds, and nobody has ever asked me if that's what I want to do with my house. It's like you're all stealing from me.'

Lena felt sick to her stomach, but she tried to keep her voice as calm as possible despite the turmoil she felt. 'Who put these ideas into your head, Emmet? Because I can't believe it's my own son saying these horrible things to me.'

He hesitated. A shadow of guilt crossed his face, but then he stuck out his chin again and said determinedly, 'No one.'

'It wasn't Malachy, surely?' She and Emmet's biological father didn't always see eye to eye, but she couldn't believe he would undermine her like this.

'I said no one.' But his eyes strayed over her shoulder in the way they always did when he was lying, ever since he was a small boy.

'Well, I think someone must have said it to you, Emmet.'

He reddened. 'Why do you always treat me like a child, like I can't have an opinion of my own? You and him always –'

She slapped her hand on the desk. 'Again, Emmet, Eli's not a "he" or a "him"! He's your dad.'

Emmet stayed silent.

Lena lowered her voice. 'It's true that biologically your dad isn't your natural father, but, Emmet, he's been there, doing what fathers do – and a lot more than most, let me tell you – since you were a baby. He played with you, taught you things, read to you. He's supported and loved you from the start, so he is your dad.'

'Well, he's done pretty well out of being my "dad", hasn't he, Mam?'

Lena stared at her son. The words hung between them, the tension mounting. 'What on earth do you mean, done well out of it?' she asked slowly. Lena's temper was something she'd had to learn to manage over the years. She didn't possess the supreme self-control of Emily or the placid nature of Jack, or even the ability to brush things off the twins had in spades.

Emmet had a wild look about him now. He clearly knew he was on thin ice with his mother, but still he ploughed on like something deep and dark was driving him. 'You had a child by a rich man, who was always going to look after me as soon as he found out about me, and now *he* – Eli, Dad, whatever – can rent out Doc's old house to all those people because you, you –'

'Because I *what*, Emmet?' Lena stood up from her chair, trembling, and took a step towards him.

'Because…'

'Say it, Emmet.' If it wasn't too early in the day to be even possible, she would have thought there was a faint smell of whiskey coming off him.

'Because you had…'

'Go on.'

He threw his hat at it. 'You decided to have sex with a rich man and have his baby to trap him.'

Lena had never in her life hit her children, but the rage, the sheer fury that he would judge her like that, cast such aspersions on her morality, insinuate that she would trap someone for the sake of their money, made her snap. She slapped him so hard, her hand left white stripes across his flushed face.

'How dare you, Emmet Kogan. How dare you speak to me like that! I thought your father loved me, and I loved him. And yes, I became pregnant, but I paid a very, very heavy price for that. Your grandfather, August Berger, told Malachy to stay away from me, called me names I won't repeat, and I hated him for it. And I hated Malachy for believing it for a long time. But to hear the same sort of name-calling from my own son…'

Emmet held his hand to his cheek, fury glittering in his eyes. 'Maybe you don't like to hear it because it's true.'

Lena's breath caught in her chest. 'Get out! Get out of my house this minute!' she shouted.

'*My* house, Mam, remember that.' He was gone then, slamming the door, leaving her shaking. The next moment, the Rover started up, and when she rushed to the window, she could see it roaring up the drive.

Less than a minute later, Eli came racing the other way up the avenue towards the house, and she ran out to the front steps to meet him. The whole story came tumbling out. Her husband listened patiently, and when she was finished, he wrapped her in his arms, soothing her.

'I don't know where's he's gone,' she sobbed. 'I'm so afraid he's going to crash the car.'

'He's a good driver, Lena, and I'm sure he'll be all right. Try not to worry too much.'

'How could he say those awful things to me, Eli? Why does he hate us so much? All we've ever tried to do is be good parents.'

Eli gently rubbed her back, then led her into the house and to the sofa in the library, where he sat her down and put his arms around her once more.

'He doesn't hate either of us, though he might feel like he does right now. But he's angry. Something is really bothering him these days. I wish I could get through to him, but he shuts down whenever I try.'

'I can't believe he could be so hurtful.'

'I know, love, and he can't speak to you like that, so I will have a stern word with him as soon as he gets home. I only have a couple of patients booked in this afternoon. Maybe the fine weather is making people feel better.' He smiled.

She sat back on the sofa, wiping her eyes. They might as well face all their problems at the same time. 'Eli, I was going to go through the accounts before talking to you, but I don't think the fine weather is the trouble.'

He sighed, 'I suppose you're talking about my run-in with the Monsignor. I know he's a vile man, but surely people aren't going to stop going to the doctor because of a man like that? I'd say it's just a temporary thing, Lena. They'll come back as soon as they think anything is really wrong with them.'

'But, Eli...' she paused, trying to think of a way to phrase this. 'People are so afraid of him, they might not come back.'

He said incredulously, 'You think they would rather risk their own health? Their children's lives?'

Lena sighed. 'Things are changing, slowly, but the Church holds massive sway with people, and the pope was clear on the stance of the Church on contraception. Monsignor Collins is a different character to Father Otawe, who had such genuine love for his congregation that he would have turned a blind eye in a case like Frances Moriarty's. The Monsignor enjoys the power over people his collar gives him, and he uses it to its fullest extent. The reality is that he's following the papal message to the letter of the law. Whatever about asking people to defy the priest – that's a huge ask, but they might – but by choosing you over him, they are effectively defying the pope.'

'What?' He laughed. 'Listen to yourself, Lena. The pope? Some old man in Rome should be telling women like poor Mrs Moriarty to have children even though it will kill her?'

'Eli, calm down. I'm not saying I agree. I'm telling you what's happening, and why. Don't turn on me.'

'I'm sorry.' He touched her hand and tried to look cheerful again. 'Anyway, I'm still sure it's only for a short time. It will be fine once the dust settles. Nobody wants to go to Dr White in Kellstown, not even the people of Kellstown themselves. And Dr Burke in Bandon is a friend of mine, and he'll tell any one of my patients who goes to him not to be so silly, and he'll send them back to me soon enough.'

Lena said nothing. She didn't want to hurt or insult her beloved husband, and what she was thinking had never come up in their marriage before now.

'Tell me,' he demanded, looking into her eyes.

She was taken aback. 'Tell you what, it's nothing..'

'Your face, though. There's something, you're just not saying it.'

He could read her like a book, and perhaps she needed to tell him, perhaps he needed to understand. 'Well…the thing is…just that it came as a bit of a shock to everyone that you aren't Catholic. I mean, you usually come to Mass with me and the children, and then when the Monsignor assumed you were Protestant, well, that would have been a shock, but then you announcing that you were in fact a Jew, well, nobody around here would ever have known a Jew before.'

Eli looked horrified, and she knew she'd hit a bad nerve. But if he was going to deal with this situation, he needed all the facts at his fingertips and that was the truth. People adored Eli, and they thought him an excellent doctor, but they would have a hard enough time getting past him being in the Church's bad books. And then to know he was Jewish as well…well, it wasn't nothing.

'And they're disgusted with me for being a Jew, is that what you're saying?'

Lena sighed. 'Eli, do you know how many Jewish refugees were allowed into Ireland during the war?'

'Well, not many, I suppose, but then there was no Jewish community here really.'

Lena shook her head. 'They didn't choose not to come to Ireland – they weren't allowed in. It's a dark thing, and something we don't acknowledge really, but we didn't let them in. There was a tacit agreement between church and state that a strong Jewish population would dilute the power of the Catholic Church, and so most applications were rejected.'

She allowed her words to sink in. It took some time.

Like most things to do with that time in his life, Eli had consigned the horrors of the Third Reich and the unwillingness of the world to help his people to the deepest recesses of his mind. He didn't like to dwell on his flight from Berlin as a child in 1940, or on the anti-Semitic discrimination he endured from the likes of his stepfather's mother, Bessie Evans, or on the lasting impact of having so many of his German relatives murdered in cold blood.

'So what do you suggest, Lena?' he said at last, in a strained voice. 'I just stand by and watch the Monsignor destroy my practice because I'm Jewish?'

'It's not just that, Eli. You challenging him in public would have raised his hackles –'

'I challenged him?' His eyes flashed. 'He came to my surgery and called me out in front of everyone! All I did was defend my right to do my job.'

'I know, Eli, but listen to me. Trust me on this. I'm completely on your side, but you need to understand what you're up against.' She watched as the realisation of the situation, the ugly truth, sank in.

'Don't despair, though. I have an idea.'

He turned his intense brown eyes towards her, his face white and drawn.

She said, treading carefully, 'I think it would be best if Dr Burke talks to the Monsignor. He's a Catholic, and maybe he can persuade the Monsignor that you've agreed not to suggest the pill to women any more, and also that it would be a bad idea to send your patients to Kellstown, to Dr White. And he – I mean Dr Burke – can say that he can't possibly take any more patients because his practice in Bandon is full already.'

'So I have to drag in a Catholic doctor to beg for me?' Eli asked bitterly. 'And how am I supposed to tend medically to people if I've to check the Catholic rule book every time I write a prescription?'

His belligerence was covering up a deep hurt, she knew. Eli was so conscientious, always going over and above for his patients. He went out at all times and in all weather on house calls, he funded tests from his own pocket if he thought people couldn't afford it, and he often didn't charge people enough. The thought of his patients walking out on him because he wasn't in their Church must have felt so painful.

'Your patients love and respect you, Eli,' she said softly. 'This will get sorted out, I promise. And when they come back to you, they'll all be so apologetic and relieved.'

'I just don't see why they have to listen to that man.'

'Eli, think. If someone told you that you were going to burn in hellfire for all eternity if you did a certain thing…well then, what would you do?'

He shook his head. 'And they really believe that God could be so cruel as to invent a place of torture like that?'

She was surprised, and realised they'd never discussed this before; they'd never compared their views of the afterlife. 'Don't you have a hell in your religion, Eli?'

He thought about it. 'Well, I suppose there are some references in legends based on biblical verses, the *Midrash* they're called, to a place called *Gehinom*, but it's not common knowledge. I think the idea is that it is where our souls go but never for more than a year. And it's not a fire – it's a sort of place where you realise all the wrongs you've done and have to suffer through that intense shame and embarrassment before you ascend to God.'

Lena smiled ruefully. 'It sounds awful, like being a teenager all over again.'

'Times a hundred,' said Eli, also with a slight smile.

'Mind you, it's a lot better than the Catholic hell. I wonder if it's true? The Monsignor will be furious if he dies and finds out that's all that happens to bad people. He definitely prefers the idea of sending us to burn in hellfire for all eternity.'

'I think Monsignor Collins could do with a good dose of Gehinnom himself,' said Eli grimly, and this time Lena didn't say anything to defend her Church.

CHAPTER 15

*I*f Emmet had known about the Jewish idea of hell, he would have thought that's where he was stuck. Never in his life had he felt such awful shame and embarrassment. He was sick to his stomach at the way he'd spoken to his mother and could hardly believe it had happened. It was like he'd opened his mouth and John Crean's voice had come pouring out, poisonous and cruel.

God, he hated that man.

He had long since stopped believing in their 'gentleman's agreement'. The solicitor's cheque had never come, and he didn't believe he was going to see any of his thousand pounds again. Even worse, he'd not just been cleaned out, but he now owed a lot of money to a dangerous crook. A man called Bunny Cotter had allowed him and Crean to bet 'on tick'. Their horses had lost over and over, and now it seemed Emmet was in debt to this Cotter for three hundred pounds.

Earlier that morning, before his row with his mother, he'd been walking up to the farm on his way to see the mare, who was completely docile around him these days. But John Crean had overtaken him on the road and stopped, insisting on him getting into the car and having a drink.

'We need that three hundred quid and quick, Emmet. The solicitor says the Park Lane money is going to take another month to come in. And Bunny Cotter wants his by a week today, or he'll send his man around to collect it.'

'Can't he wait a month, until you have it?' muttered Emmet.

'Not going to happen. Count yourself lucky I persuaded him to give us the extra few days.'

'But if you haven't got it...'

'If *we* haven't got it, you mean,' said John sharply. 'Ask your father for the money. He owes you, staying in your house without paying rent. Or ask your other father, the rich one.'

Emmet was horrified at the idea of going to Eli or Malachy. Either of them would want to know why he needed the money when he should have a post office account with a thousand pounds in it, and if he admitted he'd blown it at the racetrack... He hated to think what they would say. He'd never be trusted again, with anything.

John passed him the hip flask, and he took a long drink. He was getting used to whiskey now; it didn't burn so much.

'But if we don't have it, we don't have it. What can he really do to us?' The whiskey was making him bolder.

'You really want to know what he can do to us?' John stared grimly out at the summer rain. He had the windows wound up, and the car was hot and sweaty. 'I'll tell you what. Bunny's cousin is a fella called John Daly – he's what's known as a fixer. He's a lump of a man and doesn't give a fiddler's curse what you say. If he wants money, he'll batter you. And I don't mean a few slaps. I mean a hospital job, broken bones, broken teeth. One fella had to have his jaw wired after Daly. And then he'll tell you that you have a week to get it or he'll come after you again, and next time you might not be so lucky. Or he'll do the same to your family. He might put his eye on your pretty little sister, or your mam even – she's a fine-lookin' bird.' He turned to Emmet. 'That man will stop at nothing.'

Emmet shuddered and took another slug from the bottle, another dose of Dutch courage. 'OK then, let's go to the police.'

'No!' John's hands shook as he grabbed the whiskey back from Emmet and threw back several mouthfuls. 'That's the worst thing we could do – Daly would murder us. Look, if you won't ask your father for the money, you'll just have to take that fancy Rover of his. We can sell it in Cork and pretend it was stolen. I know a man who can move it for you.'

Emmet stared at him, dazed as much by John's suggestion as by the whiskey he'd been drinking. 'I can't take Dad's car! That's stealing.'

'So? Don't you want to keep your mother and sister safe? Daly's a savage, and if he got his hands on two pretty women like that... We need that money fast, Emmet, and this is the only way. Get the car and come and pick me up on the Cork road, on the far side of the village.'

So now, still slightly befuddled with the whiskey he'd consumed earlier, Emmet was driving towards the Cork road where John Crean was waiting for him, and then they would drive to Cork and sell the car, and he'd pretend he left it outside a shop somewhere and it was stolen.

On the outskirts of Kilteegan Bridge, he stopped and turned the car to face home again. He couldn't steal it, he just couldn't. But when he was nearly home, he remembered the dreadful Daly and thought of him doing unspeakable things to Sarah. And he turned back.

And then...on his third time driving towards home, he came to a different, bolder decision. There was one person in his life who might listen to him and understand, and even know how to help, and that was Skipper. Skipper was brave, and he was clever too, and he seemed to genuinely like Emmet.

Yes, that's what he would do. He would drive up to the farm and throw himself on Skipper's mercy, and Jack's as well – he was a good man – and maybe the two farmers would help him out without forcing him to confess his terrible behaviour to his parents.

* * *

JACK STOOD AT THE SINK, looking over the yard and waiting for the coffee to brew. Skipper's brother, Wyatt, and his wife, Laurie Lee, had sent him a present of an electric coffee machine for his thirty-second birthday. It was a feat of engineering, dripping hot water through a cannister full of ground coffee and filtering it into a jug on a heated plate.

'Just as well we got that there machine,' Skipper murmured in his ear, coming up right behind him. 'The only time I ever thought about leavin' Ireland was when I realised no one here could make real coffee worth a damn.'

'Ah, you'd never have left me, even if I made you drink tea every day.' Jack grinned. 'But you're right, the coffee dripper thing does make me feel much more secure.'

Smiling, Skipper slid his arms around him, and Jack turned to kiss him, a long kiss that transported them many miles away from Kilteegan Bridge.

The sound of the door opening came too late. They jumped away from each other, staring in horror at Emmet, who stood rooted to the spot.

'Emmet,' Skipper managed, but no other words came.

'What… Jack… Skipper… What were you doing?' Emmet's voice was raspy, shocked.

'Emmet, just listen…' Jack made a move towards his nephew.

'No, don't touch me!' Emmet shrunk away from him.

'Emmet, just listen, we –' Skipper tried again.

'You're disgusting! You're a poof, both of you are poofs. I've heard of people like you. You're perverts! Get away from me!' The boy turned and ran. From the yard came the screech of tyres as he reversed the car in a U-turn and drove fast out of the gate.

Jack and Skipper were left staring at each other in horror, the danger of their situation sinking in.

'Will I go after him?' Skipper asked. 'I'll catch him up and we'll talk. He might listen to me.'

Jack shook his head, pale with fear and hurt. 'I don't know, maybe leave it for now, leave him to calm down first. This is terrible. Will he tell anyone, do you think? Oh God, will he tell the Monsignor? That man will destroy us entirely, and whatever hope Eli had of getting back into his good graces will be gone.'

'He ain't gonna tell the Monsignor,' said Skipper firmly. 'Emmet's a good person. He just won't. He knows it would ruin us, and he loves you and he likes me well enough.'

'Loves me? He said I was disgusting, he said not to touch him. *Me*, his uncle, who's played with him since he was a baby. He called us both poofs – how could he even use that word?' Jack's voice was rough with pain.

'He just got a shock, that's all. He'll come round. He'll come back.' He tried to take Jack in his arms again, to comfort him, but Jack stepped back sharply with a scared glance towards the door, and Skipper realised the man he loved was shivering uncontrollably like one of those sad, terrified, bullied horses that owners from around Ireland brought to him to cure.

* * *

HOW COULD JACK, his own flesh and blood? How could Skipper, who was his friend – or so he'd thought? How could they be the kind of perverts John Crean had told him about? Like Daisy Davy in the jail, who attacked other men and forced himself on them. A shudder passed through him. Surely Jack and Skipper didn't do that...

And it wasn't just Daisy. John Crean had taught him to notice and avoid any man who seemed a bit effeminate. There was a slim well-dressed man who worked in a bar beside the racecourse in Killarney, and he was a bit girly, Emmet knew. Rumour was that he went with men, and John always made a gesture with his wrist whenever he turned his back, like having a limp wrist was a sign of men like that or something.

Surely his uncle couldn't be one of those. It was impossible. He was a hardworking man, and Skipper too; they weren't a bit feminine. They were farmers, they didn't care about things girls liked, and wasn't that what men like that were inside? Men with too much woman in them or something? He didn't understand, but he knew it was disgusting. And illegal. And if Monsignor Collins found out, well, he'd be horrified. He'd probably call the guards and have them both arrested.

Emmet tried to stop his brain going there, imagining Jack and Skipper in jail and all that went on there. Maybe they would even want that to happen, which was worse. They were girly men. They'd lied to him about their true inner natures. He couldn't believe he'd thought they would have the courage or strength to protect him from the likes of Bunny Cotter and John Daly.

Tears streamed down his face as he drove, the whiskey still in his veins. He was driving too fast, and before he knew it, he'd taken the bend too quickly and the car spun out of control. There was a deep ditch on the side of the road – Jack cleared it every year with the tractor because it was the way the waterfall that began high in the hills reached the sea – and now his father's Rover was half on its side in the ditch.

He sat, gripping the wheel, terrified. The sickening crunch of metal, the long hiss of air leaving a tyre – he didn't know how much damage was done, but he knew by the smashed glass of the windshield and the smell of oil that it was a lot. So much for stealing the car to sell it. And his parents would be so furious with him. He just couldn't deal with any of this right now.

He wrenched the door open and dragged himself out of the car. It was difficult because of the angle, but he managed it. He was unhurt, but the car was wrecked. The driver's wheel was off the ground, and the entire bonnet looked to be crushed. He thought about running away to England or something, but he was tired, so tired. His head hurt. He wanted to cry or scream. He needed comfort. He needed someone to be kind to him. He wanted his mother, but he had been so horrible to her that she had slapped him. He had screamed at Jack and Skipper in disgust and seen the fear in their eyes. Nellie was always off in Cork doing her beauty course, or in Bandon at the weekends, working at the hotel. The only person he had left to turn to was his father, though God knew what Eli would do to him when he heard about the car...

But no matter what, he was lost and he needed his dad.

* * *

THE WAITING ROOM WAS EMPTY, not the usual crowd, and for a bad moment Emmet thought his father must be out on call. But Margaret was there and smiled as he entered.

'Hi, Emmet. Have you come to see your dad? He's not busy at the moment, so you can go right in.'

'Thank you, Mrs Hannratty.'

She looked at him sharply. 'Are you OK, Emmet?' Something about him must have made her realise it wasn't a social call.

He kept his head down. 'I'm fine, I'm fine.' He knocked on the surgery door, then opened it.

Eli looked up and smiled when he saw him. 'Hello, son, what are you doing here? I thought you might be a patient, though that would be a fine thing these days. I seem to be down to the likes of Jimmy Piper. I'll have to buy Margaret a cream slice for listening to his endless stories that go literally nowhere. There's nothing wrong with him, between you and me, but he likes the chat. Not that I say anything – he just starts telling me the long winding tale of all of his family and their many predicaments.' Eli laughed but stopped short. 'Is everything all right, Emmet? You look pale. Are you sick?' He jumped up and placed his hand on his son's forehead.

'I'm not sick, Dad, I just have something bad I have to tell you.'

His father gestured for him to take a seat in the chair reserved for patients and perched on the desk. 'Right. First, whatever it is, we'll find a solution. Secondly, well done on coming to speak to me. I know by your face, that wasn't an easy decision. So from the start, as calmly as you can...'

Emmet took a deep breath and began with how he'd behaved towards his mother and said the most horrible things, and that he felt awful with himself. And then he got to how he'd taken the car, but not why. He explained to Eli about driving the car too fast, though he again didn't mention why. He didn't want to horrify his father about Jack and Skipper; it was bad enough he knew himself.

He got to where he drove the car into the ditch and stopped, his head down, looking miserably at the floor.

Earlier he'd been planning to come clean about John Crean as well, but the sight of the empty waiting room had shaken him. Nothing had been said yet by Lena or Eli to him or Sarah, but clearly business was bad, and suddenly it didn't seem like a good time to tell his father he owed three hundred pounds, especially with the wrecked car having to be paid for. He was due another envelope from Malachy, and maybe if he offered to hand over the whole twenty dollars to Bunny Cotter every month, that would pay off the three hundred he owed in just over a year and everything would be OK.

Eli never interrupted or seemed to show any emotion at all as Emmet spoke, but now that he'd finished, Eli pulled his son to his feet and just stood there. For a moment Emmet wondered if he was going to hit him for the first time in his life, like Lena had earlier, but instead Eli put his hands on Emmet's shoulders.

'Right, I already know about the way you spoke to your mother. She was heartbroken, and between us we think you're very upset about something you're not telling us.'

'I'm not, Dad.' His eyes strayed to the wall over his father's shoulder.

'You are, Emmet, and maybe you'll tell us when the time is right, but don't take it out on your mother again – she doesn't deserve it. The car is a bit of a disaster, but it was an accident, and the most important thing is that you're all right. Cars can be fixed, but human beings are a bit trickier, so that's all right. I'll send that Noely Crowley from the new garage to pick it up, and hopefully it won't cost too much.'

'I'm so sorry, Dad.' He wished he could offer to pay for it, but he couldn't, and he was so relieved Eli hadn't asked him for the money. The one thing he couldn't bring himself to tell his father, at least not yet, was about the huge hole in his post office account.

Eli drew him in for a hug and held him tightly. 'We all do silly things when we're young. I had Charlie bail me out of a few scrapes too. He wasn't my father biologically, but he did all the work of one, and so it's my turn now. Do you see now why I didn't want you to drive by yourself yet? The number of dead boys I saw when I was in

Cardiff… I can't tell you how glad I am that you're alive. That's all that matters to me.'

Emmet's heart filled with love for this man, his true father who cared for him more than for his car, and for the first time, he plucked up the courage to apologise for the way he'd spoken to Eli before the wedding instead of just trying to pretend it had never happened. 'I'm sorry for being horrible to you too, when we were arguing about Stanford. You are my dad, not Malachy. I just… I was an eejit and I hurt you and I know I did. It was wrong, and I'm so sorry.'

Eli released him from the hug but kept his arm around his shoulder. 'I'm flattered actually.'

'What? Why?'

'Well, when I was training to be a doctor, we had to study all sorts of things, and psychology was one. The study of the mind. And our prof, a funny-looking old chap with white hair that stuck out over his ears and big round eyes like an owl, explained that the neurological process in the brain that happens when little children hit around two – and they can have some ferocious tantrums – is caused by the realisation that the baby is a separate person to his or her mother, and that creates a neurological shift that can be very unsettling for babies and for their parents. And then he explained the exact same thing happens in the brain of someone in puberty, separating from the family structure to be their own person in the world. And it is just as hard to navigate. Sure, they aren't usually throwing a tantrum and screaming on the floor, but it usually causes frustration and upset.'

Emmet sighed ruefully. Maybe that was what had made him fight with his father in the first place. He had wanted to feel independent, wanted to go to college abroad and drive Malachy's sports cars and have one of his own.

'But here's the thing,' Eli went on. 'Young people only lash out at those they love and those people who make them feel secure. So you expressed a frustration with the world, caused by a perfectly normal and natural neurological process in your brain, and I was in the firing line for it. That's because deep down, you knew I wasn't going anywhere, that I wasn't going to abandon you or hit you back or say mean things in response. So you feel safe around me, and that's why I'm flattered.'

Emmet smiled at him. 'Is there no bad thing you can't see the bright side of?'

'Emmet.' Eli squeezed his shoulder. 'The day I knew with complete clarity that your mother was the girl for me, you came as part of the package. And so as soon as I realised I loved her, then I loved you too. And I understand you have to grow and become independent, but I'm not looking forward to the day you move away and discover the big wide world.'

Emmet sighed. 'I don't want to leave you and Mam either, but I think I'll have to one day. To be honest, I've always felt a bit of an oddball in Kilteegan Bridge.'

Eli laughed. 'You're not an oddball. You just haven't found your people yet. When you do your exams next year, and go to college, wherever that is, to study whatever you choose, you'll find so many people like you. Kilteegan Bridge is a lovely place to live, and it's a great place to raise a family, but there's a big wide world out there, Emmet, and you will find your people.'

'I don't know...'

'Trust me on this?' Eli sat back down on the desk, and Emmet perched on the examination table. 'As someone who had a hard time fitting in when I was a kid, younger than you, with a German accent in a country where the Germans were bombing their cities day and night, just trust me on this. You will fit in somewhere. It might not be here, but your mam and I will always be here waiting. This will always be your home, and your refuge and your anchor, but this world has a lot to show you, Emmet Kogan. You're just on the brink of a huge adventure.'

If Joe Daly doesn't kill me first, thought Emmet to himself. But aloud he said, 'Thanks, Dad, and don't worry – I'll always come home.'

* * *

ELI WATCHED as his son walked up the avenue to the house. Lena would be furious about the car and would probably give the boy the tongue-lashing he deserved, and that was fine. He did need to get it with both barrels for what he'd done, but Eli couldn't be the one to do it. If he'd shouted at Emmet, their relationship would be irretrievably broken, and that was not what he wanted. Despite the mess his son had got himself into, he was glad he'd come to him.

Maybe soon Emmet would tell him what was really bothering him. Until then, he would just have to keep an eye on the boy and patiently wait.

CHAPTER 16

*E*mmet turned at his father's voice at the breakfast table.

'Earth to Emmet. Your mother was asking you something?'

'What?' Emmet looked at Lena, who was smiling at him. Things between them were all right again since yesterday. He'd apologised at length for his outburst, and she had forgiven him of course. Explaining about the car had taken a little longer, but like Eli, she was so glad he hadn't killed himself that she had forgiven him for that too. And she hadn't even asked him to pay for fixing it either. He didn't deserve his parents, he knew that; he was full of such shame and guilt. 'Sorry, Mam, I didn't hear you.'

'I was asking what your plans were for the weekend?'

'Nothing really.' The fact was, this weekend was the last chance he had to sort things out about the money he owed. John Crean had reluctantly agreed to take his suggestion about paying his debt off at twenty dollars a month to Bunny Cotter, and he was praying that would work.

'Really? Nellie called up yesterday. She was looking for you. She said she hadn't seen you in ages, but you were with her last weekend, weren't you? You two went to the pictures, you said?'

His mother's tone was light and conversational, but something about her questioning suddenly put him on guard. Had Nellie given something away? They always covered for each other automatically, but they hadn't spoken for a long time, and maybe they needed to meet up to get their latest stories straight.

He said carefully, 'We did, but she's all about eyeliner and lipstick and shoes these days, so she must have forgotten. She dragged me to *Cabaret*, when I wanted *The Poseidon Adventure*.'

'Yes, she remembered you'd gone to the cinema when I reminded her, but she said you saw *Last Tango in Paris*, which I've heard isn't suitable at all, by the way.'

Emmet laughed uncomfortably. 'Ah, Mam, she was winding you up, trying to get me in trouble for watching films that would have Monsignor Collins staging a protest if he knew about it.'

'Don't mention that man's name in this house,' Eli said darkly from behind his newspaper.

'Because of the sermon he preached against you?' Thirteen-year-old Pádraig looked up from his plate of eggs and bacon, fascinated. He was a rogue, full of mischief, and the image of Lena, although big for his age, and with his father's hair and eyes. 'Don't worry, Dad, all my friends are on your side. They hate him.'

'We don't hate anyone in this house,' said Lena quickly. 'And who says he preached against your dad? Monsignor Collins never mentioned your father's name.'

'Oh, everyone knew who he was talking about,' Pádraig said, his eyes sparkling.

'Pádraig...'

'What's that, Podge?' Emmet had nicknamed his little brother when Pádraig was a toddler, and it had stuck. He was mightily relieved to have the spotlight taken off him and what film he'd supposedly gone to with Nellie. 'All your friends support Dad?'

'Yeah, they do, and they... I mean, they don't like the Monsignor one bit.' Pádraig was clearly delighted at getting his brother's approval; he idolised Emmet almost as much as he idolised his father. 'Every time Monsignor Collins came to the school last May, we were

120

all terrified in case we wouldn't know our catechism for the confirmation. He would hit you on the head with his huge hands or across the knuckles with a ruler – it was horrible. And last Sunday he dragged Daithí Kerrigan around the churchyard by the ear for messing when he was serving the Mass as altar boy, and he wet his pants in front of everyone and then he started crying –'

'Thank you, Pádraig, that will do.' Lena cut across him. Emmet knew his Mam thought the Monsignor was a bully, but it wouldn't help the situation for her children to get worked up about it, so she wanted to tone it down. Bad enough that her husband was at loggerheads with the clergy; she didn't need her children adding fuel to the fire.

'Is that why you are coming home earlier these days, Dad, because patients aren't coming to you because the Monsignor doesn't like you?' Pádraig persisted.

Eli shrugged, looking around his newspaper. 'Maybe, but I can't worry about that, and neither should you three. We'll be fine anyway.'

Lena backed him up. 'Look, lads, it's all going to blow over. Dr Burke is going down to speak to Monsignor Collins to explain he can't take Eli's patients, so it will soon be sorted out.'

'But what if he doesn't listen to Dr Burke and he keeps on saying bad things about Daddy, and then Daddy has no patients and we have no money?' Sarah was worried. 'I mean now that Emmet's practically given me Molly, he needs a new horse of his own.'

'We're fine, Sarah love,' Lena reassured her usually sunny daughter. 'And even if this goes on for a while, we have enough money, so please don't worry, pet. It will blow over. The Monsignor is just a bit old-fashioned and set in his ways, so we'll just stay out of his way for a while and not rock the boat, and everything will be fine.'

'I don't see why Monsignor Collins would want anyone to go to see any other doctor,' said Pádraig stoutly. 'Everyone knows Dad's the best doctor in Ireland, even better than Dr Burke. And Dr White in Kellstown is desperate. He told Conor McCarthy's sister that the pain in her tummy was just a bug, but she ended up having to go in an ambulance that evening to Cork for an operation and she nearly died.'

'I heard that, Podge. It was appendicitis, and that old eejit couldn't tell. Dad would never make a mistake like that,' Emmet added.

'He's not just an eejit,' Sarah chimed in. 'He's deaf as a post, so everyone has to roar their ailments out loud for the whole village to hear.'

Emmet encouraged his little brother with a wink.

Pádraig raised his voice to shouting levels, putting on his strongest West Cork accent. 'I'M CONSTIPATED, DOCTOR! NOTHING DOING FOR A WEEK! THERE'S A DESPERATE SMELL OFF MY TOE, DOCTOR!'

Emmet collapsed in laughter, and Sarah started giggling. Lena knew she should probably stop Pádraig clowning around and mocking people, but Dr White really was terrible. She knew from Eli that he helped himself to his own medications, especially the morphine. And it was good to see her oldest son laughing again. It made her realise how long it had been since he'd looked remotely happy.

A ghost of a smile played on Eli's lips. He cleared his throat and placed his knife and fork together on the plate. 'Thanks, Lena, that was delicious.' He smiled at her.

Lena loved so many things about him, and his genuine consideration for others was one of them. He never ate a meal, no matter how simple, without thanking whoever prepared it, and she'd seen several times other men, unused to doing such a thing, almost embarrassed into it by him.

'Now, boys and girls,' Eli said, pushing back his chair and standing up, 'talking of being hard of hearing, 'tis time I went to work. Mrs Weldon is coming in this morning, bless her for standing by me like Jimmy does, and she's another one deaf as a post, so I'll be roaring for the next half an hour. She only comes by to get her regular prescription, but she always ends up telling me some long story about Benjy, and then because poor old Benjy is no longer with us, she starts crying, the poor woman.'

'I think you do more counselling down there than medicine, Eli.' Lena smiled at him.

'Maybe. But if the mind is wrong, the body isn't much good to you, is it? Poor Mrs Weldon is just so lonely, but I really wish she'd consider a hearing aid. Some of them now are really great, and they improve people's lives to no end. But she can't be doing with any of what she calls "new-fangled nonsense", so we'll all just keep roaring and repeating ourselves over and over.'

'She's so nice, though.' Lena gave him his jacket. 'She goes dancing every Friday night to the Castle Hotel, she tells me – I met her in the butcher's the other day. She says she never gets asked up but she likes being there all the same. She chats to other women, though she said she'd love a man to dance with.'

'Was Benjy her husband?' Sarah asked Eli sympathetically.

'No, a border collie,' he explained. 'Her husband died years ago.'

For some reason this information sent the three children into further fits of laughter. Eli just rolled his eyes, kissed his wife and left for work.

CHAPTER 17

'I honestly didn't run up debts of three hundred pounds, I swear, but John says I did, and that I was asking for credit at the track, which I didn't do – I'm not even old enough. I'm not saying it's all his fault. I went along with it when John asked Bunny Cotter to let us bet on tick, but I honestly thought it was fifty, a hundred pounds maximum, so how I owe him three hundred, I don't know. But he says if we don't give Cotter the money in the next few days, his fixer, Joe Daly, is going to come after me, or he might even hurt Mammy or Sarah – he said he does that to women,' Emmet finished miserably.

He and Nellie had gone to the beach for a swim and a private discussion. Both of them were aware how nearly they'd got caught out with their different stories about going to the pictures, and they'd agreed they needed to know what the other was up to if they were going to be able to lie successfully for each other.

Nellie was stretched out on her towel, wearing a pink polka-dot bikini that left nothing to the imagination, drops of sea water running down her pale smooth skin. When he'd finished pouring his heart out, she sighed and shrugged. 'I can't believe you got mixed up with my uncle. He's such a crook. He's making Nana Peg absolutely miserable these days. He robbed her gold cross and chain, and you know that beautiful painting she did, the one over her fireplace? It took her months to get it finished. Well, he said he was going to get it valued because he was so proud of her. And guess what? She never saw it again. She was so upset, and then trying to make out like it was all right because she knows we'll go mad.'

Emmet groaned. 'He told me he'd only come home to look after Peggy.'

'You can't believe a word that comes out of that man's mouth. His promises aren't worth the paper they're written on, not that Jingo ever writes anything down. Daddy says he just shakes hands and calls it a "gentlemen's agreement", which is a laugh. That gobshite wouldn't know a gentleman if one bit him in the arse. I think Dad would choke him with his bare hands if Mam let him. Not that she doesn't wish Jingo gone – she just doesn't want Dad to go to jail.'

Emmet groaned, unable to believe he hadn't realised John was a con man right from the start. If only he'd talked to Nellie about this before, but she'd been off on her own business all summer, weekdays in Cork at this beauty course and weekends working at the hotel in Bandon.

'I don't know what I'm going to do, Nellie. I've suggested paying the debt off at twenty a month, and John says he's going to try and see if Cotter will agree to that.'

'He's got you calling him John, has he? Same as Nana. He wants everyone to forget his creepy thieving past and pretend he's this big property tycoon, but it's only in his head. He might have come back with a stash of cash he robbed off someone, but it was soon gone, and Dad says he's clearly lying about all his so-called properties – it's just to persuade people to lend him money.'

Emmet was beginning to regret telling his cousin anything. It made him feel so stupid compared to her. There was something very worldly-wise about Nellie these days. She seemed more sophisticated and less soft than the girl he remembered from only a few months ago. He decided not to tell her about having lost all his post office money; she would think he was beyond redemption.

'Anyway, what's *your* big secret, Nell?'

She smiled coyly, sitting up to towel her long fair hair. 'Well...you know that boy I was telling you about?'

'You didn't really tell me anything about him.' Like before, he felt a stab of worried protectiveness.

'Well, he's called Gerard, and I meet him on the weekends, in Bandon mostly. That's where he works.'

'So what's he do?' Maybe he was a liftboy at the hotel or something.

'Oh, Emmet, he's lovely.' She came over all gooey as she spoke about him. 'He's always taking me to really nice places, to hotels and fancy restaurants, like the Inisowen Arms and the Arbutus Manor – we went there for the bank holiday weekend – and people are always thinking I'm at least nineteen or twenty.' She said this proudly, though she was only fifteen. 'He's got loads of money 'cause he's a salesman. It's the only job where you can earn more than the boss of the company, he says.'

Emmet was shocked but tried not to show it. He'd assumed Nellie's boyfriend was the same age as herself, or not much older, not a man who sounded much more grown up than she was.

'And his car!' she went on. 'Oh, you should see it. It's a Ford Capri, like a sports car, and he spins me wherever I want to go in it.'

He didn't want to sound provincial or disapproving in front of her, but he knew now what it was like to be tricked by someone older and more worldly, and who was maybe a con man as well, and so he had to ask. 'And what age is he?'

Nellie waved her hand nonchalantly, smirking at the three nuns who were walking on the strand and looking horrified at her in her polka-dot bikini. She didn't care a bit what anyone thought of her. 'He's older, like, not a kid like the usual fellas who eye me up. He's a *proper man.*' She gave Emmet a knowing wink.

'How do you mean, a proper man?' He had a horrible idea he knew the answer to this one.

'We've gone all the way, you know.'

'You mean, you've stayed overnight with him, at his place?' He tried to sound casual, but he felt nothing like it.

'No, not his house – that's not possible – but at hotels. He always books beautiful places.'

'And why isn't his house possible?' Emmet asked, with a sinking feeling he knew the answer to this one too.

She lit a cigarette, another new habit, inhaled and then blew the smoke out in a thin plume. She sat up and turned on her towel to face him. She was turning golden brown as the summer wore on, and although she was his cousin and his friend, he could see how any man of any age would think she was gorgeous.

'If I tell you something, Emmet, do you promise to keep it to yourself?' she asked seriously, her blue eyes sincere. 'Like I won't tell about you running up debts?'

'Of course I promise. We never tell anyone anything we talk about.'

'I know. OK, don't go mad now till you hear the whole thing, but Gerard is forty- six and he's married.' She sighed at the shock on his face. 'Don't be like that, Emmet. His wife is horrible, so mean to him, and he's going to leave her but he can't yet, not until the children are a bit older. And also his boss is her father, so his work depends on being married to her as well. It's an awful trap for him, but he's promised me he'll break free from her family when he saves up enough.'

'Ah, Nellie...' Emmet hated the idea of this grown man taking advantage of her.

'No, Emmet, honestly, stop there. I know it sounds a bit sordid or something, an affair' – she pulled a face – 'but it's not like that. Poor Ger, she just doesn't understand him. They don't sleep together or anything – they haven't for years and years.'

'But how old are his kids?'

Nellie sucked on the cigarette, agitated now. 'They're one, three and five, OK, but the last two were all her idea. She just wanted babies, so she seduced him and he didn't really want to.' She looked mutinous. 'I wish I'd never told you now. You look like my mother, all po-faced and disappointed. Honestly, I'm so sick of this stupid town and everyone in it. You all think the world starts and ends in Kilteegan Bridge, and it really doesn't. There's a big world out there, Emmet, where everyone isn't all tied up with the rules and running to confession every five minutes.'

'I'm not judging you, or being all po-faced and whatever else you said I was. I'm just a bit…well, a bit surprised is all.'

'I know what I'm doing, Emmet. I'm not a child being led by the nose into a dangerous situation.' Clearly her implication was that Emmet was just that with John Crean.

He turned from her and stared out to sea. Her words had stung him.

'Ah, Emmet, I'm sorry. I didn't mean that. The whole Jingo thing, look, it could have happened to anyone.' She leant over and put her finger on his chin, turning his face towards her. 'I'm sorry, all right. I'm just dreading Mam and Daddy finding out about Ger, and I'm worried they won't give him a chance. If they met him, they'd love him, but it's just getting them to see him when the time comes…'

He was still hurt, and anyway, even if he wasn't, he couldn't pretend this was OK; it just wasn't. 'If they met him, Nellie, they'd see a middle-aged man, older than them even, with young children, messing around with a beautiful girl less than a third of his age. And your father would kill him stone-dead.'

Nellie sighed, and it seemed to come from her toes. 'I know. It's so unfair, but I don't think we'll ever be able to be happy here in this dump. I did suggest we go to England, leave, not say a word to anyone, and I thought he'd jump at it, but he started going on about my studies and getting my trade in the beauty business. He doesn't want me to throw away my dreams for him – that's the kind of man he is, so considerate. But I told him that I'd do it in a heartbeat if we could run away together, but he…' – she stubbed the cigarette out on the sand – 'well, he didn't think it was a good idea. He said he'd love nothing more, but it wouldn't be fair on me.'

Emmet kept his own counsel on that. Telling Nellie that maybe Gerard wanted to have his cake and eat it too would only alienate her, and he needed her to trust him if he was to keep her safe from this snake.

'You are being careful, Nell, aren't you?' he asked awkwardly.

She looked at him crossly. 'I'm not so thick as to get pregnant, if that's what you mean.'

He smiled, relieved. 'I'm sorry, but I had to ask.'

'And he's very careful too. He knows I'm too young to have a baby. We're going to wait until I'm older and he's left his wife.'

'And you really think he'll –'

'Yes, he *will*,' she said furiously, throwing a sandy strip of seaweed at him. 'And while we're talking about being careful, just remember what I said. Uncle Jingo is a liar. You can't believe anything he says. If I were you, I'd just tell him to feck off and get lost and forget about squeezing any money out of you, greedy gobshite that he is. Stand up to a bully and they'll crumble, you'll see.'

CHAPTER 18

*J*immy Piper was explaining why everyone in his family had suffered from exceptionally hard toenails, and how cutting them himself was impossible with his arthritis. His mother needed to use the secateurs that were for pruning the roses on hers apparently.

Eli knew he should send Jimmy to the chiropodist in town, but he was feeling benevolent, and besides Jimmy had stuck with him when so many other patients had left.

The whole situation with his practice had got worse after Dr Burke tried to intervene. Collins had more or less denounced the Bandon doctor from the altar, not by name exactly, but no one was left in any doubt that Dr Burke had sided with the enemy. And so the only doctor left to them was Pat White of Kellstown. Eli had stayed away from Mass since Collins came to his surgery, but Lena came home in a fury.

'You should have heard him, Eli. He was giving out yards about evil men siding with each other to thwart the Church, and he's now decided the whole place is in need of a Redemptorist mission. He was roaring things like, "I don't know what's going on here! Obviously this place is completely out of control! You'd think there was no such thing as hell the way you're all going on!" And now the whole village is going to have to spend five nights in the Church next week listening to a bunch of Redemptorist priests preach fire and brimstone at us like we're lost souls in need of saving. It's completely insane.'

'It certainly sounds insane,' said Eli calmly. 'So I take it you won't be going?'

'Of course I'll be going!' she snapped at him. 'You don't understand – everyone has to go. Except mercifully for the one night when it's only men allowed, because that's the night they preach about sex, which doesn't involve us women of course.'

'But, Lena, if you think it's mad –'

'It's not about whether it's mad or not.' He could see she was frustrated and furious with him for what she saw as his obtuseness. 'You don't understand. We've been told to go, and we have to do it. We can't just ignore the priest – we have to keep in with him. I'm trying to calm this situation down, not escalate it, and us boycotting the mission would be throwing petrol on the flames.'

He looked at her, questioning the idea that she needed to keep in with the man who was trying to destroy them, but she gave him such a pleading look, begging him not to push her, that he just hugged her and retreated to his surgery, which was a haven of quiet these days.

Except when Jimmy turned up. Today it was his toes.

'No problem, Jimmy. Jump up there and take off your shoes and socks, and we'll take a look.'

'You're a very good doctor, Dr Kogan. I tell everyone. And I was very fond of Doc Dolan too. He was very good to my father, Lord have mercy on him, when he had the gout. Oh, poor Daddy was a martyr to the gout, roaring he'd be every night, but Mammy used to say he was only roaring at the crows outside so as not to scare us children.'

Eli managed not to wince at the stench from Jimmy's feet; those socks had never been washed, he guessed. He filled a basin of warm water and added a drop of disinfectant and a bit of soap and asked Jimmy to put his feet in. It wasn't to soften the nails as he told Jimmy it was; it was more to give his feet a much-needed wash.

He let the man chat away, telling him about his parents and his family, all dead now. Jimmy had never had a girlfriend, or many friends. Possibly the endless yakking was to blame for that, who knew. But he lived a solitary life, and Eli felt sorry for him.

As always, the great thing about treating Jimmy was that it allowed him plenty of time to think his own thoughts. For instance, would he ever be able to convince Mrs Weldon to wear a hearing aid? She was coming in later for her blood-pressure prescription, and he wondered whether he should have another go at persuading her; he was sure it would transform her life. He might get one from the company as a sample and get her to try it. Meanwhile, Jimmy only required a few nods or an 'Is that right?' every few minutes.

Soon Jimmy's feet were washed and his toenails cut, and Eli even found a fresh pair of socks in a drawer that he gave to Jimmy. The man's gratitude was totally disproportionate; it was just a pair of socks, but he had tears in his eyes as he left.

'Thanks very much, Doctor. You're a gentleman, no doubt about it, and aren't these the finest pair of socks a man could have? They're so comfortable. And my feet feel like I could dance at the Lilac tonight.' He chuckled.

'Why don't you?' Eli asked absently.

'Why don't I what?' The man looked startled.

'Maybe not the Lilac, but why don't you go home and have a shave and a wash and change your clothes and go out dancing? There's a nice band in the Castle Hotel on a Friday night. You never know who you'd meet.'

Jimmy blushed. 'Ah sure, Doctor, who'd want to meet the likes of me?'

Eli thought for a moment. 'Well, you have a car, don't you?'

'I have a lovely car, 'tis a beauty, a Volkswagen Beetle.'

'Well, Mrs Weldon, you know, who lives in the terrace, she goes dancing on Friday nights to the Castle Hotel. She usually gets the bus, but there's no bus this week because Bartie who drives it is after an operation, so maybe if you called and asked her if she'd like a lift?'

'Mrs Weldon who owned Benjy?'

Eli wondered how many Mrs Weldons there could be. 'Yes, that's her.'

'But why would a fine, nice, respectable lady want to go anywhere with me, Doctor?'

He looked so confused, Eli wondered if he'd made a mistake, but he didn't think so.

'I couldn't ask her that. She'd call the guards.'

'Why would she?' Eli asked gently.

'Because...well...she's a fine person, and very nice and well got, and well brought up, and sure...'

He looked like he might cry, and Eli regretted ever starting this conversation.

'She'd be mad to want to go across the road with the likes of me.'

Eli decided he'd just bite the bullet. 'Right, Jimmy, maybe she won't, and to be honest with you, she definitely won't if you don't have a good scrub and wash your hair and put on some clean clothes. You might even take yourself up to Charlie in the barber's and get a haircut. But once you're cleaned up a bit – lose the wellington boots too, by the way – then why wouldn't she allow you to drive her to a dance? She's from a lovely family, but you tell me all the time about your family, and they sounded like great people too, and you have a fine house and a bit of land and a nice little business with the leather. And why wouldn't a respectable man of the parish offer a lady a spin when there was no bus?'

'I only have the wellingtons, Doctor,' Jimmy said sadly.

'Right. Wait here. Have you the time?'

'I can, of course. I don't have anything to do today because I was supposed to be going to Mrs Jacobs about a bag she's buying, but she had to go to a funeral in Tralee, or was it Killorglin? Her sister-in-law. And I was only thinking to myself that it was a good day for it, because the graveyard back there is up on a hill and the coffin would be hard to manoeuvre on wet ground. Though it's not soaking back there now, not like the one in Ballydehob – that's like a lake the minute the rain starts. But sure down there 'tis all bog. I used to go cutting turf on the bog back there when I was a young fella with my

Uncle Mick. Mick who went to England – remember I told you about him the last day? He had a desperate time with itching. He was a martyr to the itch. His poor mother, God be good to her, had nails like a witch you'd see in a story just for the scratching –'

'That's grand, Jimmy. Hang on and I'll be right back.'

It was probably mad, and no doubt Jimmy would return in the same state next month, but Eli wanted to do something good today. He ran up the avenue and straight to his and Lena's bedroom. Jimmy was about his size, so he quickly selected a pair of shoes and an old suit he didn't wear any more, a shirt and a tie. There was even some new underwear Lena had bought for him when she was in Cork still in the packet, so he grabbed those as well and another pair of socks for good measure. He threw everything into a paper bag and made his way back to the surgery.

Jimmy was sitting there patiently.

'Right, I hope these fit. We're around the same size. Maybe I'm a bit taller, but you can fold up the legs or something.' Eli took the suit and shirt and tie out of the bag.

'Are you giving me these, Doctor?' Jimmy was incredulous.

'I am, so go home, have a serious scrub everywhere, wash the hair, then go down to Charlie and get a haircut, and then go home and get dressed. I'll tell Mrs Weldon when I see her later that you'll pick her up at seven, so you won't even have the embarrassment of asking her.'

'But, Doctor, what if she won't go with me?'

Eli's heart nearly broke for him. To have so little confidence. He was a nice if incredibly long-winded man, and Mrs Weldon was deaf and lonely. Why not try to make two people happy? 'She will. She was saying to Margaret how she was so sad to be missing the dance but she had no way to get there, and that it's the best night of her week.'

'And will I leave her there and come back for her, if she'll go, like?'

Eli smiled. 'You will not. You'll go in with her and buy her a cup of tea or a bottle of orange or a large brandy or whatever she wants, and then you'll ask her up for a dance.'

'Will I?' Jimmy looked like Eli was suggesting he join a circus.

'You will. Although she's very hard of hearing, so you'll have to shout. Can you manage some kind of a dance?'

'Well, Mammy used to dance with me. We'd put the radio on of a Sunday night and waltz around the kitchen, but I've never been to a proper dance in a dance hall.'

'Well, now's your chance. Don't forget to fold up the legs of the trousers, though – they'll be too long.'

'I'll just quickly hem them. Mam taught me all that stuff, sewing, knitting. She used to say I was a dab hand with the needle, and sure, aren't I a leather worker as a result.'

'Good man yourself. I forgot about your stitching. Now, go and get organised, and pick Mrs Weldon up at seven looking like a new pin.'

'I don't know about this, Doctor. I mean...I...I just don't know...'

'Jimmy, what's to know about? You're giving a lift to a dance for a neighbour, and if she wants to, you'll buy her a drink and have a waltz. Nobody is asking you to propose marriage or do the funky chicken.'

'What?' Jimmy looked aghast.

'Nothing, it's a joke. Look, Jimmy, Mrs Weldon loves the dance, and she goes every week but nobody ever asks her up – she told my wife. So maybe she'd like to have a dance with a nice man who is polite and decent, and have a bit of craic, as you Irish are so fond of saying.'

'And I'm a nice man, am I?' There was no guile in his words.

'You are, and she'll be delighted, I'm sure.'

'You might be sure, but I'm not one bit...'

Eli ushered him out. 'You'll be fine. She's going to love your stories, Jimmy. You tell them to your heart's content, and I guarantee she'll nod and smile at you all night.'

CHAPTER 19

*P*eggy Crean gazed at the sun-faded wallpaper over her fireplace. The shape of her missing painting was clear to see, a slightly darker rectangular patch on the chimney breast. She'd been proud of that painting. She'd never imagined she could be good at anything like that, but Emily had seen a few little sketches she'd done on the backs of envelopes and on bits of paper lying around the shop, just doodling really, and signed her up for a night class in the school on a Thursday night without even asking her. She'd have said no probably if Emily had asked her, which was why Emily hadn't done that of course. That girl was a marvel, and the day Blackie brought her into their business was the best day's work he'd ever done.

Nellie had bought Peggy a set of watercolours for Christmas, and Blackie and Emily had bought her some canvas and brushes and oil paints, and in the evenings, she worked on her art. It wasn't much, and she didn't think she was a great talent, so she was amazed at how well they sold in the shop and embarrassed by how much people offered her in commissions to paint their favourite animals and houses. The only one she'd done that she was really satisfied with was the one she'd hung over her fireplace. It was of the village, all the businesses and the footpaths. She'd even painted Mrs Weldon and Benjy walking up to the butcher's for some bones, and the Atlantic Ocean glittered in the background. It had taken her most of a year to get it right, and she was happy with it. It represented something, her new life, the one just for her, the ocean like the possibility of something good just beyond the horizon.

But it was gone now. Her older son didn't care that it meant anything to her. He'd claimed he was taking it to be valued and said the art dealer had wanted to keep it for a bit while he compared it to similar pieces. But she knew he'd sold it and had drank or gambled the money.

She'd gone to confession last week and confessed to the sins of anger and resentment towards her son. The Monsignor had said it was the cross God had chosen for her, that she must bear the loss of her painting with grace and humility, that she must pray for strength to overcome her pride and self-regard and that she must do her duty by her prodigal son, because the Lord values a lost sheep over all the rest of the flock. That was why Peggy wasn't in Mass today; she thought looking at that Monsignor's smug face would make her feel like boxing his ears all over again. She supposed she'd have to go to the Redemptorist mission next week, along with everyone else in the town, and that would be bad enough.

Father Otawe would never have said she had a duty to kill the fatted calf for Jingo, or 'John' as he kept making her call him. Emily was so right not to have gone along with that nonsense. One of the times Peggy made confession to the former priest, the whole story of Dick and the marriage and the violence came tumbling out. He'd told her then that if she was ever in danger, she should call him and the guards, and that they would protect her, that she could come to the parochial house any time she needed, that she was not in the wrong.

Two men of the cloth, but very different. Just like Blackie and Jingo were brothers but as unalike as it was possible for two people to be.

Peggy thought of her daughter Joanne. She'd been a silent, dark little one, and when she was fifteen she took off, and they'd hardly heard a word since. Blackie barely remembered her, and she never had much to do with John. She couldn't get away from her father, the town, Ireland, fast enough. She sent a card at Christmas, but that was it. Just signed, Joanne and family, no return address. Peggy wondered if she had children, probably, but with whom, and where was anyone's guess. The stamp on the card was English so somewhere, but that was all she knew, and all she would ever know it looked like.

She should never have married Dick Crean. That's what everyone thought; she knew that. She'd made her bed, so she should lie in it. But she never did agree. She was sold by her father to Dick's father to settle a debt. They'd agreed over a glass of whiskey in the bar of the Munster Arms Hotel in Bandon. She was informed when he came home that she was to be married the following month. She met Dick once, two weeks before the wedding, and she'd prayed all the night before, hoping that God and His saints would hear her prayers, the fervent wishes of a sixteen-year-old girl, that he'd be kind, a decent man. But he wasn't. She'd known it from the start.

He'd hit her the first time on the second day of their marriage, and almost every day since. He had hit, kicked, punched, thrown, dragged her by her hair so often, it was almost second nature to him; he did it without even thinking, like breathing or drinking. He was evil, she knew it, evil to the core. The priests said all were God's children, but Dick Crean was the work of the devil himself. The day Emily went for him with the pike and he took off for England and started another family was the best day of her life.

Blackie had bought her this house, a lovely little cottage on the main street, and he installed locks and bolts everywhere, so when she got into her bed at night, she felt safe. She wished her mother could have been as lucky. Peggy's father was a violent bully. Her brother hit him a clatter with a spade one night in desperation, and that did it for him. The guards were called, but no charges were brought. They knew Jim Scannell of old, and the local sergeant, a very shrewd man, knew the world would be better off without him, so accidental death was recorded. Her mother died three months later. It wasn't fair; she should have had a bit of peace too, but it never happened.

Peggy was so much luckier than her mother had been. She had this little oasis of peace, thanks to Blackie and Emily, where she could live out the rest of her life. This little house was the first place she'd ever lived where there wasn't shouting and things broken and fear and pain.

Or at least it had been that way until Jingo turned up.

She knew Blackie thought she was daft. She should never have allowed him back in, but when she looked at him, she saw the little boy who used to come into her bed in the middle of the night for a cuddle, the little boy who, when he was only six or seven, tried to hit Dick with a hurley to stop him beating her. He'd changed when he was eleven or twelve, starting to follow Dick around and imitate all his ways, leaving all the humping bags of seed potatoes or shovelling coal to her and Blackie while he and his father shirked all the work. She didn't know much about how things were passed from one generation to the next, and she didn't know why he went like his father when his brother, Blackie, didn't, but that's the way it was.

Still, she'd had to take him in. She just didn't know what else to do. Jingo was her baby boy, her flesh and blood, and she was so grateful when he promised her he'd turned things around, that he'd realised there was a better way to live, that he was a hot-shot property developer now. She was happy for him that he was rich, but as she told him, she would have been just as happy if he'd been working on the roads, earning an honest wage for honest work.

Either way, it had all turned out to be a lie. After he'd spent the wad of cash he'd had in his pocket when he arrived, which she was beginning to suspect must have been stolen, he turned out to be the same old Jingo as he'd been before, always looking for the next scam or easy money.

Would he ever change? Maybe there was no chance of it. Maybe, like his father, he was a lost cause.

There was a loud knocking on the front door in the hall, and she decided not to open it in case it was one of Jingo's debtors, who were always coming looking for him. She didn't know who else it would be on a Sunday when all the respectable citizens of Kilteegan Bridge were at Mass except for herself and possibly Lena's Eli, who had been staying away since the Monsignor denounced him.

Jingo shouted down from upstairs for her to answer the door, but she stayed quiet and still, and after a couple more minutes of knocking, she heard him get out of bed upstairs, cursing, and something crashing over, probably that nice ewer and basin she'd placed in the spare room for him to wash his face in the morning. Broken now.

He came padding down the stairs – he wasn't wearing any shoes by the sound of it – and opened the front door.

'Well, look who it is. It's the Emerson Fittipaldi of West Cork,' she heard him sneer, his words still slurred by last night's boozing. 'What do you want this fine morning?'

'Hello, Jingo.'

Was that Lena's oldest, Emmet, speaking? Peggy sat bolt upright, listening intently, her thin hands clutching the arms of the chair.

'It's John, not Jingo,' snapped Jingo. 'Have some bloody respect. Bad enough you left me stranded waiting for you on the Cork road without a word.'

'Is your mother at Mass?' Emmet lowered his voice as he stepped into the hall.

Jingo scoffed. 'Course she is. Where else would she be? She's a right Holy Mary, never missed Mass in her life. Now what do you want?'

'I want to know what Bunny Cotter said about paying him back at twenty a month.'

There was a pause, and then Peggy heard Jingo say, 'Well, he was raging at first, said you'd soon be drinking through a straw or something, but I talked him round, said it was your first time and you were a bit thick but had learnt your lesson, so he relented.'

'Oh, thank God.' Peggy could hear the relief in Emmet's voice, and she burnt with shame. She hadn't known there was anything going between him and Jingo, but there clearly was, and she knew it was all her fault. She'd been so stupidly convinced her son had turned over a new leaf and was a successful businessman, and she'd persuaded Maria O'Sullivan to invite Jingo to her wedding. When she saw Jingo talking intently to Emmet, the doctor's son, instead of trying to put a stop to it, she'd been delighted. Jingo mixing with the quality was the golden pinnacle of all her efforts to mend her family's reputation in the town, and she'd even felt annoyed with Lena when she'd crossed the dance floor to put a stop to their conversation.

Now she could hear Jingo saying smoothly, 'But Bunny says I'm the one who has to deliver the cash. He can't be seen taking money off a minor – he'd lose his betting licence. But that's OK. I'll meet you at the post office on the day of the month your father's letter comes, and you can give the money straight to me.'

'Oh...'

'No, don't thank me. I don't mind helping out. I'm planning on staying around here for a while, I reckon, at least for the five years we'll need to pay off the debt.'

There was a long pause, then Emmet muttered something.

'What?' Jingo sounded annoyed.

'I said, it won't be five years. At twenty a month, that'll take fifteen months.'

'Three hundred?' Jingo spoke in a world-weary voice. 'Have you lost your mind? Do you seriously think Bunny Cotter would let you off interest-free? No, he and I worked it out together, and by the time it's paid off with interest – and that's at his lowest rates because he trusts me – it will be five years.'

'That's... But that's... Jingo... John... That's over a thousand pounds!' Peggy could hear Emmet's voice shaking as he worked it out. 'How could we owe Bunny Cotter so much? We never bet that much.'

'High interest rates in that end of the market, I'm afraid, kid. You shouldn't have got it on tick, but here we are.'

'But I didn't ask for tick. You were the one who asked for it.'

Jingo's voice rose angrily. 'Oh, no you don't, Little Lord Fauntleroy. You're into this up to your neck the same as me. Did I drag you by your pretty little red curls to the track? Did I? No, I didn't. You got into the gee-gees. You were the one wanting to put on bets. I never pushed you. It was all you, so don't go rewriting history here.'

Peggy listened anxiously for Emmet to answer, but he didn't reply.

When her son spoke again, his voice was triumphant; he knew he was winning. 'Anyway, you eejit, how did you think I was laying bets for you when you didn't have any money to put down?'

'But I only had no money because I'd lent you it all, everything in my account, over a thousand...' Emmet's voice was weak.

'And I've told you,' Jingo said cheerfully, 'you'll get that back when my solicitor sends me my cheque. Now off home with you, and as I say, not a word to Mammy and Daddy. Joe Daly doesn't care who Bunny Cotter tells him to batter, and he'd love a few hours with your mam, or your sister, or both if you start shouting your mouth off.'

That was it. Peggy had had enough of Bunny Cotter and his so-called sidekick Joe Daly. Dick had threatened her with those names for years after they were married, coming into the shop one night after closing and demanding money from the till, until one time in despair she refused and told him that she didn't care if Bunny Cotter or Joe Daly did use her as a punching bag or worse, he wasn't getting another penny out of the business. The next thing, she was on the ground behind the counter and Dick was booting her in the head, remarking between kicks that he was quite capable of using her as a punching bag or worse himself, thank you very much.

She stood up from her chair and went to the doorway. 'That's enough Bunny Cotter this and Bunny Cotter that, Jingo,' she said firmly.

The two of them turned in shock at the sound of her voice, Jingo in bare feet and a dressing gown pulled on over his pyjamas.

'And, Emmet, don't mind him. I'm pretty sure now that man Bunny Cotter does not exist at all, and nor does Joe Daly, or even if they do, they must be very old and toothless by now.'

'Get back in the sitting room, Ma,' snapped Jingo. 'I'm having a private conversation with my pal, and you don't know what you're talking about. You've even forgotten my name – I said to call me John.'

'John, then, leave Emmet alone. Stop tormenting him. He's a good boy.'

Jingo grinned at her maliciously. 'Emmet might be the posh son of a doctor, Mam, but he's not a good boy at all. He got me to put bets on the horses for him with Bunny because he's too young to do it himself, and he gave me money to buy him drink. He even wanted me to sell the car he stole off his father, only he crashed it before he got to me.'

Peggy glanced in amazement at Emmet, expecting him to protest his innocence, but the boy was slumped against the wall, looking sick with guilt.

Jingo was delighted. 'You see? Look at his face. It was all him, and I'm only trying to help him out of the hole he dug for himself. You always blame me for everything that goes wrong, Mam, but you should trust me more. Aren't I the son who came home to look after you? I wish you'd love me back the way I love you.'

Peggy's motherly heart felt a deep pang for her lost sheep, but she managed to hold firm. It was one thing when he was stealing just from her, but if she'd heard right, he'd already 'borrowed' a thousand pounds off Emmet. There was no cheque coming from any house on Park Lane, she was sure of that now, so it wasn't borrowing but plain old-fashioned stealing. 'Son, whatever Emmet did, I can see he is very ashamed of it. But guilt is something you've never felt in your life, so I'm certain he only got into bad ways because you dragged him into them.'

'Ah, shut up, Mam,' said Jingo contemptuously, turning away.

She raised her voice, though it trembled when she spoke. 'I will not be quiet. You're a liar and a crook, and whatever you've done to me, I'm not letting you do it to anyone else in my family.'

He spun back to face her, his black eyes blazing with rage. 'Shut your mouth, I'm warning you, or I'll shut it for you!' he yelled, and raised his hand to slap her. She cowered back, terrified, but Emmet leapt forwards and grabbed Jingo's wrist.

'Leave her alone!' he yelled.

Jingo jerked his wrist out of Emmet's grasp, snarling and showing his teeth. 'Get out of my house, you little snot-nosed –'

'It's not your house.' The boy was white in the face but held his ground. 'It's your mother's, and you need to leave here right now.'

'Leave? I'm never going to leave,' Jingo snarled, and raised his fists.

In quick response, Emmet rolled up his shirt sleeves, his jaw tight with fury. 'We'll see about that…'

Peggy panicked. Jingo was a dirty fighter, an eye-gouger, an arm-twister. 'No fighting in this house!' she shrieked at the top of her voice, and with a quick glance in her direction, both of them stood back.

At first she was surprised Jingo had obeyed her as readily as Emmet, but then she realised that although the younger lad was still growing, his rolled-up sleeves had revealed muscular arms, got from riding horses. Jingo had never played a sport, he'd started smoking and drinking with Dick when he was barely into his teens, and he'd never done a day's work in his life, so his arms were thin.

'Let me throw him out for you, Peggy,' begged Emmet.

Jingo laughed, all cocky now that his mother had stopped the fight. 'Oh, I'm going nowhere, kid. Unless it's back to bed to finish the nice dream about your mam I was having when I was so rudely interrupted…' He darted past Emmet and ran up the stairs, still laughing, and moments later his bedroom door slammed.

Emmet was scarlet in the face and obviously dying to go after him despite Peggy's strictures about not fighting. She caught hold of his arm. 'No, love, don't. He's a coward but he's desperate. He's got his back to the wall and nowhere to go, and I don't want you getting hurt scrapping with him. Now come into the kitchen and I'll make you a cuppa while you tell me your side of the story if you want to.'

He followed her into the back, still breathing hard. 'It's not a good story, Mrs Crean, though I wasn't going to steal the car. I thought about it. I was so frightened about what he said would happen to Mam and Sarah if I didn't get the money, but I realised I couldn't do it, even before I crashed it into the ditch.'

'I believe you, pet.' She smiled at him as she moved the kettle to the hottest spot on the range. 'And even if you had, it wouldn't have been you to blame.'

'I was to blame for most of it, though. I went along with everything he suggested. I thought…' His voice trailed off in shame.

She nodded sympathetically. 'I know. You thought he was the big, sophisticated property developer, and so did I. I was such an eejit. I was telling everyone how great he was. I even wanted your aunt and Blackie to give him a job managing one of their shops, can you believe. But Jingo hasn't changed. He's just got better at pretending. He's the same old waster he ever was, and I should never have let him back into our lives.'

Emmet jerked his chin towards the ceiling. 'Are you sure you don't want me to? You know, Nellie said to me if I stood up to a bully like Jingo, he'd back down, and I think it might be true.'

'No, pet, it'll take more than you to run him, big strong boy though you are. We have a couple of hours yet before the thirst comes on him and he heads out to the Donkey's Ears, so after we've had a cuppa, I'm going to call your uncles.'

'You mean Jack?' Emmet looked alarmed.

'And Blackie and Skipper as well, of course, because I think of Skipper as one of your uncles these days.' Peggy turned to take down her chipped old teapot – Jingo had stolen her good willow-patterned one that Emily had given her from the shop – and spooned in a heap of tea leaves. 'But don't go fretting. I'm not going to tell them anything about the car or the horses or your savings or anything – that's your business. I'm just going to ask them to come and do what I should have had them do a long time ago. And that's stick Jingo back on the boat to England. I'm not putting up with him any longer, Emmet. When it was just me, that was one thing, but to go stealing off you, my Nellie's first cousin, that's the last straw.'

She turned to smile at him and found him staring at his shoes miserably.

'What's the matter?' she asked anxiously. 'Is there something else you haven't told me? I promise I won't be shocked. I'm past all that.'

'No, it's just...I don't know if you should ask them. Jack and Skipper, I mean.'

'Whyever not, love?'

'I don't think they're the sort who like to fight.'

She laughed, surprised. 'Well, hopefully they're not, please God, and Blackie's not the violent type either. But I've been told Jack and Skipper came on a gang of sheep stealers last summer, and from what I hear, they gave a very good account of themselves and put two of them in hospital before the rest took to their heels, though you didn't hear that from me, of course.'

'Really?' Emmet looked stunned. But then miserable again. 'There's another thing, Mrs Crean. I had a terrible row with them recently. I mean, not exactly a row, but I spoke very rudely, so I don't think they'll want to do me any favours.'

'Oh, don't worry about that.' She beamed fondly at him as she placed her nice matching willow-patterned cups on the table; she'd been amazed to find them still in her cupboard – it seemed like a good omen. 'Everyone falls out with their relatives from time to time, but I know the O'Sullivans, and they always fall back in again in no time. You've a great family, Emmet, loyal and loving. I would have given my eye teeth to have one like yours, but it wasn't to be, although Blackie and your Auntie Emily have made it up to me. So don't you fret about Jack and Skipper. Whatever you said to them, it won't make any difference when it comes to it. They love you, Emmet, and I'm sure they know you love them.'

Emmet looked doubtful, but while he drank his tea, she made two phone calls and both times explained to the person at the other end that Jingo had been stealing off her and was now trying to frighten Emmet with a thug called Bunny Cotter, who she was almost certain didn't exist. Afterwards, she sent the boy home, because what was about to happen wasn't a boy's business. She sat down in the same chair she'd been sitting in earlier, stared at the dark patch over the fireplace where her picture should be and waited.

* * *

SHE DIDN'T HAVE to let the three men in because Blackie had his own key, but she heard the front door opening very quietly and then the rush of feet up the stairs.

A loud crash followed, and seconds later the door to her room flew

146

open and in burst Jingo, his nose bleeding and his pyjamas half torn off him.

'Mam, they threw me down the stairs!' he screamed. 'I told them I didn't do nothin', that stupid kid got himself into a mess. I was only tryin' to help him, and they come here and attack me...'

Blackie, Jack and Skipper piled into the room after him, panting, but Jingo pulled Peggy up off the chair and held her in front of him, using her as a human shield. 'Tell them to leave me alone, Mam! It's not fair, three against one.' She tried to pull away, but he wouldn't let go. He was holding her upper arms in a tight painful grip. 'Just stay still, Mam.'

So she did stand still, but she slightly turned her head to look once more where her precious painting had been.

When he'd sold that painting, Jingo had hurt her as much as he could ever hurt her, and she found she didn't care any more what he might do to her now.

He was in his bare feet, and she had her good leather shoes on; they had a bit of a heel. She stood hard with one of them on his bare toes. He howled and shook her till her teeth rattled.

She stamped on his foot this time, as hard as she could, and she was strong from years of drawing heavy bags of cement and coal into the shop.

'You've broke my toe!' he screamed, and let go of her, ready to hit her, but the minute he released her, Blackie, Skipper and Jack rushed to drag him away. He pulled and strained to get free. 'Mam, tell them to let me go!'

'I want you out of my life, Jingo,' she said quietly, facing him as he struggled. 'For good this time.'

'Don't call me that! I'm *John*, Mam, your own son, and when I get my money from the house, I'm going to buy you expensive jewellery and flowers and clothes and another, better painting for the wall, from a proper artist, a van Gogh or something...'

It was pathetic. Even at this late stage, he was trying to pull his 'John Crean' act on her, but it only showed how he understood nothing about her. She hadn't loved her painting because she thought she was as good as a real artist. She'd loved it because it was hers.

And he wasn't her John.

That might have been the name she'd chosen for him when he was a newborn baby, but he was Jingo since the day Dick was in the pub and was told his wife had had another boy. 'By jingo!' was Dick's only response, apart from assuming the publican would give him a few free drinks on the strength of it. Jingo had been almost a week old before his father even saw him, let alone held him. It probably wasn't entirely Jingo's fault that he turned out to be such a dreadful person, but then every man and woman was in the end responsible for themselves. Everyone had a conscience, and like Emily kept telling her, there were many people raised in worse situations than her son, and they managed to behave so much better than he did – like her other son, Blackie, for instance.

Her two sons had never had a bond, even as little boys. Blackie had started working with her in the shop as soon as he was able, and Jingo had started going to the pub with his father long before he should have been able. She didn't know much about how things were passed from one generation to the next, but Jingo was his father's son and Blackie was hers.

'Ma, you can't let them throw me out! It's all right for Blackie!' he screamed at her. 'He got everything, but I got nothin'. You never loved me, never cared about me, it was always just him.' He strained against the steel-like grip of Blackie and Skipper, while Jack stood between him and his mother for fear of another attack.

'You were given what little I had, Jingo, and you took more. You've stolen from me. You've said and done horrible things, not just to me but to other people too. I'm mortified of you, and that's the truth. So get out of my sight, and I never want to lay eyes on you again. You're dead to me, Jingo. I hope for your sake that you change your ways one day and try to live a better life. You're still a young man, and you have choices.'

She had found a strength that she'd never summoned for her father, nor for her husband, but she had it now and she was going to have her say. 'Stop imagining everything that goes wrong is someone else's fault. You bring your own misfortune down on your head, and I've had enough. I've suffered endless abuse at the hands of men – my father, my husband and then you – but it stops here, Jingo. I need peace, in my head and in my heart and in my home. So get out of my house and my village and my country, and wherever you end up, I hope you find a way to live a better life.'

'Mam... I'm sorry, Mam. I'll be better...' But Blackie and the others were dragging him out now as tears mixed with blood on his face.

'Goodbye, Jingo,' she said, in a voice so strong she almost frightened herself.

From the front door, she watched Emmet's three uncles bundle Jingo into the van Blackie used for deliveries. It took a while because Jingo was putting up a fierce fight, but they managed it in the end, and then they drove away down the street.

The whole place was peering from behind their curtains, she was sure, but Peggy Crean didn't care. She stood out on her front doorstep in plain view of everybody, and she took a deep breath of clean country air and exhaled slowly, then thanked God that she would never, ever again have to set eyes on Dick Crean's son.

CHAPTER 20

'So where does this Bunny Cotter live?' asked Jack calmly. He was sitting beside Blackie in the front of the van, looking over his shoulder into the back. Skipper had expertly tied Jingo's hands behind his back and lashed his feet together with baler twine, rendering him immobile. Skipper sat beside him, cushioned by some bags of peat moss.

'How should I know?' howled Jingo as his head banged off the side of the van when Blackie drove over a pothole.

'Come on, Jingo. We can drive around indefinitely looking for this thug, or you can tell us where to find him.'

'I only seen him at the races!'

Blackie glanced in the mirror as he took the next corner. 'Right then, let's head to the racetrack and you can point him out, and then as you're such great friends, I'll bring both of you to the boat and stand the price of two one-way tickets to England. You and your pal can go and find our worthless old man if you want someone new to scrounge off.'

The shower of expletives that came in response made Blackie smile, and he drove even faster, deliberately bouncing over the potholes instead of avoiding them; Blackie guessed the metal floor of the van was doing nothing to make the journey easier on his brother's body. He'd feel every bump and turn, and in West Cork, that meant every stretch of road they had.

'Do they hold race meetings on a Sunday?' Skipper asked Jack as Jingo roared in vain at Blackie to slow down.

Jack smiled his slow smile at Skipper. 'I don't know for sure, but maybe they do, and maybe we'll find this Bunny Cotter there. What d'you say, Jingo?' He and Skipper both turned to grin at the man lying trussed in the back.

'Ah, shut up, you dirty pair of poofs,' snapped Jingo, bouncing around on the hard floor.

Blackie glanced to his left to see how the two farmers took the insult. He saw Skipper's jaw tighten, and Jack turned to stare out the windscreen.

In the back, Jingo cackled shrilly. 'Ooh, I hit the nail right on the head there, didn't I? I don't know why I didn't think of it before. You're never out of each other's company. Sure Joe Daly's only going to love making mincemeat of you two.'

'Right.' Blackie pulled sharply into a lay-by, shielded from the road by a tall hedge.

'What are you doing?' asked Jack, looking at him, startled. 'Whatever it is, it's not worth it. He's just an eejit shouting his mouth off.'

'Maybe so, but I've had enough of his nonsense, and I'm doing something that should have been done years ago,' said Blackie firmly. 'And what I couldn't do in front of my mother. So you two go for a stroll in the woods there, Jack and Skipper. This is between me and him.'

His heart pumping with adrenalin, Blackie jumped out of the van and went around the back. He had been suppressing his anger on the subject of his father and brother for years, so it was true that this wasn't just about Jack and Skipper. This was about the humiliation Jingo and Dick had put him and his mother through all their lives. It was about him never being able to imagine himself worthy of a girl like Emily because of his name being Crean. It was about making sure that Jingo got the message loud and clear. His brother was like a boil, and lancing it was the only way.

He opened the doors and dragged his brother to the ground, roughly pulling off the tape that bound his hands and the twine around his ankles.

Jingo yelped. 'They're only a pair of poofs, Blackie. It's them should be kicked out of town. Don't let's be fighting on their account.'

'This isn't on their account, you worthless piece of dung. It's on mine.'

'Don't touch me!' Jingo jumped up and tried to run, but Blackie grabbed him by the collar and shook him like a rat. His scrawny brother hissed and kicked and spat obscenities, but Blackie was all brawn and Jingo didn't stand a chance.

'Blackie, don't do anything that gets you in trouble,' said Jack worriedly, appearing around the side of the van with Skipper.

'Listen to Jack, Blackie. Don't. He's right.'

'Give me twenty minutes, you two. I'll see you back here.' Blackie's tone brooked no argument, and Jack and Skipper looked at each other, shrugged and turned and went.

* * *

IN THE WOODS, they disturbed a vixen that stopped what she was doing to gaze at them for a moment, her amber eyes intense, before trotting off into the undergrowth about her business.

Skipper inhaled deeply. The sweet smell of the furze, its oils released by the heat of the late summer sun, was sweet like honey. He was brought back to that moment in the Montana woods with Jack, years ago, on the day he'd confessed his feelings for the Irish boy and found to his amazement and relief that they were returned. Now he put his arms back around Jack and pulled him tight against him. 'You all right, Jackie-boy?'

'Yeah...' But Jack was tense and pulled away. He stood facing Skipper with his hands in the pockets of his work jeans, frayed and paint-spattered with holes on the knees. 'Do you think he will realise

Jingo is right, once he stops to think about it? I don't think I can stand to see Blackie look at us the way Emmet looked at us the other day.'

Skipper thought about it. 'I ain't sure, but both your sisters and even your mama invite me to family things like I'm your person, just like Blackie or Eli are Emily's and Lena's, don't they? So I reckon the whole family knows somethin', even if they don't say it out loud. Look, Jackie-boy, things ain't never gonna be easy for us, never were and probably won't ever be, but what folks do is more important than what they say, right?'

He gazed at Jack intently

'And they accept us, you know they do. Ain't nobody in the family really thinks I'm just a ranch hand here, passin' through. They treat me like I'm one of y'all, and I feel like I am. So maybe we'll never say it out loud, but that don't matter.'

Jack nodded but then grimaced. 'Though Emmet had no idea, did he?'

Skipper's heart broke for Jack; he knew how hurt he'd been by Emmet's expression of disgust. He hugged him, and this time Jack didn't pull away but leant his head on his shoulder. 'He'll come around, Jackie-boy,' Skipper murmured in his ear, pushing his fingers through Jack's dark curls and then kissing him. 'He's a good kid, jus' a bit confused, and he'll be back. You should see the bay mare with him – she loves him more than she loves me. You might be able to fool a human, we're kinda dumb, but you'll never fool a horse. They know a good one, and she sees it in Emmet.'

* * *

WHEN THEY ARRIVED BACK to the lay-by, Blackie was sitting on the back of the van, the doors open, smoking a cigarette. His knuckles were skinned, and his shirt clung to his body with sweat. Jingo was lying inside, taped up again, both eyes swelling and his nose bleeding, dripping onto the metal floor. He had quite a few more cuts and bruises, but he looked like he'd live.

153

As Jack and Skipper came towards him, Blackie stood up. 'Tell these two what you told me,' he snapped at his brother.

Jingo was lying with his swollen eyes closed, and he mumbled something so softly, they couldn't hear him.

'Say that again!' demanded Blackie.

'There is no Bunny Cotter,' Jingo said, louder now but sullenly. 'He doesn't exist. I made him up. Well, my old man made him up actually. He used him to get money out of my mother, said Bunny would send John Daly to…do things to her…unless she gave him money out of the till.'

'Great role model there, Jingo,' said Jack contemptuously.

'He was my father. I thought he knew what he was about. I was proud of him. It wasn't my fault he led me wrong,' Jingo whined.

'Shut up.' Blackie clenched his fist. 'I'm so sick of your whingeing. It's always someone else – it's never you. You've lived this hard-done-by story all your life, Jingo, but you got what I got. And we are very different men. Now I'm only going to say this once. I'm going to drive you to Cork. I'm going to get you a suit of clothes and a ticket for the boat to Swansea. And not because you deserve it but because I'm a Christian man with a good conscience, I'm going to give you one hundred pounds. It's enough to set you up in digs for a few weeks over there, if you want to get a proper job and pay your way. I doubt you will, but I'll have given you one last chance so I can tell our mother you won't be sleeping on the streets. Now if you drink it or gamble it, you'll be under a bridge within days and so be it. That's your choice. I couldn't care less.' Sincerity rang true in his every single word.

'I don't care a twopenny damn what happens to you, but our poor mother won't sleep if she thinks you're a pathetic tramp on the street. So I'm going to tell her I've helped set you up, which is what the clothes and the hundred quid is for, and if you've a shred of decency, and I don't think you do, you'll send her a postcard telling her you're all right.' He paused and pointed into Jingo's swollen face. 'And this is the most important bit, Jingo, and I swear to God in heaven I mean this. If I ever see your face again, for the rest of my life, if you so much as put a toe on this island again, I will actually kill you. I'll make it look like an accident, and nobody will care and nobody will suspect me. Do you want to know why?'

Jingo didn't speak; he looked terrified.

'Because you are nothing but a low-life scumbag who steals and lies and abuses people's good nature. That's all you ever were and probably all you'll ever be. But despite you and my father, I made something of myself. I married a wonderful woman, became part of a great family, and when you threatened them, that was the final straw. I work hard, I'm completely honest in my dealings, I never borrow or steal, and I treat people with respect. Things like that are important to decent people but mean nothing to the likes of you. So if you turn up in Kilteegan Bridge again, it will be the last thing you'll ever do – I'll make sure of it. And I'll get away with it too, so think carefully.'

And Jingo clearly saw in Blackie's face that he wasn't bluffing and turned his head away with a defeated groan.

* * *

In Cork City, they stopped at a men's shop, where Blackie bought a pair of trousers, a shirt, socks and shoes. He even bought a suitcase and put a few other items in too, a shaving kit, spare underwear, a pullover and an extra shirt.

While Blackie bought the clothes, Jack rang Kilteegan House from a telephone box and asked Lena to bring Emmet to the phone. He told Emmet that Peggy was right, that there was no Bunny Cotter, that that was the end of it. He said goodbye and hung up while the boy was still stammering his thanks.

Once they got to the Port of Cork, all three of them escorted Jingo to the gents' toilets and supervised him dressing. Blackie did his rough best to clean up the cuts on his face, but the bruising would look worse before it got better. Nothing was broken, though.

The *Innisfallen* had been serving the people of Cork for decades, and Blackie Crean bought a one-way ticket to the Welsh port of Swansea and a connecting train ticket to London.

He handed the ticket to his brother as they stood on the dockside. Then he took the suitcase out of the boot of the car, giving that to him too. Finally he took out his wallet and counted five twenty-pound notes out into Jingo's hand.

The dockers were busy preparing to make her sea ready, and all around them, people were hugging their goodbyes. There would be no hugging for the Crean brothers, though.

'Remember what I said, and no matter what happens, no matter how bad things get, we never want to hear from you again.' Blackie's eyes blazed with intent. 'Get on that boat. Get out of our lives. And as of this moment, I have no brother.'

Jingo turned on his heel in his new leather shoes, and clasping his suitcase, he walked up the gangway.

They stood and watched as the purser checked his ticket, and moments later the gangway was removed. The crew threw off the ropes, and with a loud honk of her horn, the *Innisfallen* pulled away from the quayside.

'Are you all right?' Jack asked Blackie, who stood, motionless, his face an unreadable mask.

'I am now,' he replied grimly, and walked back to the van.

CHAPTER 21

*E*mily and Lena sat in Emily's kitchen over the shop, the windows giving a perfect view up and down the main street of Kilteegan Bridge. A trickle of men headed towards the church in ones and twos, including the Monsignor and the Mouse, who were walking together, chatting like they were the best of friends. It was the men-only night of the Redemptorist mission, where a bunch of fanatical priests would tell them how it was their duty to get their wives pregnant as often as possible, and that they'd go to hell if they had sex for any other purpose than procreation.

Yesterday, she and Emily had been in the congregation, but because all the women of Kilteegan Bridge were there as well as the men, there had been no word about sex – that wasn't the business of women somehow. There was just a lot of preaching about how the man was head of the household, about how a woman's job was to love, honour and obey him and thank God when He blessed her with another baby, and about how a good holy woman would never have any trouble in getting children and keeping them.

It had been horribly painful for Emily, who had lost so many babies, and Lena had found her crying in the churchyard afterwards.

'Oh, Em, pay no heed. They're talking absolute rubbish,' Lena said, hugging her older sister. 'And it's not like every priest would agree with them. Could you imagine Father Otawe saying anything so awful?' But she knew it was hard for Emily not to believe it was her fault on some level once any priest said it was, even a wild-eyed Redemptorist.

Her sister was in a happier mood this evening, thank goodness. 'It's slowly sinking in that Jingo is gone for good,' she announced, pouring Lena more tea. 'Blackie is going around like he's walking on air, and Peggy is in great form, painting away again. She's going to try and do a copy of that one he stole.'

'Yes, it's such a relief.' Lena still wasn't sure what had happened to change Peggy's mind about getting rid of Jingo. Her brother and Skipper and Blackie had all been very vague on the subject. She suspected it was something to do with Emmet. Emmet had been so much happier since that mysterious phone call, which came only an hour after Jingo had left in the back of Blackie's work van, with Jack and Skipper for some reason. Eli had some idea what had happened, she thought, but he said it was best sometimes not to ask too many questions. Jingo was gone, and that was all that mattered.

She hadn't pushed Emmet to tell her anything, though. She'd discussed it with Eli, and they'd decided to wait and see if Emmet came to them, the same way he'd confessed to them about crashing the car.

'And are things picking up any bit at the surgery?' Emily asked tentatively. 'I heard Mrs Logan in the shop fretting over whether to send her young one to Dr White – she's complaining of a pain in her hip for ages. I get the feeling everyone's sick of him, he's so useless.'

'Not really.' Lena sighed. 'A few have remained loyal, and some have come back on the quiet, which we're so grateful for, but we've lost over ninety percent. Dr White was called to the convent because one of the nuns was sick, lovely Sister Dympna – remember she taught baby infants? Imagine, they got that old quack rather than have Eli, who was only down the road, go to her, who might have some clue what to do to make her better.' She was hurt and outraged on her husband's behalf.

'I suppose the nuns can't defy the Monsignor, in all fairness.' Emily gave a ghost of a smile.

Lena's brow furrowed. 'I suppose not. And Eli's so good. He's more worried for his patients than he's worried for himself. He begs them to go to Mick Burke if they won't come to him, but nobody dares do that either, since Dr Burke stuck up for Eli and the Monsignor turned around and called down the Redemptorist mission on us all.'

'I still think people will keep coming back to Eli, even if it is secretly at first.'

'I hope so, but honestly, Em, I feel like we are having such a bad run of luck. Eli prescribed the pill to someone who will die if she gets pregnant again, and *he's* in the wrong?'

'Of course he isn't. Most normal people don't think that he is either, no doubt about it. And as for that...' She stopped, and Lena could tell from the set of her shoulders that she was about to say something that might upset Lena further.

'What is it, Em? You might as well tell me. It can't get much worse.'

'Have you spoken to Eli?'

'What, since this afternoon? No, he's gone to Bandon with Emmet. He's giving him driving lessons again, and they went to pick up Nellie from her hotel shift – you know she's always giving out about having to get the bus back.'

'I know, unless she's staying over with her friend Geraldine, which she does half the time. She has Blackie up and down like a yo-yo, but he couldn't do it today – he had to go to the mission with all the other men. He can't afford to upset the Monsignor, particularly since Nellie called the Monsignor a pervert. I thought he was going to call down the wrath of God on us that time, but maybe he didn't want to get into a public debate with someone like Nellie.'

Lena laughed. 'He's decided to cut his losses, I'd say. Now tell me what you were on about when you asked if I'd spoken to Eli.'

Emily sighed and looked sorrowful. 'Well, Eli came into the shop to get something, and the Mouse was in buying some nails. The revolting little man sidled up to Eli, and I heard him say, "Sorry about that, Doc, the mouse got in again." And with a cackle, he was off.'

'The mouse got...?' Lena stared at her.

'The "mouse", you know.' Emily gestured vaguely. 'That's what he calls it.'

'Oh!' The penny dropped. 'Oh God, that's disgusting. And...oh...oh no... Please, please don't tell me he's got poor Frances pregnant again?'

'I'd say that's just what he meant.' Emily shuddered in disgust, the Mouse really was repulsive.

'And he was laughing at Eli, like he'd got one over on him as well as on his poor wife.'

'Oh, this is absolutely awful. I can't believe this. We can't put up with this.' Lena clenched her fists in rage. 'I'm going to have to talk to him.'

'Who, the Mouse? Don't. He'll just laugh and take it out on Frances.'

'Not the Mouse. It's the Monsignor I have to talk to.'

Emily was wide-eyed. 'Lena, what's the point in that? You'll only make things worse for Eli.'

'I don't care. Well, I do, of course I care, but if Frances Moriarty is pregnant, she's going to have to be under the best medical care possible if she's going to survive. Eli will have to get her into hospital at the first sign of miscarriage. And I know she won't let Eli look after her without the Church saying she's allowed. The poor woman is terrified of Collins, so he has to tell her himself it's OK.'

'Lena, think about this,' said Emily firmly. 'He'll go mental if you approach him.'

'That's as may be, but he's not the law, and it's morally wrong what he's doing. Frances will die if Eli can't look after her. She might die anyway, but under Pat White, she hasn't a hope. You know I'm right about this, Emily, and I'll be sure to tell the Monsignor it was my idea to come to him and that Eli knows nothing about it.'

Her sister sighed. She obviously still thought it was a bad idea but couldn't really argue with the moral side of it. 'Well, anyway, you definitely can't do it in this sort of mood. If you must go and see Collins – and I'm not saying you should – get your best arguments together and go over to the parochial house when you know he's in. Talk to him calmly and sensibly, and whatever he says, don't lose your temper.'

Lena knew Emily was right. Even though she'd improved over the years, she was still apt to fly off the handle when confronted with rudeness or cruelty. But shouting at the priest wouldn't help poor Mrs Moriarty, who was so lovely and kind and generous – all the things Monsignor Collins wasn't.

'Fine, I'll go tomorrow and see if I can win him over by being all sweet and polite. I might even bake him a cake. If he knows it's a matter of life and death, maybe he will come around, just in this one instance anyway.'

'Poor Frances,' said Emily softly, gazing out the window at the empty street. 'It must be so awful for her, losing baby after baby. It makes me realise how lucky I am to have our Nellie. Frances has no child to show for all her pain and trouble. I wonder if she hopes each time that this time it will happen for her.'

'Maybe,' said Lena, with a pang of sympathy for her sister. 'I just hope Frances realises it's not worth dying for, that's all.'

* * *

LENA WASN'T LONG GONE and Emily was washing the cups in the sink when the door flew open and Mrs Crean stood in the doorway, looking strange.

'Peggy?' Emily was frightened; her mother-in-law looked as if she'd seen a ghost. Surely Jingo wasn't back so soon? 'Is everything all right?'

'Is Blackie here?' asked Peggy breathlessly.

'No, he went to the mission. What's the matter, Peggy? Have you had bad news?'

161

'No. Well, yes, in a way, I suppose, one would have to say yes. But no, definitely no… Oh, Emily.'

'What is it, Peggy? You're worrying me now.'

Peggy hesitated a moment longer, but then her need to tell what had happened got the better of her and she handed Emily a telegram.

Emily scanned it.

MRS CREAN. STOP. WRITING TO INFORM YOU OF THE DEATH OF RICHARD CREAN. STOP. BIRMINGHAM. SUDDENLY. STOP. MRS CREAN.

She didn't understand. 'Who's Richard? And who is this…other Mrs Crean?'

Peggy said impatiently, 'She's his English wife, of course, the other one. She calls him Richard, we call him Dick, but whatever he was called, he's dead now.'

Emily understood now why her mother-in-law had come bursting into her kitchen in such a state of shock. 'Oh, Peggy, are you all right? Do you want to sit down? Sit down. I'll make you a cup of tea. Do you want something stronger? You look like you could do with it.'

Peggy plumped down at the table, her eyes still wide and staring. 'Mm, yes. Something stronger, maybe I will. Yes. Give me a glass of that nice sweet sherry you brought back from Cork, if you don't mind.'

Emily bustled around, fetching the sherry from the cupboard and pouring out a big glass, which Peggy drank half of in one go before setting it down. 'Pour yourself a glass as well, Emily.'

'I'm fine, Peggy. I don't really like it.'

'I don't care. Pour yourself a glass, and then sit down here.'

Puzzled, Emily did as she was bid. Peggy never ordered anyone around. After pouring herself a drink, she took the chair opposite Peggy.

Her mother-in-law took a deep breath in through her nose, let it out through her mouth, then raised her glass towards Emily, indicating her daughter-in-law do the same. 'Cheers,' she said.

Emily tapped her glass gently against Peggy's. 'Are you all right, Peggy?'

'Emily, I'm absolutely fine. Better than fine actually. Now take a drink.'

As Emily sipped cautiously, with a wrinkled nose, Peggy threw back the second half of her sherry and slammed the glass down on the table with a whoop of celebration. 'Hallelujah, hallelujah, hallelujah! Thanks be to God, I'm finally free!'

CHAPTER 22

*E*mmet was worried for Nellie. She'd looked so miserable when they picked her up from work. He'd never seen her in distress before – she was such a strong-minded girl – but she seemed pale and somehow shrunken. Maybe it had been a bad day. She was all day in the hotel kitchen, and he knew it was heavy going.

He tried to make small talk, but she only stared out of her side window at the rain, leaning her forehead against the glass, and answered in monosyllables if she answered at all.

He was sitting in the back beside his cousin because Eli had taken over the driving. His father had 'joked' he didn't mind risking his own life by letting Emmet drive him to Bandon but that it wasn't fair to make Nellie risk hers by letting him drive back. Emmet had rolled his eyes but didn't argue. He knew he hadn't a leg to stand on since he'd put the Rover into the ditch.

He hadn't been back to the farm since the crash. He was grateful to Jack and Skipper for running Jingo out of town, and to Jack for ringing him to reassure him about the nonexistence of Bunny Cotter, but his uncle had put down the phone while Emmet was still thanking him, and now he didn't know what he could do to make things go back to the way they were before he'd discovered Jack and Skipper's frightening secret. It felt so awkward having to stay away from them. He wished he could have said goodbye to the bay mare, who must have gone back to her owner by now. He'd love to know how she was behaving. She was such a beautiful horse and so trusting of him. But it looked like his training days with Skipper were over.

He glanced again at Nellie and was startled to see big tears sliding down her face. He rummaged around in his pockets for a clean hand-kerchief, which she took with a small miserable smile.

The window on her side was steamed up by her breath where she'd leant against it, so he reached across her and wrote in the mist with his finger. *Talk?*

She stared at his question for a long minute, then, without looking at him, nodded.

Emmet leant forwards. 'Dad, can you drop me and Nellie off at her house? She's got a book of mine I need.'

'Want me to wait for you?' asked Eli, glancing at him in the rear-view mirror.

'No, she says it's going to take her ages to find it. I'll just walk from there, thanks. It's stopped raining now, so I'll be grand.'

After Eli had dropped them off, by unspoken agreement the cousins slipped down the side of the shop, through the yard behind and over a broken bit of the wall into the patch of wooded land where they had spent so much of their childhood playing in a tree house Blackie had built for them, a simple open platform with a peaked roof to keep it dry. He'd made it so well, it was still standing, a red-painted hideaway halfway up a big chestnut tree, with branches thickening around it.

Emmet tested the rope ladder and it was sound, so they climbed up one after the other and sat with their legs dangling from the plat-form. Nellie took out a packet of cigarettes and offered one to Emmet. He waved it away; Jingo's cigars had put him off smoking for good. She took one for herself. The breeze blew out her first match, but he helped by shielding the matchbox with his hands, and on her third try, she got her cigarette lit. 'Thanks, Emmet.' She took a puff and then went pale and retched over the side of the platform.

165

'Oh, Nellie, are you all right?'

'Yes, yes, I'm fine,' she gasped, taking another drag, this time swallowing hard to stop herself retching.

'I don't think you *are* fine, Nell. Has something bad happened?'

'No, I'll be fine.'

'Come on, stop saying you're fine. You said you wanted to talk.'

She determinedly smoked halfway down the cigarette, clearly not enjoying it one bit, but in the end, she gave up, stubbed it out on the wooden platform and threw it into the damp undergrowth below them.

'OK, I'll tell you. I suppose I have to tell someone, and I think I'd rather tell you than anyone else, although I don't know why, because you're a total eejit and you won't be able to do anything about it.' For a moment she sounded like the old Nellie again, decisive and extremely insulting, but a moment later, her face crumpled and she dissolved into floods of tears.

He put his arm around her, and she didn't shrug it off. 'Oh, Nellie. Nell, what is it? Tell me?'

'It's...Ge...Ge... It's Ger...Gerard,' she gasped brokenly through her sobs. 'He says he doesn't want a baby with me, now or ever. He says he's got enough children with his wife already.'

Emmet took a deep breath of relief. He hated seeing his beloved cousin so distraught, but he also knew, like the dogs on the street knew, that this fella was a right creep and she was much better off without him. 'Well, I can't say I'm sorry, Nell. I mean, I am sorry you're unhappy right now, but he sounds like an awful man. I was worried there you were going to tell me you were pregnant.'

'I *am* pregnant!' she wailed. 'God, you're such an eejit. Isn't it obvious? I can't even smoke a fag without throwing up.'

'Oh, Nell.' His heart sank into his boots.

She glared at him through her streaming mascara. 'Don't look so shocked. You're not my mother or the bloody Monsignor or anything, and look at the mess you got into with Jingo.'

'I know I did – I'm an eejit. I swear I'm not shocked by you being...

I mean, I...' Emmet took a breath and tried his best to sound normal. 'I mean, are you really, really sure?'

Big fat tears welled on her lower lids, dropping down onto her cheeks. 'I'm late.'

'How late?'

'Four weeks.'

So she was then. That was one advantage of being a doctor's son – he had a father who wasn't afraid to explain these things, sometimes over the dinner table while they were eating until Lena ordered him to stop. 'Gerard, does he know?'

'Oh, Emmet.' Her body gave way to wracking sobs.

He put his arms around her again, allowing her to cry into his chest and cover his shirt with mascara, and as her sobs subsided, he handed her his handkerchief again, which she used to try to wipe her face. The result was not successful. He took the handkerchief and dipped it in a small puddle of rainwater that had accumulated in the fork of the tree that held the house and handed it to her again. 'Try it now. We can't have you going back in there looking like a banshee.' He smiled, and she managed the weakest of smiles in response.

'Yeah, can't have Mam and Dad finding out.'

He hesitated, then said carefully, 'But Nellie, if you're pregnant, they're going to know soon enough anyway?'

She shuddered. 'No, I can't tell them. It would kill them. I'll be a disgrace to the family and I...I've ruined everything.'

He gave a slight smile. 'Well, if being related to Dick and Jingo Crean didn't kill your parents, I think they'll cope with this. They've risen above plenty of disgrace before. Now, have you told Gerard you're pregnant?'

'Yes, I have.' She gazed down at the ground as the sounds of laughter and chat came through the open windows at the back of the house, where her parents were innocently eating their evening meal before she ruined their lives. 'And I thought he'd be happy, that it would give him a reason to leave, and we'd live together in England or something.'

'And what actually happened?' asked Emmet wryly.

167

Her voice grew bitter. 'He said I did it on purpose to trap him. He says his wife did that, that's why he had to marry her. He says he'll pay me to have an abortion, and he'll only take me back if I do what he says.'

Emmet was speechless.

'If you're going to agree with Ger that I should get rid of it... I couldn't do that.' She looked panicked.

'I'm not suggesting anything,' he said, recovering his voice. 'You know the same thing happened to my own mother when she had me. Doc arranged for her to go to Wales. To be honest, I think she was considering adoption, but then she met Dad and everything was OK.'

She looked panicky again. 'But I don't want it adopted either. I don't want to go to one of those awful mother-and-baby homes to have the baby, where the nuns torture you and then take the baby and sell it.' Her blond hair was up in a ponytail, and with no make-up left on her face, she looked like what she was, a terrified, vulnerable girl.

Emmet had heard the horror stories like she had about what happened to girls who got pregnant out of wedlock. He'd overheard his dad one time telling his mam about a stand-up fight he'd had with some farmer who wanted to send his daughter to one of those places; Eli had helped the girl to get away. He wasn't sure of the details, but Father Otawe was involved too, he seemed to remember, on the girl's side. But Monsignor Collins was not like that.

'No one's going to tell the Monsignor, Nellie, and all the family will rally round like they did when getting rid of Jingo. We'll sort this out.'

'But Gerard said he'll tell Collins if he finds out I've not got rid of the baby.'

Emmet stared at her in astonishment. He couldn't believe she would think even a scumbag like Gerard could do such a thing. 'Sure, your man doesn't even know Monsignor Collins.'

'He does,' she sobbed. 'He's a big church-goer, and Collins was in his parish before Kilteegan Bridge. And then Gerard sold the Monsignor his car. He sells cars to all the priests. He gives them special discounts and takes them out to dinner to celebrate.'

Emmet had a hard time getting his head around the idea of this Gerard being a big church-goer. 'Fine, he knows him, but, Nellie, why on earth would any man tell a priest he got a girl in trouble out of wedlock?'

Her voice rose to a wail. 'To get rid of me by having me sent to one of those homes! And I'll never get out again, because they make you stay forever, doing laundry and stuff to pay them back. He says he doesn't care about going to confession to admit he got me pregnant, that he's going to tell the Monsignor it was me who seduced him.'

Emmet shook his head, flatly refusing to believe any man on God's earth could do such a thing and get away with it. 'He won't do that. He can't blame you – you're underage.'

She dropped her voice and muttered something he couldn't catch.

'What did you say, Nell?'

She looked desperately at him, and there was no trace of his brave, defiant cousin left in her; she was quailing like a rabbit caught in the glare of headlights. 'Ger says my being underage makes me look even worse. He says Monsignor Collins already thinks I'm a hussy because of what I wear, and because I called him a pervert for looking at my boobs.'

The surge of rage he felt nearly blinded him. 'OK. This isn't going to happen, I swear. I'll take care of it.'

Her eyes brightened immediately. 'You'll take care of it? Really?'

The grateful tone of her voice nearly broke his heart. Not that long ago, she would have mocked him for being overprotective and pretending to be the big man, but now she was clearly ready to clutch at any straw.

'I will, I promise.' And he meant it. He didn't know how he was going to go about it, but he would never let her down, ever. Even after he'd been so cruel to Jack and Skipper, they'd come to his aid. Now it was his turn to stand up for another member of his family. 'Everything is going to be all right, Nell. I won't let you down.'

She smiled and sniffed and used the wet handkerchief again to give her face another wipe. She looked feverish and unwell but not as distraught as earlier. He took the handkerchief from her and tried to wipe the worst of the make-up off his shirt.

'Sorry.'

'It's all right.' He smiled. 'I spend a lot of time with horses, so this is nothing compared to what I often have all over me.'

She giggled a bit then, and to make her feel better about herself, he confessed how he'd nearly stolen his parents' car in desperation before he crashed it, and how good Eli had been about it, and how even Lena had forgiven him after threatening to put his head through the mangle (not really true, but it made Nellie laugh a lot).

* * *

HALF AN HOUR LATER, as they crossed the yard to her back door, he asked, 'Nellie, do you think you'd like to tell my mam first, before you tell your parents? I mean, she'd definitely understand. And I could tell her first, so to give her time to get over it.'

Nellie thought about it. 'Maybe, but we can't tell any of them who the father is. I honestly think my dad would kill him, and he'd go to prison.'

'Well, then, I'll just say you didn't tell me, so I don't know.'

Nellie nodded as she opened the back door to let herself in. 'Fine. Will you ask Auntie Lena if I can come and talk to her? And thanks, Emmet. You're the best.'

CHAPTER 23

*L*ena knocked at the door of the parochial house, a fine two-storied Georgian house with big windows on extensive grounds opposite the church. A few minutes later, the priest's housekeeper opened the door and stood looking at her with her pointy eyebrows raised to her sparse grey hairline.

'Good morning, Mrs *Donegan*.' Lena smiled as she carefully emphasised the woman's correct name. A lot of people in the village called Mrs Donegan 'Mrs Dragon' because of how hard it was to get by her to see the Monsignor, and it would be a disaster for Lena to start off by calling her the wrong name.

When the Monsignor came to the parish, the first thing he'd done was to dismiss Mrs Ormond, who was still in deep despair over the loss of Father Otawe. The poor woman had to go and live with her sister, and this absolute weapon was lodged in the parochial house in her place.

Mrs Dragon treated all deputations to the priest as a terrible imposition, and she looked at the parents of babies trying to arrange a christening or young couples wishing to marry with naked distaste that they would have the audacity to assume the Monsignor would be able to perform such tasks for people as insignificant as them. Lena had heard from Emily how she would stand in the shop name-dropping like mad, Cardinal This and Bishop That, as if she and the higher echelons of the Catholic Church were the best of friends and they sought her advice and counsel regularly.

Now she looked Lena up and down like she was something she'd picked up on her shoe, and said, 'The Monsignor is not available, Mrs Kogan.'

'But his car is here?' Collins's very flash brand-new Saab was parked at an angle on the gravel. It was hard to know how a priest could afford such an expensive machine, considering the vow of poverty, though Lena had heard there was a car salesman in the Bandon area who was a real Holy Joe and made a point of giving priests a big discount.

'I didn't say he wasn't in, I said he wasn't available. He's had a great deal to do with the Redemptorist mission, and the poor man needs his rest.'

Lena fought back the urge to point out it was eleven in the morning and that the whole town had been dragged along to the mission and still had to get up first thing in the morning to work and look after their children.

'I'm so sorry to disturb Monsignor Collins, Mrs Dra...Donegan. He does such a wonderful job, and I felt so uplifted by the mission. But I do need to speak to him – it's really very important.'

Mrs Dragon looked at her with deep suspicion, but Lena summoned her sweetest smile and then held out a basket covered by a white cloth. 'Oh, and I've brought you and the Monsignor a rhubarb tart and a bottle of cream from the farm, and a Victoria sponge with homemade raspberry jam and butter icing.' She knew from Chrissy at the Copper Kettle that when Mrs Dragon and the Monsignor came into the café together, Mrs Dragon always ordered the rhubarb tart with cream and the Monsignor made a greedy beeline for the Victoria sponge and always demanded a huge slice, the size of two, while making a stupid annoying joke about being a 'growing boy'.

Mrs Dragon's eyes sparkled slightly, though her mouth remained shut tight. She took the basket by the handle but didn't stand aside, and for a horrible moment Lena thought she was going to close the door on her anyway. But then the woman said, 'Wait here. I'll tell him he's a visitor.'

A minute later, she returned and indicated for Lena to go into the sitting room, where Monsignor Collins was standing in front of the fireplace with his hands clasped behind his back. He wasn't wearing his soutane today but instead had on a black suit and shirt with a stiff white collar, and as always there was a strange air of menace around him, like he spent more time dwelling on the sins of the devil than he did on the goodness of God. The image wasn't helped by the fact the fire had only just been lit and wasn't yet drawing properly, so there was a thin cloud of smoke with sparks in it rising behind him.

'Good day, Mrs Kogan,' he said in his haughty voice. He didn't invite her to sit, not that she wanted to.

'Good day, Monsignor Collins. I hope you're well and enjoying the sunny day.'

He brushed aside her polite small talk with a flick of his hand. 'Get to the point, Mrs Kogan. Mrs Donegan tells me this is a matter of supreme importance according to yourself. Although I've noticed the citizens of Kilteegan Bridge are very prone to exaggeration, or if we dare call it by its real name, outright lies.'

Lena kept on smiling sweetly. She couldn't afford to pick a fight over the character of her neighbours right now. 'It is indeed, Monsignor Collins.' She stopped, searching for the right words. She'd had her speech all prepared – she'd gone over and over it in her head – but in the face of this cold, condescending man, all her arguments seemed inadequate.

'And…?' He arched an iron-grey eyebrow. 'What is it your husband sent you to say?'

'Oh, Eli didn't send me, Monsignor Collins. He wouldn't presume to trouble you. I'm here on my own account without him knowing about it.'

He turned slightly away from her, as if this made what she had to say even less important to him.

She ploughed ahead anyway. 'It's about Mrs Moriarty, Father – I mean, Monsignor. She's with child again, and so she's in great danger. Every time she loses a baby, it takes a terrible toll on her body. The last time she barely survived, and so she needs constant care. And I wanted to ask your kind permission to let her maybe stay at my house and be looked after by me. I'm not asking for you to change your mind about anything, just to make an exception in this one case because it really is a matter of life and death. She would not defy you, as she should not.' Lena nearly choked on the words. 'But in this case, if you were to say you thought it would be best, given how ill she was...'

He looked at her with calm, cold eyes. 'You want me to give Frances Moriarty into the care of your husband?'

She held his gaze steadily. 'Well, yes, Monsignor, him as well, just for the duration of her pregnancy, but it's mainly so I can nurse her and keep a constant watch on her, and then maybe she and the child will survive.'

He shook his head, as if in wonder at her stupidity. 'You do realise Frances Moriarty is in the best hands possible already?'

She felt a wild stab of hope. 'She's in the hospital in Bandon?'

He actually laughed, a short dry bark. 'I mean in the hands of God, Mrs Kogan. I mean Frances Moriarty and her baby are safe in the love of Our Lord. She is a devout woman, and she has acknowledged her dreadful mistake, which she was led into by the sinful and unscrupulous behaviour of your heathen husband. She has returned to the ways of the Lord, and He will reward her with motherhood, which is the highest honour any woman can have bestowed upon her.'

Lena did her best to keep smiling, to not show her disgust at the priest's arrogance and stupidity. 'Of course, and God is good,' she managed, 'and the mission has reminded me of that. But –'

'But?' he interrupted, slightly threateningly. 'God is good, *but*?'

She stood her ground. 'But she does need nursing and medical care, Monsignor Collins.'

He nodded, with a faint cool smile. 'Of course. And Joseph, her loving husband, will nurse her, and Dr White will attend her when her time comes.'

'Dr White?' Lena felt sick with anger. Whatever about the Mouse nursing his wife, which seemed the most unlikely thing ever. The idea of that useless idiot from Kellstown having anything to do with a woman who was losing her baby was reprehensible in the extreme. 'Monsignor, if you won't have Eli, then could you at least ask Dr Burke? I'm sure he'd be happy to step in.'

'Do you have a problem with Dr White, Mrs Kogan?' asked the Monsignor smoothly. 'A decent God-fearing man?'

Lena knew she should leave right now. She knew it was vital for her not to lose her temper. If she didn't kowtow to the priest and agree with everything he said and abandon poor Frances Moriarty to her fate without a murmur, then her husband would never get his practice back, and they'd have to leave Kilteegan Bridge and their lovely house.

'Yes, I do have a problem with Dr White,' she heard herself say.

'And that is?'

'He's a danger to his patients, and it's important you know that before you send any more of your parishioners in his direction. Please, Monsignor Collins, it's not just Frances Moriarty. Other people are going to die. They have already. Mrs Timlin's newborn baby had scarlet fever, and he said it was a heat rash –'

The priest sighed heavily. 'Mrs Kogan, I don't listen to idle gossip.'

'It's not gossip, Monsignor, and it's not just that he's a terrible doctor. He's also his own best customer. He uses the morphine he should be giving to dying patients.'

'Please leave, Mrs Kogan. As I've told you already, my ears are closed to idle gossip and malicious slander.'

'He said Ciaran O'Donnell had a migraine, but it turned out to be a brain tumour, and Ciaran could be alive today if he were diagnosed correctly –'

'Goodbye, Mrs Kogan.' He threw open the door of the living room. 'Mrs Donegan? Mrs Kogan is leaving now.'

'Please, please, think about what I've said, Monsignor,' begged Lena as she backed down the hallway. 'It's not gossip – it's all true.

And please find it in your heart to help Frances live. The whole town will support you and thank you.'

He followed her all the way to the door, which Mrs Donegan was holding open with a thin, gratified smile. He stood there, looking smug and condescending in his black suit, his hands still clasped behind his back and his widow's peak giving him the look of Dracula. 'It's I should be thanking you, Mrs Kogan. You've inspired my next sermon. It will be on the danger of gossip, and what a sinful error it is for a man to listen to a woman's wagging tongue.'

* * *

LENA MARCHED UP and down the silk carpet in her sitting room, between the fire and the sofa where Eli was sitting, wringing her hands with guilt. 'I tried to appeal to his better nature, Eli, and I was trying so hard to keep my temper, I really was, but now I've made everything so much worse.' She turned to face him in despair. 'Do you think I should go back to him and try to make peace?'

Her husband looked at her sympathetically, his long arms spread out either side of him on the back of the couch. 'I love you for even thinking of charging back into that lion's den, but I don't think making peace with him is an option. He's not for changing, Lena.'

'But what will we do? Poor Frances, she'll die. And he'll be even more against you now.'

'Look, there's a way through this.' He patted the place beside him on the sofa. 'Why don't you go to see Mrs Moriarty and let her know she can come to see me in secret? My surgery is out of town, and there's a path through the field and orchard. Margaret will let her in the back, straight into the surgery, without her having to even go through the waiting room.'

Lena looked relieved as she sat down beside him on the sofa. 'Yes, I'll do that. I'll slip in to see her while the horrible little mouse is in the Donkey's Ears and say it to her. And I'll tell her how a lot of others are coming back to you in secret as well, without naming any names.'

'Not as many as I would like.' Eli sighed.

'But there'll be more next week. Em hears everything in the shop, and she says with every mistake Dr White makes, the more worried people are getting. It's not even so much about themselves – it's about their children, particularly after what happened to poor baby Timlin.'

Eli shivered, despite the fire being lit. 'I can't imagine learning a lesson in a crueller way. That poor little mite and his poor parents. I'd rather lose all my patients to a decent doctor than have any other of them experience such a misfortune.'

'I know you would, but hopefully we can prevent a tragedy like that happening again. I'll call into Frances, like you said, and once we get her through this, I'm going to insist she uses her post office money to come with me on a trip to England. We'll find her sister, and maybe her sister can persuade her to stay.'

Eli drew Lena into his embrace and kissed her gently on the cheek. 'You're a kind woman, Lena Kogan, and I thank God for the day I met you.'

She snuggled against him. 'I'm so sorry about making things worse between you and the Monsignor. Did I tell you what he said to me when he was leaving?'

'No.' Eli looked down at her with an eyebrow raised.

'You're not going to believe this. He said, "You've inspired my next sermon, Mrs Kogan. It will be on the danger of gossip, and what a sinful error it is for a man to listen to a woman's wagging tongue."'

'Dear, oh dear, what will that man come up with next?' Eli shook his head, looking very concerned and serious. But then he pressed his lips together and his chest started to heave, and seconds later he burst into hoots of merriment.

'Oh, stop that.' She pummelled his chest furiously with her fists, but he grabbed her wrists and pulled her against him for a kiss, and before long she was laughing herself at the absurdity of it all.

CHAPTER 24

Gerard O'Keeffe sat back at his desk in the Bandon salesroom, smirking to himself. That new temp secretary was a right tasty piece he mused, and he'd had her blushing and giggling within two hours of her arrival at the outer office. That old bat Evelyn, who'd worked for the firm since God was a child, could look as disapproving as she liked; it's not like any man had shown a shred of interest in her in decades, the desiccated old fossil.

He'd give the new girl a few days to really warm to him. He didn't believe in going in for the kill too soon; the chase was part of the fun.

Nellie had been fun until she got herself pregnant, and he'd had to tell her he had no notion whatsoever of starting a new family with her. In hindsight he probably shouldn't have gone there. She was very young, and those ones always got a bit too clingy; and sure enough it had been all tears and dramatics when he told her she had to get rid of the baby. He'd had to threaten her with Monsignor Collins before she finally backed down.

Anyway, he didn't know why she'd been so upset. It wasn't like he was abandoning her – he was going to pay for her to go to England and get it done properly, not by one of those desperate backstreet places. He'd learnt his lesson on that the last time when the girl nearly died. And besides, he was genuinely fond of Nellie – she was beautiful and sparky – so afterwards he might even take her back.

In fact, he decided suddenly, trapping the new temp would be a bit too close to home. His wife, Marissa, was the daughter of his boss – it was how he got this job in the first place – and Barry Dowling was the driest old stick on earth. Ger had his eye on a partnership, and cheating on Dowling's daughter under his nose wasn't how to get that, especially not with that Evelyn watching him constantly; she wouldn't hesitate to tell on him. And Marissa would have his guts for garters, not to mention what she'd do to any of his other bits and pieces, if she got a whisper of what he was up to.

Yes, he'd forget the temp and focus on Nellie. He allowed himself a moment to think of her nubile young body, so inexperienced for all her confidence, and groaned. He'd go and see her and act all apologetic and loving, then take her to a hotel some night this week and promise her they'd be together in the end. And then he'd give her the money to go to England, with extra to get herself a few nice things – she loved the style – and everything would go back to how it was before.

He'd have to call to see Eimear too of course, though she was rapidly going past her sell-by date. She was almost thirty, and he'd been knocking about with her on and off for the last fourteen years. He wasn't that into her any more, but any port in a storm and all of that, and currently, with Nellie sulking, this was a storm.

Ger knew other men were jealous of his Midas touch with the ladies, and more than once he'd been asked his secret, but there was nothing to it really. You either had it or you didn't. He had it, most fellas didn't. Simple as that. Sometimes he wished he wasn't so irresistible.

He sighed. The finance application for Mossy O'Donnell's new tractor was on his desk, and he'd promised to fill it out for him. Mossy was too busy moping about his wife who'd died to cope with complicated things like applying for finance. Ger had tried to tell him to get back out there – he had a fine farm of land with plenty of road frontage, so he'd be a fine catch for a young one – but Mossy was devoted to the memory of his late missus. The big eejit.

He was about to get stuck into the form when the telephone on his desk rang. It was Evelyn.

'Yeah?' He was damned if he was going to be polite to that old bat after she'd been throwing him daggers.

'There's a client here to see you, Gerard.' Her nasally voice grated on him.

'Have they an appointment, because if they don't, say I'm busy.' He was about to hang up when he heard her say, 'Up the stairs, second door on the right.'

Ugh. The minute he became partner, he'd give her the marching orders. Put some young one in there with nice pert boobs and a curvy behind, and insist she wear a tight skirt and blouse to work. This whole firm would be his soon enough anyway. Marissa had one sister and she was in America, and Barry had to retire soon. There had been another partner, Brendan Flanagan, but he died three years ago, a massive heart attack on the golf course after that Dr White in Kellstown had told him it was just indigestion. Still, it was the right way to go, quick and hopefully painless. Barry had kept Flanagan's name on the company because they'd been friends since school – it had always been 'Dowling and Flanagan', but it was fine because Brendan had no children. He'd been too busy hitting holes in one to pay much attention to his horsey-faced wife, and who could blame him? So one day the firm would be Ger's, and he'd be on the pig's back.

He'd need it too; Marissa was not cheap to keep. She was determined to send the kids to private schools and all the rest of it, so he'd have to make sure the money kept rolling in. He'd employ a load of juniors, pay them a pittance and get them to do the donkey work. He'd look after the corporate clients. The Mossy O'Donnells of this world with their tractors could take a running jump.

He stood up to check his tie in the mirror and smoothed back his luxurious blond curls. Then he hastily brushed them forwards again to conceal his increasingly high forehead.

'Gerard O'Keeffe?'

He turned with a start. A boy of only sixteen or seventeen had entered the room without knocking. 'Who the hell are you?'

'Your secretary sent me up to you, Mr O'Keeffe.'

'Ah, of course. What can I do for you, sir?' He switched on his salesman's smile. He would have to have a stern word with Evelyn about what constituted a serious client. This child was barely out of nappies.

The boy sat without being asked and took out some writing notepaper and a pen. 'What you can do,' he said evenly, 'is write to my cousin, Nellie Crean, that you won't be going to Monsignor Collins about her, whatever she decides to do, which is her business, and tell her you're very sorry for frightening her and that you promise you'll never bother her again in any way.'

Ger swallowed. He felt dizzy. There were spots before his eyes and his pulse was racing. Never before had one of his mistakes followed him to work. The girls he picked on were always young and vulnerable, the type that the priest or their own father would send away to the nuns at the drop of a hat if they ever confessed to their sins. 'Sorry, there's some misunderstanding. I don't know anyone of that name. Now if you'll excuse me...'

'No.' The boy who hadn't introduced himself spoke again. 'I don't excuse your behaviour. Nellie is my cousin, and you've nearly broken her heart. And believe me, you should be glad it's only me here and not my uncles or her father, because they'd make mincemeat of you.'

'Look, I've no idea what you're going on about and I've work to do, so...'

'Oh, I think you do know. Among other things, you took my cousin to the Arbutus Manor on the bank holiday weekend. I've checked, and the manager remembers you, so maybe you'd like to explain that to your wife? Or to her father who owns this company? Or to both of them?'

Sweating, Ger decided a change of tack might be in order. He longed to throttle this boy with his bare hands, but he was acutely aware of Evelyn being in the building. He wouldn't put it past her to be standing outside the door right now, holding a tray of tea as her pretext for eavesdropping. His mind was racing; there must be a way to get out of this. 'Fine, I'll write the letter, but only because my wife is…em…of a rather delicate disposition and I wouldn't like any false allegations to upset her.'

The boy pushed three sheets of notepaper across the desk. 'And then I want you to write a second letter to your wife, and a third to your father-in-law, explaining how you tricked an underage girl into your bed. I will take them with me, and if you ever come near my cousin again, I'll deliver those letters to them myself.'

'But I can't do that.' He was horrified.

'You can and you will,' said the boy steadily. 'And if you stay away from Nellie, it ends here. If not, I'm going straight across the hallway to the door marked "Barry Dowling" – I assume that's your boss – and I'll tell him everything.'

'I don't believe you.' Gerard had a sudden surge of confidence; he was going to call this boy's bluff. 'If you care about your cousin, you're hardly going to go and tell a stranger she's a slut who wouldn't take no for an answer.'

The boy looked at him with such withering contempt that even Gerard felt a pang of shame. 'I'm going to pretend you didn't say that because we're trying to settle this amicably. But please don't bother to try that one again. I suppose you're hoping Nellie has a family that is too afraid of other people's opinions to stick up for her, but she doesn't. She has a family that loves her and will look after her no matter what.' The boy stood up and opened the door so anyone who worked off the corridor could now hear their conversation. 'So please write those letters,' he said pleasantly.

Ger jumped up to close the door, but the boy's grip was surprisingly strong.

'Would it help if we spoke with your boss?' the boy asked sweetly.

'Really, that's not necessary.' Ger threw a frantic glance towards Barry Dowling's door, twenty feet down the corridor. 'I can deal with this myself.'

'Good, I appreciate it. And I'm glad we understand each other.' The boy was tall enough to be on a level with him, and his eyes were locked with Ger's.

Sweating, Gerard sat down behind his desk and penned the letter to Nellie, followed by the two short confessions to his wife and father-in-law. The boy studied all three with a contemptuous smile. 'Not exactly the whole truth, but they'll do,' he said, before pocketing them and going back to the door, where he stood in the open doorway. 'Make sure you stick to your promise, and then nobody will hear from me what a slimy toad you are. But I warn you, if you ever come near my cousin again, or any member of my family for that matter, the first person I'll tell is Nellie's father, who would leave you for dead, and if he didn't finish you off, I have a feeling Marissa and her father would. So the stakes are high, Gerard, very high indeed.'

As soon as he'd gone, Gerard O'Keeffe rushed to the door and looked up and down the corridor frantically, listening for any sounds. He was sure he saw Barry Dowling's door close quietly, but maybe it was his fevered imagination. He had to get out of here while he recovered his nerve, then he'd be able to walk back in with a shrug and a smile and a plausible explanation for anything that his prudish clown of a father-in-law might or might not have overheard.

He took a slug of whiskey straight from the bottle on the sideboard – he normally reserved it for toasting deals with his best clients – and pulled on his coat. He thundered down the stairs and out of the office, past the suspicious gaze of Evelyn and the smiling eyes of the new temp, and burst out into the damp afternoon. Where should he go? The pub? A restaurant?

No, he would buy some gin and go around to Eimear's. After all, he paid for the squalid little flat that she never looked after, always hanging her wet stockings everywhere and just lounging around drinking and smoking away his money, stubbing her cigarettes out into ashtrays that were already overflowing. Pulling up his collar and lowering his head against the rain, he headed down the street, watched from above by his father-in-law, who had already decided enough was enough.

CHAPTER 25

*E*mmet crossed the yard, nervous but glad. He was going to start talking to Jack and Skipper again, like nothing had happened.

It had come on him as he took the bus back from Bandon to Kilteegan Bridge, thinking about what he'd said to Gerard O'Keeffe about family and how the O'Sullivans and the people they were married to always stood shoulder to shoulder with each other. They would never throw one of their own to the wolves. They would never banish Nellie to the nuns. They were a unit that would stand and fall together.

Emmet felt stifled in Kilteegan Bridge sometimes. And it wasn't that he didn't want bigger adventures, and maybe spend some time with Malachy; his heart was still set on doing engineering at Stanford. But he knew now that nothing could replace the bonds he'd formed here in Ireland with the people he'd grown up with, his brother and sister, his cousin, his aunts and uncles, his mother, his father, his granny and Klaus, and even Mrs Crean, who had turned out to be so brave and helpful to him in his hour of need. She'd still told nobody the full story of what happened with Jingo, and when he'd thanked her the other day, she'd said it was his story alone to tell, if he ever wanted to. He had a feeling she thought he should tell the truth, at least to his parents, but she hadn't pushed him.

It wasn't so much confessing to the gambling and drinking that bothered him – he knew his parents would be furious, but he could cope with that. It was the thought of admitting he had lost all the money in his account.

He'd not even told Nellie about that. It felt so shameful and stupid. At the same time, it was going to have to come out someday. His mother knew exactly how much Malachy sent him each month and occasionally glanced in his post office book to check he was keeping it safe, although to be fair, she hadn't done that since he'd turned sixteen.

'You doin' OK there, pal?'

Skipper's voice made him nearly jump out of his skin. He'd been so lost in his own thoughts that he hadn't noticed the cowboy leaning on the entrance to the stable, smoking.

'Er...yeah.' He stood there awkwardly in the farmyard, not sure whether to smile. 'Er...I just thought I'd come up and see how the bay mare is getting on.'

'Her owner came to take her back,' drawled Skipper, eyeing him quietly.

Emmet's heart flooded with disappointment. He'd guessed the mare would be gone by now, but it was still a blow, and he hadn't realised how much he was hoping she was still here. 'Oh, right.'

They stood in silence for a while. Then Skipper tossed the butt of his cigarette on the ground, grinding it out with the heel of his boot, a tan leather one that went halfway up his calf and was tooled with a design on the side. Jimmy Piper had made them on Skipper's instructions. No Irish man would wear such a thing, but Skipper was his own person, and somehow they looked good on him.

'Well, Emmet, is there anyone else you'd like to see, or was it just the mare you were after?'

Emmet began to wish he hadn't come. This was a lot harder than his visit to that Gerard O'Keeffe, who was a coward and a bully, and crumbled like a dried cowpat when you put your foot on his neck.

Skipper was nothing like that. He wasn't a bully, and there wasn't anyone who could push him around. 'Well, I…'

'Because if it's the twins you're lookin' for, they've gone off somewhere up the country to a ploughin' match. Your Auntie Molly is on course to win an all-Ireland medal.'

'I'd no idea.' He was taken aback.

'Well, you wouldn't. You don't ever pay them much heed, do you?'

Emmet winced. It was true. He'd always looked down on his aunts. To him they epitomised the backwardness of Kilteegan Bridge. But Molly and May were his family too. 'Yeah, you're right. I'm sorry.'

Skipper relented a little. 'Well, as you're here, why don't you come and look who we have in the stables now.'

Emmet followed him into the stone-flagged stable yard, surrounded by stalls. In a couple of them were half-mad horses, obviously new arrivals, rolling their eyes and kicking their doors repeatedly, but in three others, the horses stood, docile, heads hanging over the door, looking politely for a carrot or a lump of sugar. As he stood admiring a small but pretty dappled grey, an ecstatic neighing from the stall at the end of the row made him look up in shock, his heart missing a beat. Surely he recognised that sound…

He was right – it was her.

She was craning her elegant neck over the half-door of her stall, neighing happily, her ears pricked up and lips drawn back in excitement, favouring him with a huge horsey smile.

'Oh!' He ran to her and flung his arms around her neck. He couldn't believe how much he'd missed her; it felt almost like love. She laid her head on his shoulder so heavily, he had to push up her chin, laughing, and then he blew up her nose and she blew back, covering him in wet droplets, making him laugh harder. 'I can't believe she's still here, Skipper. I thought you said her owner took her.'

Skipper stood with his hat pushed back, scratching his head. 'He sure did, but then he brought her here again yesterday. Seems the dang animal's got a long memory, and she went wild as soon as she was in her own yard again, bitin' and kickin' the grooms all week. No jockey will go near her.'

'Oh, I'm sorry.' Emmet turned to him anxiously, one of his arms still around the mare's neck. 'Was it because we didn't train her properly?'

'Naw, that ain't it. She just remembered, and he was too much of a bully to change, so she wasn't havin' it.'

'Did you have to give his money back?'

'We came to a deal. I'm s'posed to sell her for him, thousand bucks is all he needs, and I'll put somethin' on top for myself for all the stress she caused.' He grinned and ran his hand over her neck, and she whickered happily. 'That'll be good enough for him. He's cuttin' his losses. Me and Jack's gonna go to Cahirmee Fair, and we'll sell her there.'

Emmet turned and nuzzled the bay's velvet nose with his own, partly out of love and partly to hide from Skipper the pain in his face. If only he still had the thousand in his account, the same money he'd once offered for the black stallion. But the money was gone and that was that, and he'd only himself to blame.

'What's up, kid?'

Emmet shook his head, too gutted and angry with himself to answer.

Skipper touched his shoulder in a friendly manner. 'You wanna come up to the house? Tell me what's goin' on?'

* * *

IN THE KITCHEN, Skipper took two cold beers out of the fridge and slid one across the table to Emmet. 'So shoot.'

Emmet sighed, turning the cold bottle in his hands. 'I wish I could buy her, but I haven't the money.'

'Ah…' Skipper said knowingly. 'Well, about that. I did mention to your mother about you wanting to spend the cash you were savin' on buying that black stallion before, and she was a bit surprised – she said it was meant to be your college fund. But then she softened and said it looked like Malachy was going to foot the bill for your college anyway, so it was all right by her if you wanted to spend your money on something you really wanted, if the right horse came up. And I guess this mare is it.'

Emmet pressed the cold bottle to his forehead; he was hot with shame. 'It's not about college. The money just isn't there.'

Skipper's brow furrowed in confusion. 'But you've been savin'…'

'I've been so stupid, Skipper. Me and Jingo gambled and drank our way through the lot of it, and he kept saying I'd get the money back, or at least his half of it, but it wasn't true. I know that now, and I feel such a fool.'

Skipper leant against the cold range and took a slug of his drink. 'Well, that sure is a shame, but you're just a kid, and we all gotta learn tough lessons growin' up.'

Emmet smiled weakly. 'My lesson is to stop thinking I'm too good for Kilteegan Bridge and to remember who my real friends are.'

There was a long silence in the kitchen. Eventually Skipper broke it by saying, 'We ain't never spoken about that day, the day you came in on Jack and me.'

Emmet dropped his eyes and his stomach churned.

'Jack's really cut up 'bout it all, reckons you're disgusted and that you don't really want to be round him no more.'

Emmet still said nothing. He didn't want to talk or even think about that horrible day, ever. All he wanted was for things to go back to normal and all three of them to pretend it had never happened.

'Y'know, Emmet?' Skipper took another swallow of his beer. 'You're a smart kid, and ain't nobody round here thinks you gonna spend your life on the land, so this is your last year here. Then next summer, you'll head off to college and we'll only see you sometimes, holidays maybe. Then you'll probably get married, have kids, and the years'll roll on by, and the time to put things right will be gone. Then you and Jack will be set in stone, with this thing between you two.'

Emmet felt himself colour. He just wished Skipper would stop talking.

'He needs to hear from you, Emmet, to know he doesn't disgust you, being the way he is. I know you always looked up to him, and he loves you…'

The idea of Jack loving him made Emmet shudder. And the truth was, he didn't understand why Jack was like that. Jingo's stories of the men in the prison and what they got up to with each other, the graphic descriptions he had related – though Emmet had had no desire to hear it – meant that as much as he tried, he was sure he could never see Jack and Skipper's relationship as anything but unnatural. And it was unnatural, or why else would their relationship be illegal and against all codes of decency?

'I…' He couldn't find the words.

Skipper looked at him, straight in the eye. 'But you are, ain't you?' There was a hard edge to his voice Emmet had never heard before.

'I am what?' Emmet asked, knowing exactly what he meant.

'You are disgusted by us. I can see it written all over your face.'

'I just don't understand it…'

'What's to understand? It's only about love, Emmet. You'd be a strange boy if you didn't understand about love. What more is there to know?'

'Well…' Emmet had tried to push any images of his uncle and Skipper being more than friends from his mind, but he felt compelled to ask. 'The thing is, I just don't understand…well…how you could…' He coloured. He couldn't even bring himself to say the words. 'I can't even think about it.'

'If you're talking how Jack and I are when we're alone, why *would* you think about it?' Skipper asked, slightly exasperated.

'Well, just it's wrong, and the Church and the law says so…'

Skipper sighed. 'We ain't wrong. Nothin' about what Jack and me got goin' is wrong. We love each other, and we ain't hurtin' nobody. And as for the Church, any church for that matter, well, Emmet, they don't got such a good record when it comes to decidin' what's moral. Churches all over the world supported slavery, so did legal systems. Don't make it right now, does it? I could go on and on about all the things the churches and states defended that we now think are just plain wrong, so what else you got?'

'I just can't imagine…with another man.'

'Then *don't* imagine it.' Skipper chuckled. 'Believe me, Emmet, I feel about being with a woman the way you feel about me and Jack. I can't imagine it, and I sure as heck ain't got no desire to do it, so I don't think about it.'

He came and sat at the table, opposite Emmet. 'Look, Emmet, some folks got a lot of ideas about what other folks should or shouldn't be doin'. But maybe everyone'd be a whole heap happier if they minded their own damn business. The way I see it, we all got our own lives to live. And if you do things your way, and I do things my way, don't mean we can't be friends now, does it?'

'No, but I don't really want to be involved with, you know...'

'And I ain't askin' you to get involved, to think about it or have an opinion on it. What me and Jack got is our business, just like what your mama and daddy got.'

Emmet winced and Skipper grinned.

'See what I mean, Emmet? You don't think about that, do you? I bet you'd be disgusted if you did. Or Emily and Blackie in the bedroom? Or Bill and Deirdre?'

'No, of course not.' Emmet blushed. What did Skipper think he was?

'So why would you think about me and Jack?'

'Because...well...because it's...'

'What people do in private, so long as it ain't hurtin' nobody, ain't nobody's business.'

'Mmm.'

'Good. Now, your uncle'll be finishin' up milking real soon, so why don't you take yourself over to the parlour and have a talk with him?'

'Yeah...'

'Just do it, Emmet. And if you want to picture your uncle doin' anything while you're walking 'cross the yard, then picture him giving Jingo a good kick in the you-know-where and sayin', "That's for my nephew."'

'Did he?' For the first time since the start of this awkward conversation, Emmet found himself smiling – a small smile, but it felt good.

'He sure did.' Skipper grinned. 'He'd do anythin' for you, Emmet.'

* * *

JACK WAS HOSING down the parlour, sending all the dung and spilled milk into the gully that ran the length of the building and emptied into a drain in the yard.

Emmet waited until Jack finished. His uncle never said a word as he wound the hose up and hung it on the big hook for that purpose on the wall. *This could easily be the cleanest milking parlour in Ireland,* Emmet thought. Jack insisted on the highest possible standards of hygiene because he didn't pasteurise his milk; it was so much better like that, rich and creamy.

'You all right there, Emmet?' Jack asked eventually.

Emmet nodded, unsure of how to start the conversation.

'Do you need something?' Jack tried again.

'Not really.' But still he stood.

Jack gave him a long look, but just said, 'Grand. Give me a hand getting these ladies back to their grass so, will you?'

Emmet didn't want to let it go at that. He was beginning to think Skipper was right – if he didn't talk to Jack about this now, then his chance to stay close to his uncle would be gone, probably forever. 'No. I mean, listen, Uncle Jack, I will help of course, but I've been talking to Skipper, and I know what you did for me with Jingo, and I just wanted to say that, you know, you and Skipper are... Well...it doesn't matter...for me...like...' He wished the ground would open and swallow him whole. He was making a right dog's dinner of this.

Jack had kept his head down while Emmet was speaking, but now he took a few steps towards him. 'Thanks, Emmet. Thanks very much.' He patted him on the shoulder and nodded, then took a deep breath, exhaled and raised his head. 'So now you've got all that off your chest, can you give me a hand with the cows?'

Emmet was grinning as he and his uncle let the cows out of the yard back into the field. He realised now that nothing about his uncle had changed. Whatever had happened in between, he was still the same Jack who never said anything more than was needed to be said, and sometimes a great deal less than that. But that was the way he was, a quiet man. It hadn't exactly been an in-depth conversation, maybe not the one Skipper had sent him to have, but somehow Emmet knew things between him and his uncle were all right again.

* * *

As he set off for home later, Skipper caught him up on the farm track, detaining him with a hand on his shoulder. 'Hey, you didn't say goodbye to the mare.'

Emmet stopped, his hands in his pockets, and kicked at a stone. 'It's kind of hard, you know...'

'What, because you know she ain't yours?'

'Yep.' There wasn't much more to be said about it.

'What about if I said she *was* yours?' asked the cowboy, his thumbs stuck into that ridiculous broad belt of his, behind the big sharp buckle.

For a moment, Emmet dreamed. Was Skipper really suggesting giving him the mare? But then he shook his head. 'No, like I said, I've no money.'

'And what if I said you didn't need to give me money?'

'Skipper, someone has to pay for her, and you can't buy me a horse worth a thousand pounds. You're not that rich.'

'But we make a living, Emmet, and that's down to you. I know those fields are yours, along with the house.'

Emmet blushed furiously, remembering his outburst to Lena. 'Well, my parents have it in trust for me, but even so, I'd want you to have it. You're...well, you and Jack are...you're family, aren't you?'

'Can you think of the mare as your rent?'

'No, Skipper, no way. I'm not charging you rent, and Mam would kill me if she thought you were spending a thousand pounds on me.'

Skipper took out a cigarette. 'But she wouldn't have to know,' he murmured as he struck a light.

'I can't just turn up with a horse like that and her not ask how I could afford it.'

'You can afford it. You got a thousand bucks in your account.'

Emmet felt exasperated. Was Skipper deaf or something? 'I told you, I don't.'

Skipper held up his hand, stopping him. 'Well, *you* know that, and *I* know that, and I suppose Jingo knows that, but he ain't coming back and I ain't saying nothin'. So why don't you tell your mama you paid me out of your post office account and that will take care of that end of things as well? And if you want, you can come into partnership with me with the horses and I won't pay you for a whole year, to make it back.'

'Oh, Skipper...' Emmet couldn't believe it. He had no words.

'First thing you need to do, though, is name her. Y'know, I'm tired of calling her the bay mare, but I always think it's for the real owner to give her a name.' Skipper grinned. 'So go away and sleep on it, and when you wake up tomorrow, you'll know what to call her.'

CHAPTER 26

Things in the practice had reached a kind of manageable level; around a third of Eli's list had crept back from Pat White. But they were being so furtive about it, it was farcical. They would come up the lane and walk right past the gates of the house, then double back in through the field and then the orchard. Margaret had to open the back door for them into the surgery so no one else would see them.

And then the same people would look the other way if he saw them in the village, pretending they didn't want anything to do with him. It would have been funny if he didn't feel so bad for them, torn as they were between minding their bodies and minding their souls.

Pat White was being as careless as ever. Eli had some test results for a patient, and when he spoke to that patient, saying further investigation was needed, that the tests had shown up a shadow on his lung that would need to be looked at, the man told him that Dr White had said it was just a cough. It had turned out to be TB, which was totally curable with antibiotics these days if you caught it in time. But if White had had his way, the man wouldn't ever have gone near the hospital.

He smiled when he saw Jimmy Piper walking boldly in the front door of the waiting room. Jimmy never bothered with the back door.

'Morning, Jimmy, how are you?' he asked, looking up as he straightened a few chairs before the clinic opened.

He noticed that Jimmy was much more spruce than usual. His hair was cut, and he was clean-shaven. He wore dark trousers and a white shirt, and the aroma that had always emanated from him was gone. In one hand he had a large paper bag, and in the other a burnished brown leather bag, polished till it shone, with handles and a brass closing mechanism at the top. It was a beautiful thing.

'I'm grand, Dr Kogan, grand altogether.' He was beaming from ear to ear as he stood watching Eli fix the last chair.

Eli waited for a long story about some relative of Jimmy's who lost his dentures from smiling too much, or a tale of some neighbour fifty years ago who was a martyr to a cold back or some other such random fact, but nothing came.

Puzzled, he opened the door of his surgery. 'Fine, I'll just get set up in that case. Margaret isn't here yet, but take a seat in the waiting room and I'll call you in two minutes.'

Jimmy went right on beaming. 'But I'm not here to see you, Doctor. Well, I am, but not because there's a bit wrong, because there isn't a single thing in the wide world wrong with me today.'

'I'm very sorry to hear that, Jimmy,' Eli joked, turning back to him. 'All this rude health will have me out of business.'

'Ah, Doctor, I can come in if you're in need of...' Jimmy looked stricken.

'Not at all, Jimmy. I'm only pulling your leg. I'm delighted you're feeling so well.'

'I brought you back your clothes, Doc, and thanks very much for the loan of them. I brought them into the laundrette in Bandon to be cleaned, so they're all fresh again.' He handed him the paper bag.

'You're welcome, Jimmy, but you could have kept them if you liked,' Eli said, accepting the bag and putting it behind the reception desk.

'Oh, you're very good, Doc, but I went and bought a whole new wardrobe, so I did. Shoes and shirts and pullovers and the whole shebang.' Jimmy looked pleased as punch.

'Well, not before time. You deserved it.' Eli was so pleased that whatever had come over Jimmy, he'd cleaned himself up beyond recognition. 'That's a smashing bag. Is that a new purchase as well?'

'No, Doc, I made that. It's calfskin, tanned, with a brass top frame, hand-stitched.'

Eli gave a low whistle as Jimmy handed him the bag. He was fascinated by the perfect stitching and the wonderful aroma of leather. Then he saw, just under the handles, that beside the brass clasp was a small plaque, engraved on which in beautiful copperplate was 'Dr E Kogan'.

He looked at Jimmy, who blushed beetroot red.

'I made it for you, Doc, just to say thanks, like. I saw your doctor's bag was a bit the worse for wear.'

Jimmy was right. Eli had bought it with his first week's pay when he'd qualified and used it every day since. It wasn't even real leather; he couldn't afford leather at the time. It had never occurred to him to replace it – it did the job – but this one was absolutely beautiful.

'Jimmy, I don't know what to say. My goodness, it's amazing, but please, you must let me pay you for it. It will have taken ages, the attention to detail and everything...'

'No, Doc, I don't want anything. It's a present from me to you, because you're a very good doctor and a very kind man, and you had no need to go to the trouble of cleaning me up and telling me to offer Mrs Weldon a spin to the dance. But I'm so grateful that you did, and it's just a small thing to say thank you for your kindness.' Jimmy got to the end of the clearly prepared speech.

'It went well then?' Eli had almost forgotten about his matchmaking that day.

Jimmy nodded happily. 'Mrs Weldon...' he blushed crimson again – 'Hannah...is a wonderful woman. 'Tis she took me shopping. We've gone on loads of skites, and she loves loads of things, like greyhound racing and set dancing, but she couldn't go because she'd no car. She's a bit deaf, but we manage anyway, and she says she loves me chatting even though she misses half of it, and I don't mind – it gives me someone to talk to anyway. And sure if she could catch all of it, I wouldn't be able to tell it over and over again now, would I? And she has me dancing and everything. I'm after making her a few things for the house – 'tis like a dollhouse and she loves little handmade knick-knacks. 'Tis no bother to me, and she's delighted.'

'Well, that's great news. I'm thrilled for you both, long may it continue,' Eli said sincerely.

'I'd marry her in the morning if she'd have me, Doc, and that's the truth. I never had luck with the girls. Era, I was a disaster, I suppose, and sure, who'd be bothered with me? But Hannah is different. She's a lovely, decent woman, and she seems to be happy for me to call and take her out places. We bought a tree last week in the garden centre, and we planted it near where her little dog Benjy is buried in the back. She dug his grave herself, the poor woman – she'd nobody to ask. So I'm there now doing a few bits of jobs, and she makes me a fine dinner and we sit down together to have it. I've never been happier, Doc, and that's the truth.'

'And does she feel the same, do you think?' Eli was delighted for Jimmy, but he didn't want him to be hurt if Mrs Weldon didn't see things the way he did.

'Well, she does, she says, but it's awkward because she's married.'

'Really?' Eli was taken aback. 'I don't remember there ever being a Mr Weldon.'

'Era, the husband was a bit of a quare hawk, before your time now, but a fierce serious fella altogether, never cracked a smile or a bit, only going around like the weight of the world was on him.'

'And what happened to him?'

'Didn't he decide he wanted the priesthood, but sure he was a married man and so that wasn't going to happen, but didn't he go over to England and become a vicar or a minister or whatever they have over there. She's not heard sight nor sound of him for years.'

'That must be upsetting for her.' Eli was fascinated by one of Jimmy's stories for the first time ever.

'Ah sure, 'tis pure ridiculous. The poor woman has been left hanging for decades. And, Doc, I know she won't mind me telling you, but 'twas never a marriage at all if you know what I mean. I don't want to speak ill of a man of the cloth now, Doc –'

'You'll get no argument from me,' Eli said darkly. He was certain Jimmy knew of the feud between him and the Monsignor, even though the older man had never referred to it.

'I know what you mean, Doctor. Those men are both wrong to be doing what they're doing, and I don't care who hears me saying it.' Jimmy's voice was raised now, as if the Monsignor and Mrs Weldon's errant husband might be hiding together in the bushes. 'And as for that Pat White, he's another one. He will have the whole place dead before we know it. I saw his car coming into the town on my way here this morning, and I thinkin' to meself, what poor soul he's after putting in the ground next.'

Eli decided not to be drawn about Pat White, who was, after all, a colleague, albeit an incompetent one. 'Well, thanks for the bag, Jimmy. It means an awful lot. And be sure to invite myself and Lena to the wedding now, if it ever happens.' He winked.

'If it ever happens, Doc, you'll be my best man.' Jimmy clapped him on the arm and strolled off. Eli stifled a chuckle. Being Jimmy Piper's best man was not how he'd envisaged it working out, but it just goes to show, you never really know.

The rest of the morning was busy enough, with patients creeping in and out, some like frightened mice but others quite giddy with themselves for defying the priest.

He finished at ten to three; there were no more patients to see. He left Margaret to lock up the front and back and strolled up the avenue. He hung his coat up in the hall, left his brand-new bag on the side table next to all the family photos and went to find Lena in the kitchen, where she was baking apple tarts.

'Hey!' she protested sharply as Eli cut a slice of warm tart that she'd just taken out of the oven. 'Who said you could have that?'

'Mmm...' His mouth was already full. 'Your tarts are as irresistible as you are, my queen of tarts.' When he'd finished, he rinsed the plate in the sink and then came up behind her and kissed her neck. 'Mmm, that was delicious,' he murmured.

'The apple tart?' She smiled as she turned to face him.

'If you two don't stop canoodling, I'm going to be sick,' Sarah announced as she walked in the back door from school and threw her bag on the floor.

'We're not, I promise.' Eli jumped back, hands in the air innocently.

'Sarah, where are you going? Come back and pick up your bag.'

'I'm meeting Emmet in the stables. We're going out on the horses, me on Molly and him on Chancer. We're going out with Isobel Lamkin, and don't worry, it's not a full hunt, just a fun one for beginners, no hounds. And we won't be going over any hedges, just small jumps set up on purpose, so I won't break my neck.'

'Oh, for goodness' sake.' Lena rolled her eyes. 'And Emmet said he'd prefer you'd call the mare Second Chance, not Chancer, didn't he?'

'He's always saying it, but she is a right chancer. She's brilliant for Emmet, but she doesn't trust anyone else – well, except Skipper. She nearly went ballistic when Jack tried to grab her halter for me yesterday.'

She flung her bag down by the dining room table where she would do her homework later and shot out the back door, though not before pausing to grab a slice of apple pie on the way.

'Quick, before the next child turns up,' said Eli, pulling her towards him and planting kisses all over her face.

'Dr Kogan! Dr Kogan! Come quick!' A great shouting and clattering came from the front door. Eli groaned, gave Lena one last kiss and went to open it.

A woman in a green headscarf was on the doorstep, wringing her hands. 'Dr Kogan, come quick, she's dying...'

'Who's dying?' He grabbed his coat and leather bag in alarm.

'Mrs Moriarty. She's bleeding, and it's only getting worse, and Dr White just says the baby hasn't come out yet so nothing can be done. Monsignor Collins is there, praying over her, and I said what if I fetched you, but the Monsignor told me if I did, it would be a sin. But

I've known Frances for years, Dr Kogan, and she's a good woman. She's never let me down...'

'Lena, call the ambulance for Mrs Moriarty,' he shouted to his wife before leaping down the front steps. 'Mrs Connolly, follow me.' He recognised her now; she was Frances's next-door neighbour. She'd stopped coming to him right after the infamous sermon, and one day when she'd been leaving the Copper Kettle as he came into the café, she'd made a big point of taking care not to brush against him in the doorway.

He flung open the passenger door of the repaired Rover. 'Jump in. You can tell me the story as we drive.'

'Oh, oh...' She looked as agonised as if he'd asked her to ride with the devil, but then with a determined look, she threw herself into the car, clearly deciding she might as well go to hell for a sheep as for a lamb.

He drove as fast as he dared while Mrs Connolly poured it all out, how the bleeding had started early that morning, and Frances had asked her to get Eli to come but the Mouse had turned up from wherever he'd been spending the night, the filthy little man, and wouldn't have her call anyone but Pat White. Dr White came, and it all just got worse, and then the Monsignor came, and...

She kept talking as they sped up the main street. 'And so I said I was going for you, and then the Monsignor said... And I just...well, I ran.' She was white-faced at her own temerity.

'You did the right thing, Mrs Connolly,' said Eli as he drew up with a screech outside the Moriarty house and leapt out with his bag.

The tiny room on the ground floor was empty, but he could hear the murmur of voices in prayer from upstairs. He took the stairs two at a time and came to a halt in the low bedroom doorway.

There on the blood-stained bed lay Frances Moriarty, on her back with a wooden rosary draped over her folded hands and candles lit around her, her lips white as snow. The Monsignor and the Mouse were kneeling on either side of the bed, praying, and the priest had his knees on a cushion so as not to get his trousers dirty. Eli recognised that cushion; Frances had admired its prettiness on the sitting room sofa at their house and had been so happy when Lena gave it to her as a present. 'I love pretty things,' she'd said wistfully. 'And I'm going to keep it upstairs in the cupboard and only take it out for special occasions.'

Eli supposed this was a special occasion.

Behind him, Mrs Connolly burst into tears. 'Oh, Dr Kogan, do something, for the love of God, do something...'

But there was nothing more he could do for Frances Moriarty.

CHAPTER 27

'This feels like the end of the world, Nellie, I know it does. It's a very frightening position to find yourself in, especially on your own, and if I knew who was responsible, I'd string him up myself. But this has been happening since the dawn of time, all over the world, teenage romances that get out of hand and then go wrong. You're not the first and you won't be the last. Try to get some perspective. You'll survive, and you'll live your life, and so too will this little baby. It's complicated, and not what you want, I know, but it will all be fine, I promise. It always is.'

Lena rubbed her niece's back as the girl sobbed inconsolably. Emmet was on the other side of Nellie on the sofa in the sitting room, saying nothing but quietly stroking her arm. Lena loved how he was standing by his cousin. It was amazing how grown up he was getting.

'Oh, Auntie Lena, my heart is broken,' gasped Nellie. 'I don't think I'll ever be able to lo…lo…love anyone again.'

'I know, pet. It hurts so much. I understand,' Lena soothed.

'I'll never forget him, Auntie Lena.' Nellie buried her head in Lena's shoulder. 'My heart will never stop hurting. He hasn't even come to see if I'm all right. He's not even around any more. I think he's left my life for good.'

Lena caught Emmet's eye. He was smiling slightly to himself, and she wondered fleetingly if he knew who Nellie's lover had been, or had a hand in his abrupt departure from the scene. She respected Nellie's refusal to name the boy, but she would have liked to get her hands on him. For now, though, it was just a matter of persuading her niece to come clean with her parents.

'Now, Nellie, I know you don't want to, but you have to tell your mam.'

'I can't,' wailed her niece, crying harder than ever. 'Nana and Daddy have had enough scandals to put up with, always trying to live something down – this might be the last straw. The Monsignor hates me already. He would only love to preach against the Creans, and then Mam and Dad's business will be ruined.'

Lena sighed. 'Well, you can hardly keep it a secret, Nell. You say you don't want this baby adopted, but you can hardly keep him or her hidden under your bed until they turn eighteen, so some other solution is going to have to be found.'

'I was thinking I would go and live in England or America and never come home…'

Lena jumped to her feet, her dark eyes flashing with fury. 'Nellie, listen to me now, and listen carefully. Your parents adore you. Maybe that's part of your problem – you've had your father wrapped around your little finger since you were born, and your mother too, though she won't admit it. And the reason is, you're the light of their life. That's real love, Nellie, the real love I was talking about earlier. You think your heart is broken? I can tell you, you will be over this boy in a year or two at most, but if my sister and Blackie lose their only daughter, they will never, ever recover. So you need to toughen up. It's not like you, Nellie. You're a brave girl, braver than anyone. So stand up – we're going to tell your mother right now.'

Nellie was so shocked at Lena's stern words, her tears dried up completely. 'But I…I…still think she'll kill me,' she said mournfully, wiping her face.

'Well, I'll kill you myself if you ever talk about running away again,' said Lena crossly. But then at the sight of Nellie's woebegone face, she relented. 'Come on, you big eejit, nobody's going to kill you. You've got a rough couple of hours ahead of you, that's all.'

'She'll go mental...'

'Oh, I think you can expect that. But don't get too distracted on what gets said tonight – tempers and emotions will be high. But even if your mother is very upset, I'll be able to calm her down. You're not alone, Nellie. You have a big loud family, and I'm, not saying they'll be thrilled, but they will stand by you, and together we'll find a solution.'

Nellie stood up humbly, and Emmet stood up as well and gave his cousin a big close hug. 'Don't look so worried, Nell. Mam will take care of you. She speaks her mind, but she's the best and will never let you down.'

CHAPTER 28

*M*aria and Klaus walked arm in arm into the Pavilion Café, which was in the same building as the cinema on Cork's Patrick Street. She and her husband had taken to going to the movies once a week. Maria would take the bus in and meet him after work, and they would go straight to the cinema, watch a film and then go to the café, and Maria loved it all.

The dawning realisation that life was something she could choose rather than be tossed around on the waves of her illness was something new to her, but it gave her such joy. She'd never felt empowered before. Her parents had ignored her. Paudie had loved her but needed to protect and manage her because of her illness. But now, Klaus just asked her what she wanted, and she found she wanted a lot from life.

There was more than one screen in the cinema, and they took it in turns to choose the film. The funny thing was, she always chose films she thought he would like and he did the same. The only movies they never went to were war films. Klaus had served in the Wehrmacht in France and on the Eastern Front, then spent from the winter of 1942 until 1950 in a Russian gulag after being captured after the Battle of Moscow. He was sent to chop wood every day for the field kitchen, and he'd told her about barely surviving on three hundred grams of stale bread a day and hot tea in the evenings. Stalin wanted to replace all the men lost in the war with prisoners of war, whom he simply worked to death. Klaus had survived, but he didn't know how. Sheer luck, he called it.

The café was busy. Lots of customers had arrived now that the film was over, and it lent the place a lovely friendly buzz. Klaus pulled out a seat for her at a window table overlooking the street below, with people hurrying through a shower, and went to order their usual coffee and cakes. She watched him affectionately. He was as different to Paudie as it was possible for two men to be. But he had the same gentle streak, and she thanked God every day for sending her not one but two wonderful men to marry.

The years after her first husband's death were mostly a blur; she'd been worse than she'd ever been before. Periods of frenetic activity, where she couldn't do things fast enough or with enough enthusiasm, followed by a crashing low and a deep despair that nothing could shake.

Doc tried his best to manage her illness, and God knew the people in St Catherine's were saints, but nothing had really worked. It felt wrong, the way her children had had to endure her when they'd lost their father, and instead of her being a mother, being strong and capable, they had to care for her too. She knew it wasn't her fault, that she never chose it, but all the same, she wished it had been different.

These days things were so much better. The lithium suited her, and so far in her marriage to Klaus, she'd not had the need to go to St Catherine's.

Her children were doing brilliantly as well. Jack was smiling all the time, him and Skipper were forever coming up with new ideas on the farm, and Lena and Em had fine husbands and lovely families.

Molly and May, once her poor neglected little girls who never knew what a wonderful man their father was, had grown up so strong and capable. They were also attractive in an unconventional way. If they made any bit of an effort, they could be very pretty, but neither cared a hoot for such things; they barely brushed their hair. There was a time when it might have bothered Maria, but not now. She was just glad they'd turned out all right and had grown up happy and confident, when her parenting certainly hadn't contributed in a positive way to that. They were still talking about going to New Zealand for a few years to study sheep farming. She'd miss them if they did, but she hoped they'd find a couple of strapping young farmers out there who liked their women to be independent, and not just there to cook their dinner and have their babies. Though neither Molly nor May seemed to have the slightest interest in boys. She wondered sometimes if, like Jack, they were a bit different. Nothing was ever said outright, and she could be wrong, but she knew her sweet, sensitive son had grown to be a gentle soul and that Skipper and he were very close.

Klaus arrived back bearing a tray with two frothy coffees and two slices of Victoria sponge with fresh cream and jam. She smiled at how he so loved his treats. For a man without an ounce of spare fat on him, he adored cakes and sweets.

'Now, my darling, I asked if they had the apple crumble you like, but alas it was sold out, so the only other option was fruit cake. I thought you would prefer this?'

'This is lovely, thank you.'

He sat opposite her and ate quickly, finishing every last morsel, then scraped the last crumbs off his cake plate and ran his finger round the edge to collect any remaining jam or cream. It always fascinated her to watch him eat. She often joked that there was no need to wash up; she could just put his plate back in the cupboard and use it the next time.

'So what did you think of the film?' she asked, picking up her fork to tackle her own slice of cake. They enjoyed the weekly post-film analysis almost as much as the film itself. This week it had been *The Godfather* with Marlon Brando.

'It was good. I liked Brando,' Klaus said absent-mindedly but didn't elaborate further.

Maria was immediately anxious that something was wrong. He normally loved dissecting each performance and hearing her thoughts on plot and twists and all of that. Maybe he was worried about something? Now that she thought about it, he had been a bit quiet when she went to meet him after work, but they'd been running late and had to hurry to get to the cinema on time.

'What's wrong, Klaus? Did something bad happen to you today?'

He smiled. 'Nothing bad. Everything is fine with me, Maria. Please, do not worry.' His still slightly accented English soothed her, and she relaxed and smiled back at him.

She had come to love his thin face, the grey hair and the silver beard. His skin was wrinkled from working for years in all weather, suffering terrible nutrition, but there was something attractive about him. She didn't feel the deep passion she had felt with Paudie, a longing that had frightened her with its intensity sometimes. What she had with Klaus was not like that; it was slow and gentle and kind.

And the balance was different. Klaus looked after her, but she also took care of him. He had lost everything of himself in the war and his captivity. While his body had survived, he told her he'd been sure his spirit was dead. Then he'd met her, and it had ignited a spark in him, and he saw a future and a life and a reason to go on. He still had nightmares sometimes; she would hold him as he screamed, and he would cling to her. And she felt for the first time in her life that she was of some use to someone rather than a burden.

'But there is something?' She knew it, sensed it or something.

He sighed and gave in. He knew how good her instincts were for when someone wasn't telling her the whole truth. 'Yes, you're right as usual, there is something, but I wanted to wait to tell you until we got home.'

'What is it, Klaus? Please tell me now, or you know I'll get panicky.'

He nodded and reached across the table to take her hand. 'Maria, *Liebchen*, it's about your brother, Ted.'

'Ah…' A warm sea of grief rose in her heart, but she also felt relief. 'He's dead, isn't he? I've known it for years. It's the only way he wouldn't get in touch with me. But I'm glad you've found out for sure – it feels better to know.'

She was actually surprised how calm she felt, after having spent so much of her life crying over Ted and longing for his presence and coming up with wild plans to go looking for him after the war. Years of therapy, and the calming effect of lithium, meant she now knew that her desperate need to find him, while born out of love for him certainly, was also born out of terror. He had been her only sibling and her saviour during her long and lonely childhood. He was the one who could talk to her when she was in despair. He was the only person in her world who seemed to love her, who cared what happened to her. The idea that he was gone, even after she was married to Paudie, had made her feel rudderless in the terrifying waters of life.

'Maria, he's alive,' Klaus said quietly.

Maria slowly put down her fork. The hum of the café, so pleasing to her ears just moments earlier, was now intrusive, too loud. She tried to take in what he had said. But it couldn't be true. How could Ted be alive, and never have written or come to see her?

'No,' was all she could manage.

'Yes, Maria. I thought, like you, that there was no chance. So many years have passed, and there were so many of us taken prisoner by the Russians. And believe me, we were so meaningless to them, you can be sure nobody would document the death of a German soldier. It was an hourly occurrence, and the bodies just left in the snow, so I didn't think there was any hope. Also, I didn't know if he had served, or if he had, what division of the military he would have been in. So the whole thing was like looking for a needle in a haystack. Edward Hannigan never appeared, wherever I looked. So I had all but given it up, the search.'

'Then how...?' Her voice sounded like someone else's, raspy and far away. She was still unable to believe what she was being told. Ted was alive? Her beloved brother? Had she heard Klaus properly?

'It was Rosa who helped me, Eli's cousin who's now living in New York, the one who turned up ten years ago.'

'I know Rosa.'

'Yes, of course you do. Well, her family was from Leipzig, and she's spent years asking questions of anyone she runs into from there, she's a lawyer but she specialises in reparations and seeking information for Jewish families – she's still looking for her own immediate family, you know. And that's how she ended up speaking to someone who knew your brother's wife, who was also from Leipzig. We already knew she was called Christiana Kloch, and we know her father, Gunther Kloch, was an officer in the Abwehr, the German military intelligence service. Christiana died in 1945, no cause of death listed, but a Christiana Kloch from Leipzig is buried in the parish of Bad-Wimmenhof, outside Dresden. Her death was on February 14th, 1945, and Dresden was more or less flattened by the Allies between the 13th and 15th, so the person who knew her assumes she was killed in the bombing.'

'But surely it can't be the right Christiana. Would she not be listed as Christiana Hannigan, not Kloch?' Maria asked, confused and doubtful.

Klaus nodded. 'I was surprised too at first and thought perhaps they had got divorced, but then I got thinking. Kloch was a name to conjure with in Nazi circles – the whole family were big supporters of Hitler from the start. And Gunther entered the Abwehr in 1938 at a position of considerable influence, despite having no previous experience, so he must have had good contacts. And it even looks like he was connected to Canaris himself.'

Seeing Maria's blank look, he explained. 'Wilhelm Canaris, the chief of the Abwehr, was never a fan of Hitler and was often accused of trying to undermine the Nazi ideals. He did his job nonetheless but was apparently often heard to say that Germany couldn't win the war, which of course wasn't the healthiest attitude to have in the Third Reich.'

'But what has this to do with Ted?'

'You see, Maria, I began searching for your brother once more, but this time for Eduard Kloch, not Edward Hannigan.'

'You think he changed to his wife's name?' The whole story seemed so unlikely.

Klaus extracted an envelope from his inside jacket pocket, and from the envelope, he pulled out a grey-green book with the Nazi symbol of the swastika and the eagle on the front and the word 'Soldbuch'. And inside that was a grainy photograph, stuck in the top right-hand corner.

Maria's heart turned over and the café swum around her. The photo was aged and yellow and grainy, but there wasn't a shadow of a doubt that it was of her brother, barely older than the Ted captured in the photograph on her dresser, taken just before he left for Germany with his new German girlfriend, Christiana, whom he was planning to marry. She scanned the writing. It was in German, but this was clearly a document containing his details. The date of birth was correct, but the name was 'Kloch, Eduard'.

'Where did you get this?' She studied the photograph again, trying to grasp the significance. It was definitely Ted.

'I've had it for a while,' admitted Klaus. 'But I wanted to know as much as possible before I showed it to you. I mean, at that stage I still imagined he was dead, and so nothing important had changed. I thought, well…I thought you might not want to know.'

'Might not want to know what?'

Klaus looked sad. 'This is a soldier's record book. It lists all his service, promotions, awards, injuries, everything to do with his career. Ted was in the Abwehr, like his father-in-law. In fact, I think Gunther Kloch got him in.'

She stared at him. 'My brother was a soldier in the German army?'

'Well, yes and no. The Abwehr were responsible for things like intercepting messages sent by wireless, and infiltrating foreign military or intelligence operations, trying to intercept saboteurs from the various resistance groups, that sort of thing.'

'He was a *spy*?'

Klaus considered her question. 'Mm…the Nazis had spies of course, though Hitler hated the idea, felt people like that couldn't be trusted.' He added to himself, as if the idea had only just occurred to him, 'Though maybe that's why there's no reason given on the Iron Cross citation, because Eduard Kloch's work was covert.'

'On the citation for *what*?' This was getting more unbelievable by the minute. 'You're trying to say Ted got the Iron Cross?' Even she had heard of that medal; it was the highest award Nazi officers could get for their services to the Third Reich.

'I'm so sorry, Maria.' Klaus looked at her with enormous sympathy, and she knew that he understood how much she'd always believed in her brother. She'd told him often enough that even if Ted had been drafted into the German army, he would never have joined the Nazi party.

Klaus took another sheet out of the envelope, clearly copied from the original.

'What is it?' she asked fearfully.

He read it to her, translating from German. '"In the name of the führer and of the supreme commanders of the military command of Germany, I present to Eduard Kloch" – and it lists a regiment here – "the Iron Cross First Class." I can't make out the signature, but you can see it's the rank of Obersturmbannführer, which was a para-military rank awarded within the Nazi party. People like Adolf Eich-mann got it. Its military equivalent in Ireland would be something along the lines of lieutenant colonel.'

It was preposterous; it just couldn't be true. 'You're saying Ted got a medal from Hitler? No, no, don't be ridiculous.' Panic gripped her chest, and her breath got shallower. She tried to remember the breathing exercises Eli had taught her: in for four, hold for four, out for four, hold for four. 'It's not possible. That would make him a committed supporter of Hitler.'

'On the face of it, yes. If he got the Iron Cross, he must have been held in high regard by his Nazi superiors. They didn't just throw Iron Crosses about for nothing.'

She seized on what sounded like a hint of doubt. '"On the face of it"? Do you think these documents might be falsified or something?'

Klaus furrowed his brow before answering carefully. 'I don't know. Not really. But in some ways, these documents don't add up. I don't know – it looks a bit strange. For example, generally in a citation, there is a note explaining the reason for the commendation, what specific act over and above duty kind of thing, but there is nothing. And the other thing is that regiment he's listed in. I can't find a record of it. It could exist – as I say, I'm not an expert – but it looks odd to me, that and the name change. I don't know. Finally, and this is the strangest thing, there is no record of his being awarded the Iron Cross in his Soldbuch – that's very irregular. But then it might have been the end of the war when everything was chaotic.'

'Or maybe someone used his photo to make a fake ID after the war?'

Klaus shook his head with a sad smile. 'A fake document to claim they were a Nazi, after the war? I doubt it. No, Maria, I'm sorry. This is Ted's Soldbuch.'

'But how can you be sure? You can't be sure?'

Again, he looked at her with huge compassion. 'Well, you see, Rosa has been helping me in my search, and a while ago an Australian friend of hers, a fellow psychiatrist, also a Jew, told her he knew an Eduard Kloch who was living in Victoria. He visited and befriended Eduard and took a photo, and it arrived at the university this morning. And it's him, Maria, I'm sure of it. Which is why I couldn't keep this from you any longer.'

Once more he reached into the envelope and this time pulled out a large coloured print of a very slim, tall, silver-haired man, his skin burnished a dark copper and with bright-blue eyes. He was standing on the veranda of a large ranch house, wearing farming overalls, and even though this photo was taken recently, he somehow looked even more like the Ted in her imagination than the grainy photograph in his Soldbuch, or even the black-and-white photo of him before the war.

'Oh, it is him,' she breathed.

'He's married to a woman from there and has two daughters, aged seventeen and nineteen.'

'I have two nieces?'

'Yes.' Klaus took out the notebook he always carried and flipped through the pages. 'They are called Sophie and Annamaria. They ride racehorses. And his wife is called Gwenda. They met because Ted was a drover and Gwenda was some sort of sheep trials champion, and they own a huge ranch in Victoria.'

Maria shook her head in bewilderment. It seemed to her that this was a bizarre dream from which she was about to wake up. Racehorses? Sheep trials? These images were a million miles away from the ones that came into her head when she thought of Nazis, the horrors of the war in Europe, the concentration camps, everything she'd heard and seen about the awful things Hitler had done. How could Ted be a Nazi, even to the point of getting a medal from the führer, and then go on to live an idyllic life, a rancher married with a wife and children?

A small voice whispered to her that August Berger and Phillippe Decker were also Nazis, yet they'd ended up in the peaceful Irish countryside while pretending to be members of the French Resistance. It was even carved under Berger's name on his headstone – *Auguste Berger, A hero of the French Resistance* – enraging Maria every time she passed by the Fitzgerald plot on her way to see Paudie. But the Nazi who had murdered Paudie had been a hard, cold man, nothing like Ted.

Maybe Ted changed, whispered the small voice.

You're wrong, she argued back in her mind. *Ted would never change – he was too kind and honourable and true.*

Aloud, she said firmly, 'He can't have been a Nazi, Klaus, he just can't.'

'Well, I'm not saying he was necessarily working in the camps.' Klaus attempted to console her. 'And his rank in the Soldbuch is not a particularly elevated one, so he might have had a very mundane job in the Abwehr. It's impossible to tell. And maybe he got the Iron Cross because he was a small cog in some successful piece of surveillance.'

She felt steadier now; the breathing had helped. And thanks to the lithium, a piece of news that before would have driven her over the edge now seemed manageable. 'Klaus, I'm not saying you're wrong, but I know there's a different explanation for this, however bad it looks. I still don't understand why he hasn't written to me...'

He's ashamed of his past, whispered the small, persistent voice. *He didn't want you to know who he was, what he did.*

'But there's got to be a good explanation. Maybe his letters went to my old house and my parents didn't bother to pass them on. So I'm going to write to him and ask him right out what he did in the war.'

'Maria.' Klaus put his hand on her wrist. 'Dear Maria. I understand you wish to write to him. But can I make one small request? Give Cork University as the return address – that way he won't know where you live. So if you don't like his reply...'

'I *will* like his reply, Klaus,' she said firmly.

Though the small, persistent voice said, *No, you won't.*

CHAPTER 29

The Mass hadn't started yet, but the church was already packed. Everyone in the village was there; all the pews were crowded, and people were standing at the back. The only spare seats were in the pew where Lena was sitting with her family. Eli had come to Mass for the first time in ages, and people were still afraid to go near him in public.

Maureen Parker, of Maureen's Fashions, made a large display of squeezing her enormous bottom into the seat in front where there wasn't enough room rather than sit beside the Kogans. Poor Jimmy Piper was wedged in at the other side because she shoved everyone along the pew.

Maureen should have been called Nosey Parker. People went into her shop as much for the gossip as for the rather dull cardigans and knee-length skirts, which were the very opposite of 'fashion'.

On a normal day, Lena would have found it hard not to laugh. But laughter was the furthest thing from her mind today.

Frances Moriarty's coffin was being brought to the church this morning from her tiny little house across the road, where her corpse had been waked for the past three days by the Mouse and his friends from the Donkey's Ears, who had spent the whole time drinking whiskey to 'drown their sorrows' and scoffing all the free soup and sandwiches that the likes of Mrs Connolly brought in to them.

The outpouring of grief was genuine. Frances Moriarty was born and raised in Kilteegan Bridge, and there were few families she hadn't helped. The packed-to-capacity church was a testament to how well liked she was. Her marriage was a match. Her mother was afraid she'd never find a husband and arranged the pairing with the Mouse rather than have a daughter on the shelf.

Frances must have arrived, because the organ wheezed into life, played by Chrissy's daughter from the café, and the church choir launched into 'Soul of My Saviour'.

Eli squeezed Lena's hand as the coffin was carried up the aisle. Lena was relieved to see it was being shouldered by six sober neighbours, who had obviously insisted on taking over from the Mouse and his drinking companions. The last thing poor Frances needed now was to be tipped on the floor by a bunch of drunks, a further indignity in death to be added to the shambles of her life.

The Mouse stumbled after the coffin, sobbing loudly and pitiably all the way, and collapsed into the front pew reserved for the chief mourners, where he sat alone.

Monsignor Collins swept out onto the altar in his white and green vestments and waved his hand dismissively at the choir in the gallery. The hymn petered out, although Monica Devlin, the town solicitor's wife, held on the last note longer than anyone, slightly off-key.

The priest began the Mass.

Lena hoped he would keep it short and dignified, and for a while it looked as if he might. In his homily, he made a few general comments about how Frances Moriarty had been a 'devout woman, much loved by all her neighbours, always ready to help anyone who was in need, a woman who had taken Christ into her heart and who was assured of her place in heaven'.

But there the Monsignor paused and fixed his flock with his cold, steely gaze. 'And let no one here be in any doubt,' he carried on in a ringing, triumphant voice, 'that the Good Lord will forgive Frances Moriarty her sins, for she has repented and begged His forgiveness. We should never presume to judge our brothers and sisters, nor cast the first stone. It is for the Lord to pass judgement on those who offend him.' Here his eyes strayed briefly to the Kogans' pew. An icy finger ran up Lena's spine, and she clutched Eli's hand in dread of what might come next.

'Frances was born a child of Christ and died in His grace as was her destiny. In life she was a loyal and faithful servant of the Lord, and of her loyal, loving husband who grieves so much today. She now sits at the right hand of the Father. We must not question the ways of the Lord, for He is all knowing.'

'OK, that's it,' said Eli, rather more loudly than perhaps even he had intended. He stood up from the pew, all six feet four inches of him, stepped sideways past Lena into the aisle and started walking out of the church.

Her heart racing, Lena stood up to follow him, whispering to Emmet and Sarah and Pádraig to stay where they were. She wasn't going to drag her children into this; they had to live in Kilteegan Bridge, and she didn't want them ostracised along with their parents.

Emily, who was sitting behind her, caught her hand. 'Lena...' Her eyes were panicked.

Lena answered her without lowering her voice at all. 'I'm sorry, Em, I can't stay. Poor Frances died for lack of proper medical care, and it is for God alone to judge the men who allowed that poor sweet woman to bleed to death rather than call the ambulance that might have saved her life.' She headed up the aisle after Eli, her heart beating even more wildly, and she was conscious that the whole church was silent, watching her go.

Out of the corner of her eye, she saw Emily make a move, together with Blackie, and she shook her head at her sister fiercely. Emily had enough on her plate with Nellie without getting herself involved in a row with the Monsignor. Jack and Skipper were on their feet, and she gestured at them to sit down as well; the last thing they needed was to draw the Church down on top of them.

As she neared the back door, she heard feet right behind her and glanced over her shoulder. To her alarm she found her three children had followed her, and Molly and May were with them, grinning their heads off, and Emily and Blackie and Nellie, even Peggy Crean...

And there were others as well, joining her family in the aisle.

Loyal Jimmy was there, with that nice Mrs Weldon. Deirdre and Bill Madden and their daughter, Lucy, were right behind them. Margaret, Eli's receptionist, was pushing her way towards the aisle, as were Mrs Shanahan and Katie, who had been the children's nanny until she got married. Several of Eli's patients, the ones who normally blanked him in public, were also getting up to leave, including the man Eli had cured of TB and the woman whose toddler he'd diagnosed with meningitis after Dr White had said it was a common cold. Mrs Ormond, who had been Father Otawe's housekeeper, followed too. Kieran Devlin, the town solicitor, seemed to have no qualms about attracting attention either; he was stepping over people's knees to get to the aisle, and Chrissy and Imelda from the café were following suit.

Up ahead, Eli waited for her in the church doorway, and Lena joined him, taking his arm. But instead of walking out into the churchyard with her, he stayed where he was, because everyone who had followed behind her started shaking his hand on their way out, murmuring that they knew he'd rushed to save Frances Moriarty as soon as he'd heard. One of these was Mrs Connolly, the woman who had risked the fury of the Monsignor by running for his help and who had already told Eli she would never forgive herself for making that decision too late.

Maybe it was the sight of the humble, devoted Mrs Connolly going over to the devil that was the last straw for the Monsignor. He had been preserving what he clearly imagined was a dignified silence, but now he went fiery red and slammed his fist on the pulpit. 'Have you no respect for the dead, Kilteegan Bridge? Have you all gone mad, to walk out of God's house on this sacred occasion? Kneel and confess your sins to the Lord or never darken the doors of my church again!

I'll have you all excommunicated, and the doors of heaven will be closed to you forever!'

Here and there a few members of the congregation who had been getting to their feet hastily knelt down and bowed their heads to avoid his furious gaze. About half the packed church had stayed in their seats all along, and now they also knelt. But Kieran Devlin, the solicitor, who had just then reached where Lena and Eli were standing, turned back towards the altar and said clearly in his soft country voice, 'Kilteegan Bridge does respect its dead, Monsignor Collins – it's just the air in here is hard to take. But we will be waiting at the graveside to pray for Frances because we are all Christians.' He also shook Eli's hand as he left and winked at Lena.

'Good speech, Mrs Kogan,' he murmured. 'And you're right, let God be their judge.'

From above in the gallery, Monica Devlin, Kieran's wife, could be heard suddenly singing 'Nearer My God to Thee', and the rest of the choir joined her. For once, because they'd adjusted their voices to hers, she sounded in tune. Chrissy's daughter even managed to play a semitone low on the organ, so it all came together beautifully.

* * *

TWO MORE ROWS of graves had been added since Lena's father had been laid to rest in the Kilteegan cemetery, followed a number of years later by her godfather, Doc. The chestnut tree that waved over them both had turned September gold, the sky was blue and hazy, and the sea sparkled below.

Mrs Frances Moriarty was buried near the sea-facing wall, into a grave that had been dug by the same neighbours who had carried her into the church. The Monsignor, still red with rage, almost spat the prayers as she was laid to rest, and the Mouse barely paused to throw a clod on his wife's coffin before he sneaked off with his drinking partners to the pub to 'drown his sorrows' once more.

Then the people who had really loved and cared for Frances Moriarty filled in her grave, and despite all the tears and shock and sadness, there was a strange sense of healing in the air, although little was said. Even Maureen Parker joined them at the graveside.

Emily caught Lena's eye, they were thinking the same thing, Nosey Parker was running with the hares and hunting with the hounds as their father would say. She wouldn't alienate any customers for something as meaningless as moral courage.

CHAPTER 30

*M*aria found it hard to sleep these nights. She was so worried that Ted wouldn't reply, and then even more worried that he would. Around and around the fears would go. *What if he's different, what if he did awful things, what if he is the kind of Nazi monster that hides from justice?* But then she would remember him as they grew up, kind, funny Ted. And she knew there was no way he could be the sort of man to be awarded a medal in the name of the führer. She'd never told anyone about Klaus's discovery; she wanted to see what or who she was dealing with before involving her children.

Many times she watched as the dawn crept in around the curtains in their bedroom, Klaus sleeping peacefully beside her. Sometimes she never slept at all. But more often she drifted into unconsciousness at five or six in the morning and never even heard Klaus wake and get up to go to the university.

This was such a morning. It was after eleven when she woke, got up, pulled on her dressing gown and went downstairs to take her medication and have a cup of tea. She stood at the sink and gulped down a large glass of water. The drug for her manic depression caused her to be a lot more thirsty and gave her a slight tremor in her right hand, but it was a small price to pay for the peace it had provided her mind. Almost anything would have been better than those awful days of euphoric highs, where she'd be convinced she could do anything, to the crashing lows that felt like they went on for years.

She was careful with the dose. Eli told her that fluid and salt could impact the effectiveness of it, so she made sure to drink a lot and not use too much salt in her cooking, leaving others to add more if they wished.

Lena and Eli, with Pádraig, and Jack and Skipper were coming to dinner. She had invited Emily and Blackie as well, but they were busy looking after Nellie, who wasn't well. Now she had to plan the menu and go shopping for ingredients. Skipper loved her bread-and-butter pudding and Jack had asked her to make roast lamb with mint jelly, so she'd take the bus to the English Market to get a nice joint.

There was a single yellow rose from the garden in a little vase on the kitchen table, along with a note from Klaus saying he'd be home by four, a little earlier than usual, to help with the dinner. He was always attentive and kind but never more so than in recent times. He knew she was worried about the Ted situation.

But if he had been a Nazi, did she even want to hear from him? Her son-in-law was Jewish, and most of his family had been murdered in Germany. Jack and Skipper... She pushed away the thought, but deep down she knew men like them were murdered in the concentration camps, like the Jews. Only they wore pink triangles instead of yellow stars. How could she love Ted if he'd been involved in such crimes? Did it matter that the blood of two people neither of them cared for ran in their veins?

She gazed in the mirror that hung on the kitchen wall. She looked tired and pale, and her blue eyes were made azure by the dark circles the insomnia had brought. There were deep lines either side of her mouth and bewilderment in her expression. She had been used to seeing that face in the past, but not for a long time now, and it shocked her to see that woman back. What if by writing to Ted, she had thrown a grenade into the hard-won peace she'd finally achieved?

She put the kettle on the gas ring and waited for it to boil. Outside the kitchen window, the garden looked lovely. She loved roses, and was growing some hydrangeas and azaleas, a few lambs' ears and a magnolia and a camellia in the glass house, protected from the frost.

When the kettle whistled, she scalded the pot and then added tea leaves; she liked it strong. And because she should eat with her medication more than because she was hungry, she cut a slice of bread from the loaf and toasted it under the grill.

A little thrush, with a beautiful gold and brown speckled breast, came to perch on the bird table that Skipper had made for them as a housewarming gift. Blackie had given her some suet balls, which she hung from hooks on the table, and the birds loved them. She buttered her toast and went to sit at the window, looking out at her garden. She'd never had a garden like this. The farmyard came up to the back door in Kilteegan Bridge, so growing plants just for pleasure rather than for food production was still a great novelty. It was something both she and Klaus enjoyed, and it gave them such pleasure to see the flourishing shrubs, often grown from slips of things they would cut on their many walks.

The house too was as different to the farm as it could be. They'd put in a brand-new kitchen, with gleaming white cupboards and grey linoleum on the floor. The surfaces were clear, and everything had its place. Klaus disliked clutter and loved clean lines and clear surfaces, and she agreed with him.

In the front of the house was a living room, and here too they'd chosen whites and greys, creams and beiges. The colours were restful to her, and while it would not have worked on the farm, with people coming in in muddy boots and sick lambs being bottle-fed by the range, there was nobody to drag in dirt or animals here and so it stayed clean and calm and soothing.

She could hear children playing, a dog barking, desperate to join them in their games, the distant engine of a motorcycle.

The house was on a lovely street, and she and Klaus had got to know their neighbours a little bit. A nice young couple with two children, little boys, lived across the road, and to their right was an elderly lady and her pet poodle, Orso, the dog that was barking now. The house on the left was rented to three doctors from the Middle East. It was nice to be somewhere she had no past. Nobody knew of her manic episodes, and she was treated, maybe for the first time in her life, as a normal person. They said hello to their neighbours as they went in and out, she'd taken in parcels for the doctors when they were away, and she had returned Orso one evening when he decided to chase the birds in their garden. The little boys across the road chorused 'Hello, Mrs Rizzenburg!' happily when they met outside.

Mrs Maria Rizzenburg. Was that who she was now? She'd never felt like a Hannigan, her father's name, then for years she was Maria O'Sullivan, and now she was this strange name. She knew Klaus, inasmuch as anyone knew anyone else, but she knew nothing of any other Rizzenburgs. She had the name of people she'd never met and never would meet.

She and her new husband had held a dinner party one night for his friends from the faculty. She'd been so nervous, but Klaus assured her that her cooking and her hosting were wonderful and that everyone was raving the next day about Mrs Rizzenburg's lemon mousse, which she'd served for dessert.

She pulled out a sheet of paper from the pad in the drawer by the telephone, picked up the pen neatly placed beside it and made a list of things she would need for the dinner. It was probably just as well Emmet and Sarah had gone show jumping in Galway, as she wasn't sure she'd be able to fit a big enough joint in the oven; it was smaller than the enormous range she'd had in the farmhouse.

The twins weren't coming either. They were going to a seminar on moving to New Zealand put on by the consulate in Dublin. Molly and May had come up two weekends ago to watch Cork play in the Camogie final, and she hadn't cooked for them, knowing they'd buy fish and chips after the match, but they'd had a lovely evening.

* * *

WHEN SKIPPER and Jack arrived around six, she was relieved to see them. Klaus hadn't shown up at four as promised. He'd called her to say he'd been delayed, and his vagueness about why had troubled her. It wasn't that she didn't trust him – she did entirely – but it was strange for him to be so evasive.

She'd been cooking all day. The evening was still warm enough to keep the back doors and windows open to rid the house of the lingering smells of cooking.

'Mama Maria, I have missed this.' Skipper sniffed the air appreciatively as he sat down at the kitchen table. 'Jack can kinda cook, and so can I, a little bit, and as for the twins, well, if it was up to them, we'd be eatin' hay or silage, so we miss you.'

She ruffled his hair. Skipper always took his hat off at the table, and she presumed in bed, but everywhere else he wore it. 'You're a good cook, I seem to remember. I always loved your pancakes and maple syrup anyway.'

'My repertoire has expanded since you left, Mama. Pasties is what me and Jack are eating these days.' He smiled up at her.

'And I must say, they're delicious,' Jack said, mashing the bowl of potatoes that Maria had passed to him and seasoning them with salted butter and fresh chives. 'I'd never had anything like them before Skipper introduced me.'

'Pasties?' asked Maria, curious.

'It's a Montana thing,' Skipper explained to her. 'Laurie Lee's mama, Darlene, she's a sweet lady, used to make 'em for Wyatt and me 'cause she felt so bad that nobody was doin' no home cookin' for us, and when I was a kid, goin' to her house for supper was one of the best things ever. She'd make these meat pasties, sometimes beef but elk or buffalo too, whatever Laurie Lee's daddy had hunted, and they were so delicious, covered in gravy. Boy, a guy would eat his fingers.' He grinned at Maria. 'I was feeling a bit blue one day. The rain was not lettin' up so we couldn't do much, and Jack here asked me what food I missed from home. I told him about Darlene's pasties, and there and then we set to fixin' 'em. Deirdre helped us with the recipe even though she ain't never heard of 'em before, but I described 'em and she took a guess, and they turned out pretty good. And we've had them regular ever since.'

'Skipper says they came to Montana from Ireland and Cornwall,' said Jack. 'Miners used to hold onto the plait of pastry round the edge and eat all the rest of the pastry with the meat and vegetables inside, then throw away the plait because it would be dirty from their hands.'

'That's right. They came from Ireland and England to the mines of Montana, and they knew that the traces of lead or copper on their hands wasn't no good for 'em, so it was a good way to avoid poisonin' yourself. But I always thought that was sad, 'cause the crust is the best bit.' Skipper laughed. 'And I also made mac and cheese...'

'Ugh, don't talk about it,' said Jack.

'Jackie-boy, you ain't got a single clue. It's like angels dancin' in your mouth.'

'But what is it?' Maria asked, laughing.

'Well, I asked Laurie Lee to send me the recipe for that, and I made it for Jack, but it was too sophisticated for his primitive palate,' Skipper mocked.

'It's awful, kind of a flour and water dough covered in a white sauce that smells of socks.' Jack wrinkled his nose.

'Hey, don't you go disrespectin' my culture now, y'hear?' Skipper chuckled.

Jack laughed. 'I'm sure there are lovely things to eat in America – I had some delicious food there when I visited all those years ago – but I draw the line at the sock sauce and wet dough.'

'Well, it was good enough for Thomas Jefferson, so it should be good enough for you. He brought pasta and noodles back to the States from France, and boy, did we love it.'

'You brought back the best thing, Jack.' Maria smiled at Skipper. It was a running joke that she preferred him to Jack.

'Here we go again.' Jack rolled his eyes.

'Well, I will have to find out how to make pasties, but I've made some extra bread pudding for Skipper to take home. If you keep it in the fridge, it will be fine for a few days.'

Skipper whooped for joy. 'She might be your mama, Jack, but it's me she loves the best. You know that, right?'

'I was never in any doubt about that.' Jack grinned.

Lena and Eli and Pádraig arrived at that moment, and after hugs and kisses were exchanged, all Maria's guests settled in around the table while she got to peeling and slicing onions to make a sauce to go with the lamb.

'So is Nellie feeling any better, the poor thing, she's never sick.' asked Maria of Lena.

Lena looked slightly uncomfortable. 'Ah she's grand I think, just a bit of a cold.'

Lena put on a bright smile and changed the subject.

'So Jack, when are you two off to Montana?'

'Not sure yet. We've to sort out a few things,' said Jack.

'Oh, I'm so envious. I've never left Ireland, and I don't suppose I ever will now.' Maria sighed.

'Why not?' Eli asked, putting down the glossy cinema programme that he'd picked up from Maria's hall table and joining in the conversation. 'You can go anywhere you like.'

Maria stared at him. As her doctor, he'd often advised her in the past against travel because of the stress. But of course, she realised now, it had all changed. Her medication was working, and perhaps she and Klaus could travel.

The thought of leaving this quiet little house to go further than Cork made her heart race uncomfortably for a moment, but she breathed in and out slowly until she felt calmer. Maybe fear was the only thing that bound her. All her life she had feared people finding out about her madness and locking her up. She had a terror of dying alone and abandoned in an institution. Maybe this fear was all that was still governing her life; maybe she could begin to question it now. 'You're right,' she said wonderingly. 'Perhaps we will go somewhere.'

'Nana, when are we eating?' asked Pádraig, staring hungrily at the joint of lamb resting on the kitchen counter.

'Shh, Pádraig, Klaus isn't here yet,' scolded his mother.

'But I'm starving...'

'Pádraig!'

'No, Pádraig's right, we should eat,' said Maria. 'I'm sure Klaus will be here any minute – I can't imagine what's kept him. Let's just get started, and if necessary I'll put a plate aside for him. Eli, will you carve, please?'

While her son-in-law sliced the rich joint of lamb – everyone wanted as much gravy as possible – she served up the buttery mashed potatoes, baby carrots and peas fresh from the pod, along with rich onion gravy and applesauce.

Klaus still hadn't returned by the time they'd finished their first course, but as she was getting the bread-and-butter pudding, golden and studded with currants, out of the oven, the doorbell pealed.

'That will be him now,' she said. 'He's always forgetting his key. Will you let him in, Lena?'

'Sure.' Lena wiped her mouth on her napkin and went out into the hall. Maria heard her greeting Klaus at the door, and Klaus's voice rumbling softly in reply. And then…

'So you're Maria's daughter?' asked an oh-so-familiar voice.

It was just as well she'd already set the bread pudding on the table or she would have dropped it. For a moment, dark spots appeared in front of her eyes, and Eli jumped up to steady her as she swayed. 'Maria, what is it? Are you faint?'

'I…I… Oh…'

Klaus had appeared in the kitchen doorway, Lena behind him, and with them was a tall, slender, silver-haired man, his skin burnished a dark copper and with bright-blue eyes. Only this time, instead of farmer's overalls, he was wearing a lightweight cream linen suit and a blue shirt, open at the neck.

'Ted.' Maria stopped swaying and walked straight towards him as if in a trance, and without another word, brother and sister were wrapped in an embrace. She didn't know where they came from, but tears rolled down her face, and when she pulled away, she saw he was crying too.

'I thought you were dead,' she managed to whisper.

'I thought you were too.' His voice was the same deep baritone she remembered, and he smelled of citrus, as he had always done.

'How? Why?'

'I wrote to our mother, and she told me you'd been locked up in an institution by your husband and died there alone by your own hand. And she said that Paudie hadn't even gone to your funeral, that he'd said the Hannigan blood was cursed and that he wanted nothing more to do with any of us.'

Maria didn't recognise the sound that came from within her, and she clung to her brother again in darkest horror. The end she had always feared for herself, to die alone in an institution, unloved by anyone, that end had been dreamed up for her by her own mother. How cruel, how impossibly cruel...

The unfathomable coldness of her mother was something she'd tried hard to understand over the years. Maybe Irene was just so ashamed to have a child as strange as Maria. Maria had even tried to convince herself that her parents had only considered having her locked away for her own good. But this, to tell Ted his little sister had died, and by her own hand, knowing it would separate brother and sister forever when they'd always been so close to each other, it was unfathomable.

'I can't believe you're here. It's really you,' Maria said in wonderment. All fear about his past or what he might have become dissipated in a moment.

'I... If I'd known, Maria, I would have come back. I would have tried...' He swallowed and tried to steady himself as the family gazed in astonishment. 'When I got your letter, I was going to write, but I realised I just needed to see you, to talk to you.'

'All these wasted years. Why would Mother have done that? I don't understand.'

Ted held her tighter. 'I don't know. It's impossible to understand. And I felt so guilty. I thought you committed suicide because I'd abandoned you. I was so angry with myself, thinking you'd be safe with Paudie.'

'And I was, I really was,' she reassured him. 'Though all the time, I was so upset and worried about you when you didn't write after the war.'

'Hearing from you, I almost collapsed. I couldn't believe you were alive, after all these years. I cried tears of joy but also of sadness – I'd missed so much of your life.'

'I've been hoping you'd write back. I can't believe you came yourself,' she said, drawing away and feasting her eyes on him lovingly.

He smiled. 'Well, I decided I could get here as quickly as a letter could, and I needed to see you with my own eyes, hold you in my own arms, to be sure it was true, that you were alive. I only had the university address, but you told me about Klaus, so I tracked him down as soon as I got off the boat. I'm sorry I made him so late. He was showing me all the documents he had about me, the Soldbuch saying I was in the Abwehr, and the record of my receiving the Iron Cross.' He looked fondly at Maria. 'Which explains why your letter asked me so anxiously about what I did in the war.'

Maria put her finger to her lips. She wanted him to be quiet, not to spoil this wonderful moment, but already she could feel the shock waves going around the room. Eli stood up abruptly, scraping back his chair. Jack and Skipper had gone pale.

Lena hurried to her husband's side. 'This is my husband, Eli Kogan,' she said fiercely, glaring at Ted. 'He is a German Jew.'

The atmosphere could be cut with a knife, but Ted merely nodded. 'Yes, Klaus told me. It's good to meet you, Eli. You got out of Berlin in 1940?'

Eli was unreadable, but his voice was steady. 'Yes, with my mother and uncle. All the rest of my family were murdered by the Nazis.'

Ted didn't flinch. 'I'm glad you survived, and my deepest sympathies on the loss of so many of your people. We tried. I tried.' He looked down into Maria's frightened face. 'I'm sorry, Maria. I have already explained to Klaus, but of course you and your family are not mind-readers.'

'You should start again at the beginning, I think,' said Klaus, taking his seat at the table. 'Why don't you sit, Ted?'

'Perhaps later, but for now I'd rather stand until the other people at the table are more comfortable with my presence.'

'I'm sure there's no need –'

'I think maybe he's right,' said Eli, remaining standing himself. He looked very coldly at Ted. 'You are my wife's uncle, so if you have an excuse for what you did in the war, especially as an Iron Cross recipient, I would be very interested to hear it.'

Ted remained standing, looking serious, and Maria took a seat beside Klaus. 'I think, despite Klaus's advice, I will begin at the end, not the beginning. I should tell you that as well as the Iron Cross, I got the George Cross, awarded by King George the Sixth, for services to the Allied war effort.'

'You mean you were a double agent?' asked Eli, bristling with rage.

Ted smiled slightly. 'No, a British agent.'

Young Pádraig gasped. 'So you were like James Bond? Wow.'

'But how… I don't understand. Weren't Cristiana's family very involved?' Maria asked.

Ted nodded. 'It's true, my former father-in-law was a high-ranking Abwehr officer, and he hauled me into the service on his coattails, and so as far as the top brass were concerned, my credentials were exemplary. I spoke fluent German as well as English, and as an Irishman, I had a vested interest in Britain being beaten. Not only that, but I'd married into a family that wholeheartedly supported the führer and saw the Jews as a scourge.' He caught Eli's eye; Eli's face was still a mask. 'The truth was, I despised the Nazis – I thought they were ignorant thugs. But speaking out in our social circle would be literal suicide, so I decided to play the long game. I joined the Abwehr and was enthusiastic about it all, and once I was established, I convinced them to send me as a spy to London. And within a day of arriving, I went and volunteered as a British agent.'

'They mustn't have believed their luck?' Skipper asked, intrigued.

Ted laughed. 'Quite the opposite. They told me they had no interest in me as an agent for them but that they would be monitoring all of my communications, and if I made contact with Germany, I would immediately be arrested. So a less than successful start.'

A slight ripple of amusement eased some of the tension in the room, and even Eli looked interested. 'So what next?' he asked coolly.

'Well, they wouldn't meet with me again, but I was desperate to convince them I could be useful, so I sent a telegram to the man who interviewed me. I said I would communicate to my German handler that a flotilla of Royal Navy was headed for Malta that weekend, and to watch what happened. I sent the communication to Berlin, and sure enough, the Kriegsmarine were deployed and German forces in the Mediterranean were put on high alert. By then the British had cracked the Enigma, though the Germans didn't know it, so intercepted communications backed up what I was saying. It was enough to convince the British that I did wield some power, and so I was brought in for an interview again.'

'Go on.' Like Skipper and Eli, Jack had been drawn in too.

'So now I was living in London, reporting back to Berlin about troop movements, industry, munitions, anything really that was of interest. And so much of what I reported was accurate. I won a great deal of trust and admiration back home because what I said was going to happen always did. But the truth was, I was working for the Allies, so everything I told my masters in the Abwehr was designed to detract attention away from something of much more importance, or more often what I told them was important but came too late to be of any use.'

'How did the Germans believe you knew so much?' probed Jack.

'Well, I set up an imaginary ring of spies reporting to me, all over the country. They didn't exist, of course, but I would say, for example, that a large shipment of food or supplies was coming into Liverpool. I told them I had recruited a docker, and then U-boats would be on alert, watching for it, when in fact the cargo was coming into Bristol.'

'But what if they wanted to meet one of these imaginary people?' Lena wanted to know; she was also becoming fascinated.

'Well, if my German handlers got too interested in a fictitious person, I would have them killed off. The British would arrange for an obituary to appear in the newspaper, I'd send a clipping, and so they accepted that such and such, a vital cog in the machine, was no more.

It was wartime and bombing was constant, so it wasn't a stretch. By early '44 I had twenty men and women, figments of my imagination obviously, working for me – and being paid, I might add, from Berlin.'

'And you kept doing that for the entire war?'

'What I didn't realise until the end was that while I did some useful things, and fed some information that may or may not have saved lives, I was being kept in reserve by the British for an important mission. They knew the Germans trusted me completely by now. They sent me to Lisbon a few times to meet with them on neutral ground, and it was clear the Abwehr believed everything I said.'

Eli was listening closely. 'So what was this important mission?'

'It was D-Day. Eisenhower was clear. He needed three full days without the full force of the Germans on his neck to get a foothold in Normandy, and so my job was to convince the Germans that the Allies had a million-man army waiting in Dover, ready to descend on Calais, hundreds of miles from Normandy.'

'What? Are you serious?' Jack was flabbergasted.

'So that's why the 15th Army and so many of the more important panzer divisions were kept back? They never believed that Normandy was it?' asked Skipper excitedly. As an American, the beaches of Normandy were a huge part of his history, and he was well read on the subject.

'Yes, that was because I, and others of course, were all feeding them the same intelligence. That the Allies were only drawing them out, trying to pull their firepower to Normandy to clear space for the main invasion. Eisenhower asked for three days, and we, along with the work of the resisters who hampered the German movements at every turn, gave him weeks.'

'And because of that, the Allies won the war,' said Eli quietly.

Ted shrugged. 'It helped. People often assume that the Normandy landings were the end, but there was bitter and hard fighting for every square kilometre after that. Despite all the Allies in concert, it was still a huge feat.'

'But they must have found out you'd tricked them? The Germans?' Lena shook her head in amazement.

'I presume it became obvious in the end, but once I'd fed them as much as I could – and the war was on the final stretch by then – the British decided it was time to kill me off as well.'

'The British tried to kill you?' asked Pádraig, with huge indignation. 'That's awful, after all you did for them.'

Ted laughed. 'No, no, not for real. They just pretended to. They barged into my flat, dragged me out for all to see and put me on public trial for being an enemy agent. It was in the papers, but they never used my real name, just the alias the Abwehr gave me, Hans Schmit. I was found guilty, of course, and sentenced to death. They even went so far as to lead me to the yard where my death by firing squad took place. Shots were fired, and prisoners saw me die. I didn't, obviously. They were blanks, and I just fell to the ground, but they made sure reports of my trial and death were widely reported. It eliminated the risk of a reprisal killing by some overzealous Nazi who was going to avenge my deception, though the British authorities were more worried about that than I was, to be honest. To my mind, anyone who survived was only interested in saving their own skin, not in coming after me. Anyway, to be safe, I was sent to Australia and given a job as a drover. And that's how I met my wife, Gwenda, and now we have two girls, Sophie and Annamaria. And that's my story.'

'Ted,' said Eli solemnly, pulling out the spare chair beside him. 'You're still standing. Please sit down with us.'

Lena smiled and reached over for her uncle's hand. 'Welcome home, Uncle Ted. We've waited a long time for this.'

EPILOGUE

aria and Ted sat in the office of the flushed, red-haired
solicitor, hardly able to believe what they were hearing.
Earlier that day they'd gone to the church where their parents
attended Mass and, with the priest's help, had gone through the book
of death notices. George Hannigan had died on the fifth of September,
1958, and Irene Hannigan had died on the twenty-first of April, 1965.
Afterwards they had gone to see their old house on Wellington Road,
just to walk past it in each other's company and remember the better
bits of their childhood, the happier times when they were playing
quietly together. Maria hadn't set foot on this street since she'd eloped
with Paudie, all those years ago. The house looked much the same,
although there was a 'For Sale' sign strapped to the front gate. As they
stood gazing up at the familiar windows, a professional-looking
young man came out of the Georgian front door and down the steps,
and asked them if they were Mr and Mrs Fitzpatrick.

When they told him no, he checked his watch and rolled his eyes.
'They were supposed to be here half an hour ago. I should get back to
my office in case they phone. Unless… I don't suppose you want to
view the house yourselves?' Seeing the puzzlement on their faces, he

laughed and said, 'Oh, I beg your pardon. I'm the auctioneer. I'm in charge of selling the place. And I can see it caught your eye, and I'm here now, so would you like me to show you around? It's a beautiful Georgian property, and it has a lovely long garden at the back, very overgrown but with definite potential.'

Maria looked at Ted, who nodded slightly. It was a tempting offer, and now that their parents were dead, they could afford to revisit the past without too much pain. She smiled at the auctioneer. 'Well, I don't think we're looking to buy, but if you've got five minutes, we'd love to have a quick look around. You see, we used to live here. This is my brother, Ted Hannigan, and I'm Maria.'

'Are you serious?' The young man seemed astonished.

Maria smiled at his incredulity. 'Yes, we grew up here, but we... well, we lost touch with our parents and –'

'You have to get to the solicitor,' he interrupted her. 'You have to get to the solicitor, right this minute. It's...'

He rummaged in his pockets, burbling breathlessly to himself. 'This is the most... I mean, I've never... No one's going to believe... Here!'

He thrust a card at them as they stood in stunned silence, with Maria beginning to wonder if she'd finally met someone as peculiar as herself. 'Take this. Go there now. Gunn and Gunn, 38 South Mall. Don't stop on the way. No, wait! Have you a car? No? I'll take you there myself. We haven't got a minute to waste.'

And now here they were, sitting in the office of the red-haired solicitor who seemed jubilant at their sudden appearance.

'It is most fortunate that you went to see the house,' he was saying. 'My uncle, God rest his soul, Alfred Gunn Senior, he tried his best to find you, Mr Hannigan, but your mother told us she didn't know your address, didn't even know what country you were in. She said you moved around a lot. And as for you, Mrs Rizzenburg, well...' – he coloured – 'your mother said you were dead, so of course my uncle didn't even try. It's so remarkable you've both turned up with only eleven days to go.'

'But eleven days to go to what?' asked Ted, looking as bewildered as Maria felt.

'Oh my goodness me.' The solicitor shot a startled glance at the young auctioneer, who had insisted on accompanying Ted and Maria right into the book-lined mahogany office. 'Didn't Arthur explain to you?'

'I thought I'd let you have the pleasure, Bill.' The young man grinned. 'Not to spoil things for you, as it was your uncle who set it all up. Right, I'll leave you all to it.' The young auctioneer withdrew.

'Well, well...' Bill Flannery wiped his flushed pink face with a handkerchief and looked quite pleased.

Maria said faintly, 'Will someone please tell us what is going on?'

'Of course, apologies. It's just... I mean, eleven days later, even ten...' The solicitor, who still had beads of sweat on his forehead, consulted a file on his desk. 'And you'd have lost everything to the Redemptorist order.'

'I'm none the wiser. Please, can you just explain, from the start? I'm assuming this is something to do with my parents' will?' Ted was clearly bewildered, and this man wasn't casting any light on why they were there. If anything, he was adding further confusion.

'Yes, yes, of course. Right so.' He inhaled and seemed to settle himself. 'My uncle, William Gunn, God rest his soul – I inherited the firm from him, wonderful man – well, your late mother was his client. He also served your late father before her. If you'll forgive my candour here, your mother did not wish to bequeath any of her considerable estate to either of you, choosing instead to leave it to the Redemptorist order. My uncle knew that was not your father's wish, and they had known each other for years, so he didn't care for what your mother was doing. He suggested the will could be challenged if you, Mr Hannigan, got wind of it, so he convinced her to specify that if Mr Hannigan hadn't turned up to claim the properties and other assets within ten years of his mother's demise – this was on the assumption that you, Mrs Rizzenburg, were dead – only then could they go to the Church.'

'Inheritance?' asked Ted, reaching for Maria's hand and squeezing it as if trying to make sure all this was real.

Flannery was riffling through the file, and he produced a typed sheet of paper and cleared his throat. 'The assets are the house on Wellington Road, and also a house in Tivoli – it is occupied by tenants, but of course, you may wish to give them notice and liquidate the asset. There's also a substantial property overlooking the sea in Ardmore, County Waterford – it was the family home of your maternal grand-mother. It is being run as a private convalescent home these many years but has been maintained in good order. The shop on Patrick's Street, Cork, is still trading, and again is in the hands of a tenant. The term of the lease is to be renewed every five years on a rolling basis, so you may have to wait until the current term has expired should you wish to sell, but I might suggest you do not as it provides a very good income in terms of rent. The tenant is a very capable individual, and the business is running smoothly. Also, there are various accounts containing sums of money, as well as investments in the form of bank bonds and shares. All detailed and held by Gunn and Gunn. Oh…' His eyes fell on the file again. 'And I have this letter from your father as well, not to be opened until both he and your mother were laid to rest.' He produced an envelope and passed it over to Ted.

Together the brother and sister looked at it, stunned. It was yellowed with age and addressed to 'Ted Hannigan' in their father's large and loopy handwriting. Maria remembered the look of that handwriting well; their father would pore over the ledgers for his gentleman's outfitters shop every evening when she was a child, filling in things in that hand. Immediately she conjured up his image. Perfect, small and neat, never a hair astray. His thinning hair combed across his white head, skin shiny. He would sit at his desk every evening in silent solitude. If she went to him for any sort of help, he would seem almost afraid to touch her or show her any affection. 'Maria, I'm busy,' he would say. 'Maybe ask your brother.' She could hear his voice now, neat and clipped like himself. Such an odd fish.

'Will you read it out loud?' she said softly.

'Are you ready?' Ted asked.

'As I'll ever be.' She exhaled.

'I'll give you a moment.' Bill Flannery left the room.

Ted tore open the envelope, extracted a sheet of paper and held it in shaking hands.

'*Dear Ted,*' he read aloud. '*I am writing this only to you because as you know from your mother, your sister has died. It is a terrible thing, but she passed away in St Catherine's soon after her husband, Paudie O'Sullivan, rejected her, and Irene tells me she was buried by the nuns in the patients' graveyard. I wish I had known Maria was ill; maybe I could have seen her one last time before she died. Still, maybe it was for the best. It all happened so quickly. She was admitted, and the next morning she was dead. She was buried in the patient's cemetery and it was all over before I knew anything about it.*'

Ted glanced at Maria to see if she was all right for him to continue. She nodded. She wanted to know everything, even the worst things. She was strong enough now to hear it, with Ted at her side. Klaus made her feel so safe, and Eli was a wonderful doctor, but to have the rock of her childhood beside her was what she needed at this moment.

Ted looked back at the letter and continued. '*I have a confession to make to you, Ted. The truth is I am your father, but my wife, Irene, is not your mother. I had a relationship with a woman called Ellen Traynor, which lasted for many years both prior to and after my marriage to Irene. Irene and I were a match made by our parents. I repeatedly implored my father to release me from the engagement, but a deal had been struck. Both families were wealthy and sought a consolidation of assets. Irene and I were part of the bargain.*

I was involved with Ellen at that stage, but I was forced to abandon that relationship and marry Irene. I realise now I should have simply refused, but my father threatened to cut me off without a penny. The manner in which I conducted myself in the following years was reprehensible, but I continued the relationship with Ellen until her death from TB. To further complicate matters, Ellen bore me two children, yourself and Maria, who had nobody to care for them when she died. She made me promise I would care for you both. She loved you with all of her heart.

I regret many things about my behaviour throughout my life, but I would like the record to show I never for a moment regretted my connection to Ellen Traynor. She was a wonderful woman, and I was so lucky to have known her. I loved her and I still do. She is buried in St Finbarr's cemetery in Cork should you wish to visit. There will be flowers there – I have arranged for a wreath of roses and lilies to be placed there every week.

Realising my children would be raised in an orphanage if I did not intervene, and because I promised Ellen I would care for you both, I confessed everything to Irene and begged her to accept you and your sister into our lives. She and I had never had children, and I hoped she would come to love you.

To avoid any scandal, she finally agreed, but I feel she never fully accepted either of you, and I was afraid to show you or Maria any affection because it distressed her greatly and only made matters worse between you and her.

I know she could have been a better mother to you and your sister, but you were fed and kept warm, and I feel I did my best by you both. Irene often wanted to send your sister to an institution, and I did wonder if Maria would have been happier with the nuns. But you stood by her always, Ted, and now that she has died, alone and unwanted, I feel glad that you postponed her eventual fate. You were always a good boy, Ted.

I hope you have lived a fruitful and happy life, wherever you are.
George Hannigan.

* * *

ELLEN TRAYNOR 1895–1921
  Loving mother of Edward and Maria
  May she rest in peace.

Maria stood reading the inscription over and over again as her brother stooped to lay an armful of daffodils on Ellen's grave. A wreath of roses and lilies was already propped against the headstone, along with a card that read succinctly, in large loopy handwriting, *I love you. GH.* She wondered how many of those cards her father had written out, to be left week after week for so many years. A man she had thought had a heart of ice. It was a strange world.

'I don't know what to think. Do you?' she asked Ted.

He shook his head as he straightened up. 'I know. It's hard to believe that man loved anyone.'

'I'll never understand it. But I'm also so glad Irene wasn't my natural mother. I could never understand why she hated me, always poking and pinching me when our father wasn't looking. It makes so much sense that we weren't her children. We were just daily evidence that her husband loved another woman.'

'And George thought he did his best, keeping us.'

Maria shrugged. 'I wonder, would we have fared any worse in an orphanage?'

'Probably. We'd have been hungry and freezing, and pinching and poking would have been the least of our worries. Besides, we wouldn't have had each other.' He tucked her arm into his. 'And knowing we had a mother who loved us is nice, isn't it?'

'We have some making up to do, though, for all the lost years when you thought I was dead.' She sighed. 'And you'll be going back to Australia soon.'

'I was thinking I might bring Gwenda and the girls over for a while? Gwenda has always talked of wanting to travel, and the money does change things. Our ranch is gone – the drought finished us. Gwenda is taking it very hard. It was in her family for generations. So maybe a break is what she and the girls need. And it would be lovely for them to meet their cousins. And I could become Ted Hannigan again. What do you think, Maria?'

As the sun set over St Finbarr's cemetery, over Ellen's grave, the grave of the mother who had loved them and didn't want to leave them, Maria put her arm around her brother's waist and let waves of calm and joy wash over her.

'Welcome home, Ted Hannigan.'

THE END

I SINCERELY HOPE YOU ENJOYED THIS BOOK, IF YOU DID I WOULD REALLY APPRECIATE A REVIEW ON AMAZON.
IF YOU WOULD LIKE TO JOIN MY READERS GROUP, AND GET A FREE NOVEL TO DOWNLOAD, JUST POP OVER TO WWW.JEANGRAINGER.COM AND TELL ME WHERE TO SEND IT. IT IS 100% FREE AND ALWAYS WILL BE.
FINALLY, THE NEXT BOOK IN THIS SERIES, WHEN IRISH EYES ARE LYING IS AVAILABLE TO PRE-ORDER NOW FOR DELIVERY IN JANUARY 2023
JUST CLICK HERE TO PRE-ORDER:

https://geni.us/whenIrisheyesarelying

ABOUT THE AUTHOR

Jean Grainger is a USA Today bestselling Irish author. She writes historical and contemporary Irish fiction and her work has very flatteringly been compared to the late great Maeve Binchy.

She lives in a stone cottage in Cork with her husband Diarmuid and the youngest two of her four children. The older two come home for a break when adulting gets too exhausting. There are a variety of animals there too, all led by two cute but clueless micro-dogs called Scrappy and Scoobi.

ALSO BY JEAN GRAINGER

The Harp and the Rose

Roaring Liberty

Standalone Books

So Much Owed

Shadow of a Century

Under Heaven's Shining Stars

Catriona's War

Sisters of the Southern Cross

The Kilteegan Bridge Series

The Trouble with Secrets

What Divides Us

More Harm Than Good

When Irish Eyes Are Lying

The Mags Munroe Story

The Existential Worries of Mags Munroe

Growing Wild in the Shade

Made in the USA
Las Vegas, NV
29 November 2022

60602946R00152